Praise for Frederick Schofield

"Schofield is fun. He's entertaining. A storyteller."

—*The Press of Atlantic City*

"Grabs you from the first page."

—*Book Dealers World*

"Recommended reading!"

—*The Tampa Tribune*

"Captivating stories."

—*Writer's Life Magazine*

"A great tale about our town."

—Pinky Kravits
WOND-AM, Atlantic City

Also available

by

Frederick Schofield

A Run To Hell

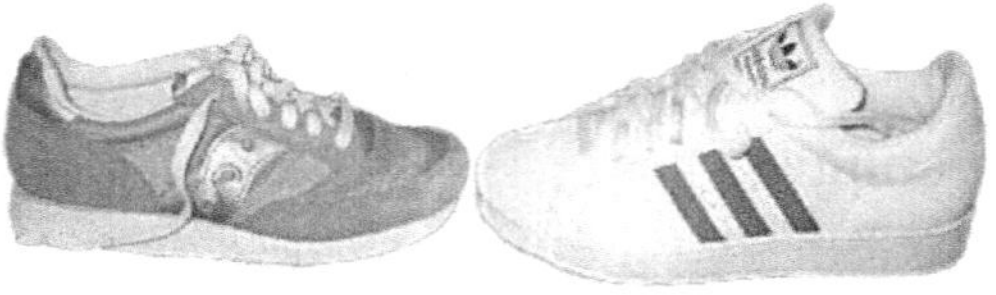

Second Edition with Epilogue

In Print, LARGE Print, Audio and E-Book

Frederick Schofield's

The Board~walkers

Second Edition Redux

BEACH BOOKS PUBLISHING, LLC

The Boardwalkers

Second Edition

ISBN: 978-1-7347024-9-1

Library of Congress Catalog Card Number: 1-73470-249-4

Published by Beach Book Publishing, LLC
Email: Publisher@BeachBookPubishing.com
Web Address: BeachBookPublishing.com

Titles for year-around pleasure reading.

Warehoused by Ingram

Available in print, e-book, and audio book.

Printed in the United States of America

About the Author

SAVOR A DREAM. In it, legal thriller king John Grisham mates with romance genre queen Nora Roberts. Later that night—because it's only a dream—she wraps with mob master Mario Puzo or is it thriller titan Tom Clancy? Anyway, the child they spawn creates easy reads: entertainment that's perfect for any beach, hearth, or comfort zone.

Frederick Schofield delivers those tales. The former trial lawyer, who colorfully prosecuted and defended, is a U.S. Marine combat veteran. He shares a wealth of tales in light reads that are flavored with intrigue, mystery, suspense, a smidge of romance, and a dash of humor.

Frederick

Schofield

THE

BOARD-
WALKERS

For Annmarie

Preface

Enter a City by the Sea

TWO-HUNDRED MILLION YEARS AGO, a small and spineless life form crawled from the sea onto the shore that was to become Atlantic City. It shook its legs on the left side of its body and paused. It shook its legs on the right side and paused. Then, a slug ate it in one gulp.

It was the first floor show in Atlantic City. Two-hundred million years of evolution can't change some things.

A lesson to learn, my new friend, then stroll by these sands. Savor each moment. Live, love, and look over your shoulder. You're joining *The Boardwalkers*.

Antonio "Quick Fish" DeBona

Part I

Chapter One

Close Your Eyes

SARAH STOOD IN SILENT SURRENDER. Eyes cast low, she turned over cuffs that would tenderly restrain her wrists. Welcoming their familiar touch, she stroked satin straps that would bind her. Sarah's hands joined behind her back. Cuffs closed. A cord wrapped her body like a comfortable second skin. Ankle restraints nuzzled silk stockings drawn taut over willowy legs. She felt secure.

Tawny skinned, firm bodied yet lithe, she was alone in her world until a feather caressed her cheek, then swept auburn curls from her brow. The sensation consumed her with promise. Gently, she was lowered to sit in cramped quarters. The quill kissed bare breasts, yet only for moments, raising her coo and arching her back for erect nipples to converge with soft swirls. Eyes closed, she longed for the next loving stroke.

Chilled by a touch then warmed by light spillage over constricting abdominals, her sensations peaked, and curiosity stirred. Sarah opened her eyes and screamed as the razor-sharp blade cut her again. Gashes followed, slow and unyielding. She howled, knowing no one would hear. Blood oozed down the modest curvature of long legs, stained her stilettos, and pulsed across the floor.

Air rank with the odor of alcohol and thick with cigarette smoke filled her lungs. As her heart pounded its final beat, she thought of him. Knowing he'd be accountable for her death was Sarah's only satisfaction. Her iniquitous compulsions would send him on a journey he hadn't the soul to take.

Laughter echoed in her mind, ricocheting off the walls of her skull, until all that Sarah was . . . was gone.

The telephone ring broke wintry stillness. Carol reached for her night table lamp even before opening her eyes. One week out of four she served on rotation, taking night calls as a member of the major crimes unit. Seasoned with twelve years' experience, she was an Atlantic County Assistant Prosecutor. Getting roused in the dark was an occupational hazard, and that kind of call churned her adrenaline.

"Miz Resnick."

"What time is it?"

"Three fifteen, Ma'am, and we have a murder on Brigantine Island.

Instantly upright, tossing blond hair off her face, she leaped from bed. Within five minutes, she held a cup of black coffee in her hand, dressed in a black suit with a tailored skirt and pumps. The Mistress of Major Crimes, as the homicide cops nicknamed her, was on duty.

Carol drove thirty minutes to the sleepy resort town on a barrier island just north of Atlantic City. Spotting the crime scene was easy. The population of Brigantine Island was seasonal. Only half its residents lived there year-round, working in casinos across the bridge or in the casino-support industries. Summer residents were long gone, leaving the island to feel deserted, indeed, people needy.

Carol spied activity from blocks away: top light bubble-gum machines spinning on a half dozen police cars and an ambulance, all parked before an oceanfront home. She pulled up to them and stared. Emergency personnel—some scurrying, others wandering or pondering—filled a semicircular driveway that looped from the street to steps ascending to a whale of a beach house. She leaped from her county car and whistled a catcall.

"Somebody has big bucks," she muttered.

Her words escaped lips on breath that steamed in frigid air. With crashes of waves filling her ears and salt air penetrating her nostrils, she pinned a county ID badge on her jacket. Carol hardly needed it. Every cop in the county knew her on sight or by reputation. She was tall as all of them in towering heels and had a take-charge demeanor, whether at a crime scene or in a courtroom.

"Good evening, Miz Resnick," an officer at the door addressed her.

Carol nodded cursorily, then followed two more cops up a winding staircase to the second floor. At the stair top a forensic investigator from the Prosecutor's Office waited.

“I arrived a few minutes ago,” he greeted.

She was glad it was Harry Chang’s night on duty. Harry is an adaptation of the name Hao, meaning “very clever,” that came with him when he had immigrated from China. He lived up to his namesake with a trained eye that missed very little. Wearing a Polo shirt, khaki trousers, and running shoes, he kept his pen and clip board by his side. Rounding out his wardrobe was a work belt holding plastic gloves, markers, chalk, tape measure, dictating recorder, camera . . . a seemingly limitless array of forensic equipment.

“What do we have?” Carol said.

“A corpse chained to a toilet,” Harry began. “Dark complected female—

“Black? Carol interrupted.

“Possibly mulatto, maybe a Latina. Early to mid-thirties, I’d say. Attractive. Chained nude with knife wounds running across her torso and most of her body. Face left alone. The coroner’s in there now. We snapped pictures. When the doc is done, we’ll go back for prints. You’ll find her in the master bathroom. . ..”

Harry’s voice trailed off as Carol moved toward the body.

She quickly noticed that someone had built the house to satisfy expensive tastes.

Carol wondered, *Is this a bathroom or a ballroom?*

Floor-to-ceiling mirrors ran the length of expansive walls. Intricate inlaid marble flooring depicting icons of the zodiac were bathed in crimson blood pools fed by streams emerging from a separate water closet. In it, walls were blood spattered and streaked. Still chained to the toilet was the upright corpse. A contorted death mask froze her horror for eternity.

"What can you tell me, Doc?" Carol called to the coroner.

The busy little man didn't take time to look up. His hand reached for the back of his neck. He massaged himself and twisted his head around as he spoke.

"She's been dead no more than three to four hours. Died slowly. The wounds were deliberate and spread across her body. She was probably tied down before she received the first. Her hands are cuffed behind her. Also done before she was cut. Then, she struggled. You can tell by the bruises around the wrists where she tried to tear free from the cuffs."

Like many, who form death's cleanup crew, his tone was dispassionate, his words precise. Carol had never fully mastered the knack of removing her feelings from that kind of scene, yet emotion never interfered with duty. She keyed on details that uncovered valuable leads.

"Police issue cuffs?

"No," Doc replied. "They're the kind you find in a porn shop: pink-painted steel with fur lining. Take a look."

The coroner tipped the body slightly forward causing more blood to flow from the open torso before continuing.

"Her ankles are chained to the bottom of the toilet bowl with S & M restraints. They match the handcuffs, more pink and fur. They're joined by a steel chain that wraps around the bottom of the commode."

Carol tried thinking it through and pondered: *What kind of monster could have done this*?

"Did some sadist dive too far into a scene?"

"Maybe." Doc replied. "Look at the incisions. Symmetrically made. Wounds on the left wrist identical to the wounds on the right. Incisions on the torso are evenly spaced, equal length, running horizontally. They stripe her from the navel to just above the breasts."

"What's on top of the toilet paper holder?"

Carol pointed at two small blood-covered mounds.

"Those," he said, "are her nipples."

A chill ran the length of Carol's spine. As she stepped back, her heel slipped in blood, and Doc extended his hand to catch Carol from falling. She straightened and he continued.

"The amputation was done with technical precision to remove just the nipples from both breasts. The areolas were placed on the toilet paper dispenser where she could see them. Someone took their time carving her."

"No one heard her scream?"

"Nobody around, not for blocks this time of year. No one heard her but she screamed alright. Must've yelled plenty. She was tortured. This woman didn't die of any single wound. She succumbed from loss of blood that poured from the gashes. Whoever did this sliced away her body, piece by piece."

Carol couldn't remain in the room any longer. She went back into the hall, sucked and expelled a deep breath, then grabbed the senior detective on the scene.

"Sargent, who called this in?"

"Anonymous tip to the local cop shop," the plainclothesman said.

Carol knew what to do immediately and issued the order.

"Make sure we get the nine-one-one tapes. Have the local cops bring them out to our office first thing in the morning."

"No can do, Carol."

"Why not?"

"The tip came into the police station on a back line. It didn't come in on the nine-one-one or main line. Someone knew the number for an inside phone line at the police station. The caller's voice was disguised, and the cop who picked up the call couldn't even tell whether the caller was a man or a woman."

"The cop didn't know if a murder call came in from a man or a woman?" Carol's eyebrows arched.

"You got it," the detective replied. "The cop, who answered, thought it was a spouse calling for an officer on the night shift. He was half-awake and wasn't expecting anything like this on an unpublished phone line. The caller gave an address and said they would find a body on the throne. The phone clicked dead. That was it. No audio recording and no way to trace the call."

Carol didn't like what she was hearing. Someone with inside information at the local police station had made the call, someone who either worked there or knew it well. Anyone who had access to that police station was a suspect. That included law enforcement officers, people arrested and detained, all those who had ever entered the place. Anyone who acquired that phone number from a local cop was also a suspect. Whoever made the call knew enough about law enforcement to avoid having the call traced or recorded for use in voice identification. The anonymous caller wasn't so anonymous anymore. The scope of targets in the investigation was already narrowing. Carol returned her thoughts to the crime scene and grabbed Harry.

"When the Doc is finished," she instructed, "go back in there. Take more pictures and get every fingerprint."

"Lifting prints from the water closet bloody walls and floor will be rough."

"There are handprints on the stall walls in blood," Carol said.

"Already took pictures of them."

"I want better. Get a crew in here to cut out the dry wall. I want each handprint separately preserved. Mark each piece of wall so they can reconstruct that water closet back at the lab. And Harry, be good to me. Don't miss a goddamned thing."

Carol peered around the living room. It was an upside-down house. That's what they call them at the seashore with the living room, dining room, kitchen, and master suite upstairs to take advantage of ocean views over beach dunes. The glass wrapped living room faced eastward displaying a lush sea scape and southward toward Atlantic City across an inlet. Downstairs cops were watching television in a den.

"Nobody comes up here again without my approval," she shouted down. "Understood?"

"Whatever you say, Miz Resnick," the cop at the front door shouted back.

Carol peered at a framed photo on the fireplace mantle. "Christ Almighty," she whispered as she lifted it.

They stared at the photograph of an attractive couple side-by-side on the beach. The woman tied to the toilet was with a man both recognized. Those ice-cool blue eyes were his signature, framed by neatly coiffured dark hair, and punctuated by an expression that always seemed to display self-assuredness just on the kind side of cockiness. That confident aura somehow made him taller than his average size and stronger than his average build. Instantly, that photo told them who owned the house and the identity of the corpse.

"The woman chained to the toilet," Carol said, "is Paul Cameron's wife."

Harry looked up at the twenty-five-foot cathedral ceiling.

"Paul's been living pretty nicely," he observed. "This place reeks of friggin' opulence."

"Well, Paul's one of the top trial lawyers in town. He's won a lot of big cases over the years I've known him. Guess that brought him some big bucks."

As Carol surveyed the room, words rolled off her tongue as if an automatic reaction.

"This place is cold. Aside from a single snapshot, it seems . . . impersonal."

She scanned fruitlessly for homey touches until Harry hit a homer.

"Gruesome murder," he said. "This could have been a special gift."

"What do you mean?"

"What's the date, Counselor?"

"February 14, 1989."

At first it passed her mind, then Carol's eyes bulged. "You're saying this is a warped Valentine's Day gift from an estranged spouse?"

She turned from Harry and speculated: *Could a man of Paul's reputation torture and slay his estranged wife that way*?

Carol had trouble connecting him with the bloody corpse in the next room. She studied the picture again. Paul's imposing stature, thick chestnut locks, and light blue eyes drew attention in courthouses. Often, they had been courtroom adversaries . . . and there were times when she had wished for more. During more causal encounters at County Bar events, she sometimes sensed he felt the same, but timing had never been right between them. Both had hesitated to take casual flirtations further.

Harry interrupted her thoughts.

"Grender will target Paul in this investigation."

Carol knew the investigator was right. Her boss would move fast, and the first murder suspect is always the victim's spouse.

Harry pressed.

"Does Paul do drugs?"

The thought startled her, but that kind of question demanded an answer.

"Not that I know."

"Does he drink?"

"Scotch," Carol recalled. "You're suggesting he went nutty on Cutty?"

"Listen, he was separated from his wife. Could have been depressed, maybe manic. You know manic-depressives. Medication can control their conditions. Then, they think they're fine, take themselves off their drugs, go nuts then slice, slice, slice," Harry said, while thrusting his empty hand in vicious stabbing motions.

"Another scenario," Harry offered, "could be he was taking heavy doses of a prescribed drug like Prozac, then mixed it with alcohol or street drugs. Could have set off a wild reaction—especially if he's bipolar. Whoever carved that woman was whacked."

"Possibly." Carol didn't like where their discussion was heading. "We'll check him for an alibi."

"Even if he can place himself somewhere else at the time of the murder, we can't rule-out a contract killing. He's a criminal lawyer: that means he knows scum bags. Has he ever worked for organized crime?"

"Can't say. Paul's never appeared in a big mob case but rumors fly. For years, we've suspected some association with Tony DeBona's people."

"DeBona? That could be the connection to a hired hit."

"Could be," Carol mused. "On the other hand, an informant told our drug task force there's bad blood between Paul and DeBona. Maybe pinning a murder rap on him is the mob's way to even a score."

"When will you bring him in for questioning?"

"The boss make's that call."

"This is a murder case. That makes it your decision, doesn't it?"

Carol peered far into the ocean. Grey sea started to blend with blue sky as the sun rose, silently exploding like a fireball. Whitecaps glistened from horizon to shore. She turned southward toward the Atlantic City boardwalk skyline. One at a time, garish exterior lighting on each casino dimmed as the glitter domes slipped into slumber. A passing seagull with wings spread wide to ride an ocean breeze gave a cry like a lonely lament, as if sharing Carol's feelings.

"Whatever happened here," she voiced in a long breath, "Paul is waking to tough days ahead."

Chapter Two

Phantom of the Opera

THE POUND OF A GAVEL RESOUNDED through the oak-paneled courtroom, ending a long session on March 15, 1989. Paul congratulated his client, packed his briefcase at the defense table, then turned to leave. The blue eyes that had peered so incisively across the courtroom, as he had argued his case, found a form that drew attention.

Paul watched Carol enter the room. While he beamed, her face darted down, her long hair framing a troubled frown. Commotion erupted behind her in the hallway. Murmurs turned to shouts. Four police officers entered the courtroom purposefully, scattering the milling crowd. As the cops approached Paul, his eyes darted toward Carol and his mind sped.

Could she have known this was going to happen?

The thought stung him as she disappeared behind the sea of blue uniforms engulfing him.

"Paul Cameron, you're coming with us," an officer barked.

"Hold your hands out, now," demanded another.

His arms extended slowly. Handcuffs came down fast. They swung him round and slammed him against the wall. A plainclothes officer too anxious to do his duty kicked the back of Paul's legs and sent him to his knees.

"Whoa, Smitty," a cop whispered. "Not here. Too many witnesses. Just read him his Goddamned rights."

Officer Smith grinned. His rosy cheeks flushed crimson. The ball on the tip of his nose twitched and shimmered.

"You have the right to remain silent. You have the right to an attorney. . .."

Paul's head reeled yet he thought clearly. Court personnel and spectators watched in stunned disbelief; all save the big man in the rear of the courtroom. Paul saw DeBona smiling.

"What are the charges?" Paul shouted.

"No charges, yet," said one cop. "You're being detained for questioning. Time to talk about your wife's murder."

"What the. . .."

Paul fought to regain his composure. They didn't have to make an arrest to question him. That smelled of Hoss Grender, the county's top law enforcement officer. Paul's stunned eyes scoured and the thought flashed.

Where's Carol?

He couldn't spot her. Instead, Sarah's face, like a heckler from hell, flashed in his mind . . . making him wish memories of the dead could be buried with them.

"Move," a cop commanded.

An officer propelled him toward the courtroom doors, the shove reminding him that the departed can haunt the living.

Just one person knew how badly and irreparably his life had shattered. Paul saw him following along. DeBona must have known they would arrest him that way. Maybe he even arranged it. As a cop pushed Paul toward a waiting squad car, he saw satisfaction shine in the eyes of Tony "Quick Fish" DeBona. The head of the Atlantic City crime family delivered what he promised—vendetta.

The man, who in some circles was referred to as the "Boss of the Boardwalk," had a large and powerfully built frame. At maybe eighty years of age, Paul figured, the man was just more than twice Paul's age. His olive complected face—at first glance so intimidating and worn—still bore traces of handsomeness in youth, a time when his thin silver hair must have been full and dark. Old eyes that glared so menacing must once have shined with aspirations of youth. Yet now, the black pools of those pupils bore into Paul's pale eyes. For a flashing moment, it was as if only the two men existed . . . each knowing what the other was thinking.

DeBona wanted him dead and Paul would strike back. He would have to take on the older man as well as the county legal system. A murder charge would carry the death sentence and he'd fight to stay alive.

Old man, he thought, almost as if conjuring, *be damned along the way.*

As a cop opened the squad car rear door, Officer Smith lowered Paul's head to shove him through, but not far enough. Paul was helpless to protect himself with his hands cuffed behind his back as his head was smashed into the car's roof. Until then, the lawyer had only heard about Smitty's trademark arrest technique from battered clients.

Dazed, he slumped in the car where a splash of vomit, no doubt a memento from an arrested drunk, made his stomach churn. He was just as sick knowing innocence can mean so little. Paul, more than anyone, knew what forces were at work. The web that snared was as sticky as the seat cover.

The roar of pounding surf filled old ears. Waves rushed to shore from afar, indeed far as his eyes could see. Tony Quick Fish had returned to the place he loved, standing on the boardwalk, sucking in sweet ocean air that invigorated like a potent elixir. His deep breaths stopped when he spotted movement from the corner of his eye.

A boardwalker, wearing baggy pants and an oversized sweatshirt, strolled close and braked. Tony realized the man's loose-fitting clothes could conceal a weapon.

This is how easily death can come, he thought.

The guy stuck his hand into his pocket, but another man moved faster. Bobby "Brains" Rubino, Tony's loyal underboss, watched his back from across the boards. Young for the position, yet quick-witted and fast-fingered, Bobby whipped his pistol from its shoulder holster. He cocked the hammer, then sighed when the stroller took a handkerchief to his schnoz, blew a blast, and moved along.

Tony nodded to the stocky associate he was grooming as a protégée. Bobby returned the gesture, while holstering the gun under his coat. He slicked back his hair, as if the fast pistol movement had disturbed his heavily greased 'do, then soberly stared up and down the boardwalk on guard.

Pivoting back to face the sea, the old man's thoughts returned to his former lawyer. Like Tony, Paul Cameron was gazing at the sharp teeth of death's open jaws. Tony had seen that the brutal murder would destroy Paul. He and the younger man had maintained quiet dealings. Tony had liked the lawyer from the start but the *avvocato* had crossed him and would pay the price.

The Boss of the Boardwalk had ordered his people to keep their distance from the official investigation.

"You know nothing," he had told them.

Once charged, Cameron would find little help. Tony chuckled knowing the murder case had all the glitz, glamour, and trash that made Atlantic City what it was. News of the lawyer's arrest would spread faster than the town's fifty-dollar hookers.

Nobody better knew what happened on or under the boardwalk than Tony DeBona. More than a historian, he was a slice of Atlantic City history, a role he recognized for what it was: thrilling and ugly all at once.

Old men should have more time to recollect the past, he thought, *perhaps a second lifetime for quiet reflection*.

But rumination was a luxury he could ill afford. Public hearings centering on his crime family were too well focused. Criminal investigators, who normally couldn't see with bifocals, delved into his organization with x-ray vision.

How? He again wondered.

At the same time, a tough Asian gang was moving into territory his crime family had controlled since prohibition. Even as Tony gazed at the sea, his men were dealing with them on the street.

Carmen Dog Face felt his pulse beat faster and his blood pressure rise. The muscle guy in Tony's crime family could be a lovable mutt of a man. Yet his floppy ears and droopy eyes hid a murderous nature that Dog Face loved to unleash. He watched his target and fought the urge to kill the man on the spot. The job was designed to send a message. Tony's *capo*, the mob captain with a ruthless reputation, had special plans.

Customers gathered round the young Chinese hood they called the Phantom. His dark hair was cropped short on the sides and hung long in back, flipping up like a duck's tail. Wearing a black leather jacket and an ear-to-ear smile, he greeted his buyers with high-fives. Phantom stood a block from their school yard, just outside the "drug free" zone where the law would double his prison sentence if cops caught him peddling his wares. He handed out small paper strips. Comic book heroes imprinted on them attracted young eyes. They helped him collect cash in small denominations that quickly multiplied.

"Cool," one youngster said as he passed Carmen's way.

Dog Face stopped the boy and took the paper strip from him. The kid's angered expression quickly turned worried as he looked up at the adult who had caught him red-handed.

"Here," Carmen said, handing him the ten bucks he had just spent. Dog Face shook his head and uttered advice. "Buy yourself real fuckin' candy."

As the kid sprinted away, Carmen studied the strip. They sweetened that kind of candy with LSD. Dog Face and his crew would stop the sales, but not from a sense of civic duty. True, it was. Tony's family forbade drug sales to children as an *anti famigilia.* But their business was territorial and organized drug trafficking incursions were *concorrenza non consentita*, competition unallowed.

Carmen gave his men the signal. As they moved, the Phantom spotted their trap, and darted across a vacant lot. He was almost around a bend when a larger pursuer tackled and pummeled him. The *capo* relished the enthusiasm that his wiry young buck showed but had to stop him.

"Vinny stop it for Christ's sake," he called out. "You're gonna kill him in the open. Just tie his hands behind his back and stick him in the car."

Carmen and the rest of his boys surrounded the Phantom and lashed his arms behind his back. As they lifted him to his feet, Dog Face looked around.

"Christ," he wheezed, spotting a school crossing guard walking their way. "A fucking witness."

The old woman came directly to them, a small stop sign on a stick used to direct traffic still in her hand. Her grand-motherly face was stenciled with concern. The Phantom smiled, no doubt realizing the men, who had captured him, would have to let him go. Carmen turned his head to avoid identification in case she called cops, but the woman tugged on Carmen's sleeve until he faced her. Close enough to smell coffee on her breath, he wondered.

What's she want?

The crossing guard answered without being asked.

"Slaughter this slime-ball," she said. "He's been selling dope to kids all year. Everyone's afraid to stop him."

Dog Face looked down with puppy eyes.

"We'll see he's not a problem anymore."

The woman turned to the drug dealer and raised her stop sign to wallop him. Carmen grabbed it as she pulled back to strike.

"Not necessary," he simply said.

As she returned to her crossing post, Carmen noticed he still had the stop sign in his hand. He played with it as his men shoved the Phantom into the trunk of their car. Desperately, the man shouted for help.

"I can't drive through town with this guy screaming," Vinny complained. "Why don't we just whack him, now?"

A howl broadcast from the closed trunk.

"Gag him," Carmen ordered.

"Ain't got nothing to gag him with."

Carmen held his temper in check. The young soldier was eager but dim witted.

"Use your socks," he directed.

Vinny removed his shoes. Sweaty socks proved to be a perfect mouth fit. The trunk closed and silently they drove away.

No one ever said one thing about Carmen Dog Face. No one ever said his bark was worse than his bite. Dog Face had nasty choppers. But he loved opera so Puccini's "*La Bohème*" blared from a boom box in an empty warehouse while his men worked methodically, using a crowbar to beat the Phantom, a street name he used to deal drugs in their territory. Phantom was blindfolded with a damp cloth and strung from the ceiling by heavy ropes that wrapped his wrists as they addressed their concern for his misdeeds.

Accompanied by a full orchestra and chorus, Pavarotti belted, "*O soave fancilla. . ..*"

The Phantom's wails were only a whisper under the great tenor's signing performance.

Stop a fuckin' minute and listen to what's coming," Carmen called to Vinny "C," the abbreviated and better way for the surname of Cissarelli to unfold.

With their pause in behavioral correction came a stellar performance.

"Just like you, Vinny, this is where Luciano hits them amazing high C notes. A lotta tenors can't hit them notes; they go to B-flats."

"Boss, can I get back to what we're doin' here. We're supposed to be kickin' ass."

"First, you listen. Then, you kick more ass."

Dog Face was right to insist. Pavarotti tossed off every high C in the short aria with the same astonishing brilliance that his men displayed teaching their lesson to the Phantom—and to every other dealer who might think about crawling onto their turf.

"Electrifying," Carmen noted, "ain't it?"

Vinny "C" struck a pose, stroking his chin as if in deep contemplation, then made an inquiry.

"Got any Milli Vanilli or Paula Abdul on that boom box? Like 'Forever Your Girl' or maybe—"

"Christ All Mighty," Dog Face snapped. "Get back to what you were doing."

The tape still spun, the tenor's singing voice filling their car when they dropped off the pusher, broken-boned and glassy-eyed. They had administered an overdose of his own medicine.

The Phantom laid in the gutter where his friends would find him. Glue affixed strips of paper, which were imprinted with comic book heroes, to his naked body. They rested him faceup, eyes still covered by the cloth wrapped around his head. Dampened with a gonorrhea solution collected from an accommodating source in the Frank Sinatra wing of Atlantic City Hospital, it would assure vision loss yielding blindness over time.

They shoved a stick deep into his throat. In his drugged haze the man's teeth somehow clenched it in place. The other end of the stick conveyed a message to his Asian crime family.

It read: "Stop."

Tony watched Dog Face joke with a handful of their boys in the Fairmont Tavern. Their crime family owned the joint, despite a straw man's name being on the deed and liquor license. The seedy dark-in-the-daytime bar in

Atlantic City's Duck Town section was the perfect place to bask in that kind of afterglow. Yet, detached from their exuberance, Tony knew retribution would follow. When the telephone behind the bar rang, one of their boys grabbed the call then whispered to Dog Face. The capo reported to his boss.

Tony saw droopy eyes and knew what news that call brought.

"Who?" he said.

"Vinny C."

Tony looked away. The young man was reckless. He had let his guard down to become an easy target.

"How?"

Dog Face rocked back and forth, filled with emotion.

"How?" Tony repeated.

"Tied down and carved. They peeled his face with a paring knife."

"Your man, Carmen. Did he have a family?"

"A girlfriend. They have a kid."

Tony shook his head. "See that the mother of his child has a little money. Just get her through the next couple of weeks. After all, this Vinny wasn't a made man."

He had never been initiated into the family. Besides, Tony figured, the young woman had their child out of wedlock like a prostitute. Tony had a heart for whores but morally children and marriage go hand in hand.

The quickness of the strike surprised him. He knew whose work it was. The Asians had contracted a special assassin to send their own message: they were ready to take on his small family. Tony had fought those wars in his youth. The cagy old Boss of the Boardwalk wondered if he still had the stamina. A breath came from deep inside, expelling air that was unnaturally thick and heavy.

Mio Dio, he thought, praying to God for strength.

Paul garnered his every ounce of resolve. Everything was happening so quickly that life seemed to blur. He was still getting accustomed to Sarah's death. Surely, he had reasons to wish her dead—her promise to raise a family that she refused to fulfill, her infidelity, her inability to truly love anyone but herself. The marriage had come too fast, as if she had been on safari to capture a man, who could afford her lavish tastes. Pulse-raising good looks, feigned affection, and steamy sexuality had been bait to snare him. Then, with an attention span short-lived and self-focused, Sarah tired of the relationship. She compelled Paul to leave their home while her divorce attorney litigated over marital assets.

Failure in personal life was a painful disappointment to a man accustomed to professional success. An unaccustomed feeling of guilt for the aborted marriage crept deep into his bones. It rounded the sharp edges of his animosity toward Sarah and opened the door to remorse when she died. His compassion came with recognition that he had entered the marriage too quickly. Passion had overcome prudence in a way he had never known. Raised to be cautious in affairs of the heart, Paul chided himself for letting down his guard. He hadn't taken time to spot her character flaws until too late. Besides, Sarah's death hardly freed him of the misery his life had become with her. It left him facing questions he couldn't answer.

A pock-faced plainclothes officer approached from the other side of the police interrogation room. He didn't speak so much as roar.

"Where were you when your wife was murdered?"

Paul looked around the stark place where he had so often represented clients. Now, it seemed smaller, bare walls ominously close and bearing in. He knew what he had to do.

"I need to place a call to counsel," Paul said.

"Who's your lawyer, Counselor?

"Lee Gunther."

"Gunther," the man grunted. "It figures. One high profile mouth maggot knows another.

"I'm exercising my right to counsel," Lee retorted. "You know what that means. Stop questioning."

The cop's eyes widened, then narrowed on his target.

"You're going to fry either way. Might as well talk."

The cop raised a cigarette to his lips and blew smoke into the lawyer's face.

"Where were you?"

Paul was too stunned to listen, not so dazed he'd talk. So quickly, he realized, life's treasures can be stripped. He had attained a measure professional respect, a wife whose beauty dazzled just enough to shade untamable flaws, and damn near every cliched trapping of success. Collected like so many baubles on a career rocket ride, he had moved too fast to see how riches can arrive at the price of spiritual bankruptcy.

Paul's thoughts turned. He reflected on where it had all begun, so far as he could tell—the path he had followed on that first trip to the Atlantic County courthouse. Like so much in life that happens at inception, his first criminal trial as a young lawyer commenced without considering consequences.

His inquisitor roared again,

"Tell us where the hell you were when Sarah Cameron was killed."

Paul tuned out the cop. He recalled the scenario that had cast his fate. The cop's mouth moved but Paul didn't hear him. Instead, he heard the fiery rhetoric of the Righteous Reverend Rich, who had clamored some six years earlier.

Chapter Three

Ain't No Tiny Virtues in Sin

"CLEOPATRA'S BEDCHAMBER was luxurious with pillows piled high and linens encased in jewel-studded silks from the Orient," the Reverend read in a booming voice. "Her attendants left with the wave of her hand, all but the brawny, bronzed man she commanded to remain. With huge pectorals and skillful hands, he wrapped her wrists in magical silk sheathes brought from the farthest reaches of the eastern domains. No words passed their lips as he anointed her bare flesh with mysterious oils that intoxicated her senses. The Queen of the Nile so softly sighed. She knew only he could quench the inferno burning in her loins."

Cleopatra moaned.

She's a tad horsey for a casino cocktail waitress, the Rev thought.

In 1978, when legalized gaming houses initially opened their doors in Atlantic City, higher standards governed hiring. Five years later, what laid before him in the dank and dirty hotel room was living proof that any cow in heels could land the job.

The Reverend placed his steamy novelette on the night table next to a reading lamp noticeably tilted left. He removed his pants and stood to face his queen. As he began to remove his clerical collar, she stopped him cold.

"Leave it on," she said in a deep, breathy voice, "and read me more."

He stood before her in his black shirt with white clerical collar, his deep-brown and muscular legs looking as if they didn't quite belong to his certainly not fat but, oh, assuredly barreled midsection. Garters held socks high above glossy patent-leather oxfords.

The skilled knots-man had tied her wrists to the headboard with a polyester sash from her uniform. She worked the night shift at Cleopatra's Barge inside Caesar's Casino on the boardwalk and that night she had called in sick to meet Reverend Rich for another clandestine rendezvous. She'd told her husband she'd be working late and, as usual, avoid waking him when she came home.

It's easy to fool a fool, she knew.

The Reverend turned a page in the well-worn paperback he had purchased on a visit to Philadelphia. For a moment, he wished it was easier to find a little harmless porn, something he could never be seen acquiring in his own community.

Ah, that day will never come, he mused before continuing in deep and resonating tones.

"The Queen of all the known lands had no choice but to accept his embrace. His powerful arms encircled her. The scent of his manliness filled her."

The Reverend hastened his pace, sprinting on the home stretch, as she laid naked, bound, quaking with pleasure from the fantasy that always fired her desire.

"Touch me," she pleaded. "Touch my breasts. Touch me and fill me."

Reverend Rich ignored her pleas, reading with greater fervor.

"The sight of his firm arousal weakened her. Her manservant would pound her with beastly strength . . . as the regal beauty shrieked in animalistic passion and submitted to her own insatiable desire for the secret lover."

The Revered steamed underneath his clerical collar, breathing fast, one hand grasping the tethered pages and the other wrapping his engorged member. He readied to leap upon the pasty flesh of his writhing wildebeest with force enough to collapse the rickety bed.

"Take your Queen," she pleaded. "Fill her love box with the seed of your jewels!"

"Lord," he cried, "I'm goin' in!"

Like a cannon blast, the outer door exploded from its frame. Flash bulbs from cameras blinded him. City police officers and investigators from the Atlantic County Prosecutor's Office burst in fighting for the best vantage points. A high-pitched voice screamed above all the commotion. At first the Reverend was uncertain whether the voice rose from a man or a woman. Then, a fat, slovenly wretch of a man stood before him. The squealer directed a newspaperman and a camera carrying detective.

"Take more pictures of the broad before we untie her."

Then, the demon screamed to police officers.

"Grab that little book and dust it in the lab for fingerprints."

Finally, he turned to the Reverend.

"Whatcha doin' with your pee stick, Padre?"

The Reverend had instantly deflated but remained too stunned to shove his flaccid organ under his shirt. Evidence of carnal intent remained in hand.

"Ain't no tiny virtues in sin," the fat man blasted.

The Reverend's head spun as he watched the man, whom he now deemed to be a demon, continue to bluster.

"Reverend Melvin Richards, you're charged with theft in the second degree. You have the right to remain silent. You have the right to an attorney. If you cannot afford. . .."

Righteous Reverend Rich, as he was fondly known, heard nothing else. How could he? Life just crashed on him. Respect he'd garnered among Atlantic County citizenry, particularly in the black community where he had risen from poverty in local housing projects, instantly vanished.

Rev thought of the movement he had helped spawn—"The Forgotten Children of Atlantic City." He'd been seeking funding for neighborhood youth educational and recreational activities from the New Jersey Casino Development Authority. The program was garnering support. National activist, Reverend Al Sharpton, was preparing to join a community march. All that Reverend Rich had hoped to accomplish, and all emoluments earned while long serving his community and the Lord, were laid waste.

He could think to do nothing but lower his head. He closed his eyes and reached for God.

"Hey, Rev," the man in charge called, "are you praying for forgiveness . . . or for a good lawyer?"

Just more than year later, the Reverend's Philadelphia lawyers focused on his defense.

"I can't try the case," Lee Gunther declared.

He ran his hand over blond hair, pulled back tight in a ponytail. Lee's tailor-made suit was his battle armor. Long hair and a polished look gave the lawyer the appearance of a rebel who'd fight for clients. His slight limp was rarely detectable yet caused the tall and lanky lawyer to think twice before leaping—a credo that manifested more than physically: Lee scrutinized courtroom adversaries before striking. He stroked his chin then laid out their imbroglio.

"Our client looks guilty as sin and the judge is on a rampage because we've already postponed this trial five times."

"Let's think this through," his law partner, Alphonse, responded less passionately.

Lee's dramatic flair was always counterbalanced by Al's subdued comportment. Together they were Mister Inside and Mister Outside, Lee championing causes in courtrooms while his counterpart cradled their books and records.

Al mused then then laid it out, covering familiar ground, to see if there wasn't something they may have overlooked.

"Our client is a respected bible-thumping black minister who's been boning his deacon's wife. The deacon learns and looks for a way to dick our guy back. Our guy is flashy. He seems to spend more than he makes. So, the deacon checks the church books and they show a discrepancy. Over time, our Righteous Reverend Rich has apparently snaked his way into one-hundred thirty-five thousand dollars from congregation collection plates.

Lee sat silently as his partner covered the problematic fact pattern that was so troubling in framing a trial defense. Sometimes rehashing spurns new notions.

"What's the deacon do about it?" Al queried. "He's patient. Waits to make his move until the Rev arranges another tryst with his wife in the same fleabag Atlantic City hotel. Bingo! The deacon has the County Prosecutor bust him for theft, nearly under the sheets with an adulterous wife."

Al tugged on both ends of his bow tie, huffed for air, and marveled.

"You gotta admire the good deacon's thoroughness. He provides the Prosecutor's Office with records to land a major larceny conviction in exchange for having the Reverend busted as embarrassingly as possible. The deacon will probably get to dump his trampy wife all in the same stroke. Nice touch."

"That wasn't the deacon's notion," Lee said flatly. "Atlantic County's chief prosecutor lives for these moments. He arranged to conduct the arrest with local press on scene. The guy's savvy enough to even bring the reporter who offers his office the best 'law and order' coverage."

"You know this prosecutor well?"

"Horace Grender? We attended Penn State at the same time. He was a legend even then. They caught him in the back of a Ford, parked outside a fraternity party, with his rod up the rear of some prom queen. She screeched so loud half the frat ran out to see Hoss with a world-class grin. Afterward, they bestowed a moniker: Horace Grender the Rear Ender. Still has a reputation for finding working women in Atlantic City who'll cater to his needs."

"He also has a reputation as a hell of a prosecutor."

"Hell of a prosecutor—and hell of a sodomizer."

The two seasoned lawyers paused. Al adjusted thick horn-rimmed eyeglasses that so often slid off the tip of his pug nose. His coat jacket was on the back of the chair, exposing paisley suspenders matching his bow tie. He maintained accounts of the firm's affairs, knowing Lee preferred keeping everything in his quick brain rather than on paper. Differing approaches made for valuable discussions: one perhaps spotting what the other overlooked, though Lee tended to miss very little. They employed lawyers—young men and women—who performed less entertaining scutwork that makes a law firm function.

The firm's reputation for achieving excellent results was their bread and butter. Nobody walked into a law office because they heard about unhappy outcomes. Knowing that made the Reverend's case, well, a pig of a file.

Worse was knowing the Rev failed to cough up his fee. He had promised to deliver cash and Lee had repeatedly postponed the case so the Reverend could find funds. After all, payment up-front is the Cardinal Rule of criminal law. Clients can't pay when the case is done, if they're rotting in jail. And, when a case is won, clients don't need their lawyer anymore, so their prevalent thought becomes: Why pay for what you don't need?

The seasoned counselors considered their quandary, knowing the unavoidable trial was fast approaching.

"All rise," the bailiff cried.

The judge swept into the room with his black robe whisking behind as if in a breeze.

His court crier called out: "On this day, the tenth day of April, nineteen-hundred and eighty-four, Court is now in session, The Honorable Edwin C. Hastings, Judge of the Superior Court of New Jersey, presiding."

Lee apprehensively peered up to the bald jurist, who was string-bean lean, humorless, and stone-faced. This was one of those times when Lee found it annoying to take that upward glance. By design, courtrooms elevate a judge's bench to make participants subliminally aware, if not wholly cognizant, of their lesser status to the jurist above them.

Equally disconcerting, Lee knew Hastings' predisposition. As a former a prosecutor, he favored the prosecution . . . just as some judges, who ascend to the bench from the defense Bar, naturally orient themselves to the defendant's side of issues. What wasn't natural was

Judge Hastings extreme attitude. He tolerated neither real nor imagined lack of respect from defense counsel.

At the prosecutor's table, Lee envisioned Hoss Grender as a bag of bloat in a nearly stretched-to-its-limit suit, topping scuffed shoes. Lee wondered if being slovenly was an advantage. Grender hadn't changed or aged. Well, how would anyone notice if he did?

"The bailiff will call the trial list," the judge began.

A court officer sang out: "The first case on your Honor's trial list is the State of New Jersey versus Melvin Richards."

Judge Hastings looked toward Grender.

"That's the case against Reverend Melvin Richards, is it not, Mister Prosecutor?"

"Yes, it is, your Honor." The pudgy prosecutor beamed. "The state is ready for trial."

"Very good. Defense Counsel, enter your appearance. We can pick a jury later this morning."

Lee rose and cleared his throat. "The defense isn't ready for trial, Sir."

The judge's neck muscles bloated; his face flushed. Spittle flew from his mouth with his words.

"Mister Gunther, this matter is at the top of my trial list because it's one of the oldest untried cases in our county. He paused, then called to his court clerk, "What's the arrest date on our docket entries?"

"More than year ago, your Honor," the woman answered, as she shifted through neatly stacked paperwork until finding the date and announcing, "Exactly fifteen months ago . . . to the day."

Judge Hastings lifted his gavel, lightly pounded his palm and shot: "Counselor, why can't you pick a jury today?"

Lee couldn't explain that his client needed more time to fleece his flock, so he approached the issue another way.

"We're waiting on a key defense witness to arrive, a critical witness we expect to appear given a thirty-day continuance, your Honor."

"Who's that, Mister Gunther?"

"Mister Green, your Honor. The defense is waiting on Mister Green."

Judge Hastings grabbed his gavel and slammed the open palm of his hand. Soft raps on his flesh came more quickly as if the mallet and his brain were working at the same speed. His movements generated a smile that filled the prosecutor's face the way jelly fills a donut. Lee felt a sinking sensation, as if the floor were melting. At last, Grender's high-pitched nasal drawl arrived like a rope thrown to Lee while being swallowed by quicksand.

"Your Honor, the prosecution doesn't object to the defense request for a continuance to produce their witness. The State merely wants to see justice done."

Lee knew what Grender was doing. He was sunning in the glow of good publicity from prosecuting a local-celebrity defendant and he'd muster more self-promotion when they re-listed the case. Lee surveyed his surroundings. The full courtroom showed just how much public interest the case engendered. The Righteous Reverend's fiery sermons were renown as the horse that dove off the Atlantic City Steel Pier into a water tank. They had to blindfold that horse to get it to leap. Lee felt like he could use one, too, as Judge Hastings exploded.

"Counselors come to sidebar! We're going off the record."

Lee approached from behind Grender. Then, Hastings spoke in the low tones of sidebar conversation that travel no farther than the hearing of the attorneys before him.

"Mister Gunther, do I correctly infer . . . you want this case postponed because your client hasn't paid his fee?"

Lee nodded. The judge's eyebrows twitched, his cue-ball head making bushy brows more prominent as they moved in high gear.

"Sir, I'm aware of your reputation as a fine litigator so I'm inclined to grant a final adjournment. But Counselor, I warn you. If this trial doesn't start when it's rescheduled, you'll spend time where I'm sending your client after it's over."

Hastings turned to his court reporter and blustered.

"Trial starts in two weeks—whether defense counsel secures his witness or not. Call the next case, Bailiff."

Lee returned to the counsel table and grabbed the Rev's shoulder.

"Deliver your retainer to my office next week," he admonished.

Then, Lee stormed from the courthouse. Stiffness from his bad knee couldn't slow him. Lee pointed his white Corvette toward the Philadelphia expressway and floored its accelerator. The powerful V-8 sped through bustling Atlantic City streets.

He barely noticed the attractive young woman, who screamed at him. Lee just caught a quick glimpse of her in his rearview mirror. What he saw nearly enticed him to return. That kind of woman always brought a man back.

Chapter Four

Show and Tells

PRELL LEAPED AWAY FROM the white sports car that sped like an ivory bullet.

"Slow down, you son of a bitch!" she shouted.

The Corvette just missed hitting her as she crossed the street. Still catching her breath, she watched it race from the county courthouse toward the expressway.

"Somebody's in a hurry to get back to Philadelphia," she correctly surmised.

The bundle afire was eighteen and loving every minute of it. A mop of dark locks surrounded what she had confidently decided was the sweetest face on the planet. When she smiled, she observed, the world did, too. She lived her cliché inside a lithe body with great, though hardly child-bearing hips that completed her petite portrait. When you know what you have and how good it is, confidence exudes from every pore. Prell perspired poise and self-assurance without knowing how quickly and cruelly naive notions are sometimes stripped away.

She paraded to her day date, catching appreciative stares from heads atop quickly craned necks. Her service had lined her up with an elderly gentleman, who liked watching young women do themselves. That's fine. She would move and moan in bed, using adult toys stuffed into her oversized handbag. Prell could even enjoy herself, while her date found pleasure peering. She liked show and tells.

Prell arrived just before noon, and knocked on the casino hotel room door, donned as directed. Well nearly so, in a faux-leopard skin coat—instead of the mink he requested, and she could ill afford—and in high heeled boots that made her tower over the diminutive senior citizen who answered her raps.

"Mister Bonavich?" she engaged with her warmest smile to assure she had found the right room.

"No," he answered. "Call me Daddy."

Prell entered the suite and Daddy closed the door. She felt old eyes soak in her youth. Perhaps the warmth left in their fading glow made it easier for her to overlook their age difference. Daddy was wrinkled and frail, yet nattily attired in his blue blazer and orange "Princeton Tiger" necktie. And, those grey eyes were beginning to sparkle with the fire of an eager, young stud.

When all else goes on 'em, she reflected with an understanding beyond her years, *appreciation shows in their peepers, not their peters.*

She wasted no time, declaring: "It'll be five hundred dollars, Daddy."

"Five hundred bucks!" His voice crackled. "Young lady, why do you need so much money?"

She dropped her coat to the floor, donning only earrings and boots. His stare warmed pert nipples that jutted upward from dark areolas.

"Daddy," she teased, "I need money because I don't have any clothes."

Prell and Daddy passed their morning in the suite bedroom, then spent the afternoon clothes shopping for baby. By dinnertime, he even slipped a tip into baby's coat pocket, as she cooed.

"Goodbye, Daddy-kins!"

"I Love being a Girl," Prell hummed, as she exited the casino, just as always. She headed for the rear casino service doors to avoid vice cops and casino security personnel, who checked for working women at main entrances.

There, she came across the large frame of a well-dressed gentleman. He smiled, as he courteously held the door for her, and gave a knowing wink. He seemed to know why she exited through the service door.

Yet how, she wondered, *did he*?

Prell and Tony Quick Fish went their separate ways.

Chapter Five

Burdens of the Unrepentant

RIGHTEOUS REVEREND RICH FELT THE BURDENS of Job weigh on his shoulders. He couldn't collect any cash. After his arrest, parishioners kept his hands off the church coffers. Despite uncertain feelings toward local law enforcement held by some members of his congregation, his flock was evenly divided: half hated their Reverend for stealing from them, while half hated him for seducing the deacon's wife. Dodging stones cast for his sins naturally crippled his livelihood and love life.

Over time, folks might remember the good he had done in a long and mostly selfless career. His kind words had touched every community member, whether on the birth of a child or death of a beloved family member. He was a good man, accused of having done bad. Until they could forgive him, the Rev did what he did best. He preached. Reverend Rich vociferated from the pulpit, reminding his flock that flesh is weak and to forgive is truly divine.

His lawyers demanded to meet with him, ominously Rev felt, on Friday the thirteenth. So, broke he couldn't afford bus fare, the Rev sneaked onto a free casino bus returning a junket to Philadelphia from a day trip. Days before his trial would start, he arrived without Mister Green.

Shawna greeted the Reverend from behind the reception counter, holding a nail file in mid-air.

"Mr. Gunther would like you to take a seat," the young black woman said. I'll be glad to handle your fee payment, while you wait."

The customarily vociferous Rev could only turn his head from side to side.

"Oh dear," Shawna sighed, "that's never good."

She joined the Rev, also swinging her head from side to side before returning to square her ballerina nails.

Intuitively aware that Judge Hastings was greasing a skillet to fry him, perspiration dripped into an uncomfortable pool in the Rev's undershorts.

"What will I do, he panicked, *if my lawyers refuse to represent me?*

Lee and his partner racked their brains in a mahogany-paneled law library.

"We can't get out of this case," Alphonse said as he flipped through the Cannons of Ethics. He poked his finger at the controlling rule. "Drop the case, now, and you'll get a disciplinary reprimand at least—and probably a suspension—when His Holiness, out there in our lobby, gets convicted and thrown in prison."

"I can't walk back into that courtroom, Al." Lee's hands lifted his leg from the chair where he had propped it. Wincing, he continued, "The trial judge is certifiably nuts and hates my guts for not trying the case sooner."

"Are you sure there's no plea offer we can take?"

"Grender knows he has a conviction coming. The only offer he's made is to lock up the Reverend for the maximum term on the offense. There's a lot of local interest and Grender feeds off this kind of case to assure reappointment to the chief prosecutor position."

Alphonse groaned as Lee called their receptionist on the intercom. "Shawna, please bring Reverend Rich into the law library."

"Should I offer him another cup of coffee?"

"Offer him a shot of bourbon and a beer chaser for the news we've got for him."

"For real, Mister Gunther?"

Lee thought for a second.

"No," he finally answered, "but later bring it for me."

The Rev entered the library and sat at the other end of the long conference table. Alphonse probed for a way to set their account straight.

"Where are your counsel fees?"

The Reverend didn't answer.

Lee rose and spoke with near theatrical force that came naturally from trying cases.

"Rev, let me see your wristwatch."

Lee took the watch from the Rev's wrist and held it up to the ceiling light.

"That's a beautiful Rolex."

Lee slipped it onto his own wrist and continued.

"You remember what I told you when we first discussed your case, don't you? Take good care of your lawyer and your lawyer will take good care of you."

The Reverend nodded affirmatively.

"That's the Golden Rule in the legal profession and you broke it. That's worse than banging your deacon's wife, worse than stealing from your church, and worse than any sin you can commit before God Almighty."

They all paused as a young associate walked into the room.

Paul Cameron had just graduated law school ranked in the middle of his class. He took solace in the lawyers' adage that the "A" students in law school become law professors, the "B" students become judges, and the "C" students make all the money. The road to fortune, however, is paved with heavy dues. As the firm's youngest associate, he slaved from sunup past sundown pursuing menial tasks. Unseasoned associates only entered courtrooms when a senior lawyer needed someone to carry a brief case.

He walked to green volumes of statutes he had come to research. Paul noticed the three men in the room were looking at him as if he were the answer to a prayer.

"Rev," he heard Lee say, "you know, there's a first time for everything in life. I bet you remember the first time you gave a sermon. We all remember the first time we got laid. I bet those first times turned out better than any of us expected."

Then, Lee introduced Paul to the Reverend as his new trial lawyer.

"Good luck," Lee said, as he patted the Rev's back, and ushered him out the door.

Paul knew they'd both need plenty. And, while most young lawyers would've quaked, he eagerly grabbed the Reverend's file. Even if Paul didn't know all the law, he would study every relevant fact. Lee uttered comforting words of advice to him before leaving for the day. Then, anxious to prepare, Paul turned the file upside down and waited for its contents to pour onto his desk.

Nothing fell out. Puzzled, he looked inside to find two pieces of paper—a handwritten IOU from the Reverend and the criminal complaint accusing the Rev of major larceny. True to form, nothing was in Lee's file. Everything was in his head and that quick-thinking noggin was nowhere in sight.

Paul suddenly realized how much trouble he and the Rev would face in the morning. He worried, but not for himself. Loyalty ran deep in his blood. He would fight hard for his client yet doubted that would be enough. Paul looked into the file folder again hopefully and found nothing.

How, he wondered with wide eyes, *do you win a case with nothing*?

Chapter Six

Wide Eyes

HALF A CENTURY EARLIER, Tony DeBona had been young and wide eyed, like so many others who came as immigrants to the United States. Italians opened New Jersey's first Roman Catholic church and its first spaghetti factory at the turn of the nineteenth century. They wrote to friends in the old country who brought rosary beads, meatballs, and a wealth of human spirit. Thus, the meatball met the meatloaf in the melting pot. For the next 150 years, they came filled with wonder, youthful Antonio DeBona among them.

His family emigrated from the rugged Gargano peninsula, a mountainous region on the southeastern spur of the Italian boot. The journey commenced by sailing west on a rig to Salerno, just north of Sicily, where they booked the lowest level steamer passage to the New World.

Opportunity abounded, they heard, in Atlantic City, a town chock full of gentility and crassitude all at the same time. There, the elegance of grand hotels attracted visitors. The boardwalk, originally constructed as a narrow mile-long promenade, had been rebuilt after each major storm washed it away. Upon his arrival, it existed as it would remain, forty-feet wide and four-miles long with an array of luring attractions. The town had something to offer every taste: pristine beaches, amusement piers, boardwalk shops, stages for the biggest stars, and dark dens for more ribald entertainment. Though the Great Depression of 1929 had brought hardship to America, the city by the sea prospered.

Relatives in the town's small Italian American community found Tony and his father labor assisting brick masons building a new hotel on the boardwalk. They had no skills but could carry bricks and mortar. To get the work, Tony's father told the job boss, who wasn't an Italian, that the men in his family had been master brick layers for generations. An Italian would have known those skills were rare in their province, but he easily fooled the big German immigrant.

The man stroked his square chin. With short-cropped blond hair he looked like a master sergeant in the Prussian army.

"How old's your boy?" he asked Tony's father.

Tony was fifteen but looked older. Already larger than his father, he was approaching six feet, and was broad shouldered. Thick dark locks folded down over his brow. His dark eyes were alert.

"My son's eighteen, Sir."

The foreman cast a disbelieving glance.

"Well, if he works for me, he'll get old fast enough," the man drawled. "You'll work from sunrise to sundown every day except Sunday. The pay's twenty dollars a week, but you'll give half back in employment taxes."

Those taxes were divided between the big German and the Black Hand—mobsters with roots tracing back to 1750 in Naples and Sicily, who engaged in extortion and other "protection" schemes, preying mostly upon the Italian immigrant community.

"Do as you're told. A thousand guineas would swear off pasta for these jobs. Am I understood?"

"Of course, Sir," Tony's father said with eyes meekly cast down. "We're indebted to you."

Tony turned from his Papa. He couldn't bear to see him grovel, but knew the family had to eat.

Italian brick workers called their foreman "the Kaiser" behind his back. He ran the job site with iron knuckles wrapped around his fist. The work was hard, but Tony and his family ate, while many other Americans suffered ravages of the harsh economic times. Tony took to his labor and new life at the seashore. The town of passions stirred his blood; its virtues and vices becoming his own—and some so sweet.

On a warm Sunday afternoon, the sweetest of all enticed. Tony wore his only suit, strolling the boardwalk with friends from the construction site. They tipped their skimmers at passing young ladies, then set the fashionable straw hats back on their heads to engage in earnest appraisals.

"Such *melones* on that one," a young man proclaimed in tribute to two of God's grandest adornments.

Many beauties graced the boards but for Tony there was only one.

What a vision, he thought.

She, like Tony, was an Italian immigrant yet they were so different. He had grown brawny lifting bricks, while she was a delicate beauty, olive-complected and raven haired.

That day, she walked with her family, all decked in fineries. On the Sabbath, the promenade became a fashion show with boardwalkers adorning their "Sunday best" to stroll between attractions or ride in hundreds of wicker and wooden pushcarts. Cart operators paid a license fee to the city and a cart tax to the Irish mob that controlled the town, while permitting the local Black Hand to perpetrate their malpractices among the Italian immigrant community and allowing a Negro gang to work among their own.

Tony was infatuated.

"Who is she?" he asked his *paisans*.

"Forget her, Tony," one young man sighed. "Her father is the master chef at the Saint Dennis Hotel. They're from Casale D'Avellino. Their noses ride too high for a lowly mortar man."

"They're Italian," Tony responded indignantly, eager to meet the young woman, yet knowing his companion was right. Unlike Tony's poor roots in the Italian countryside, she came from a sophisticated town in the Provence of Salerno. Her parents would see him as unsuitable for a daughter with such charms. He watched them leave the concert hall at the Million Dollar Pier, then left his friends, following close behind the family, all while hoping for the impossible: a way to meet her.

As the summer sun beat, Tony overheard the girl's father call for a glass of Brighton Punch to cool his palate.

Before the "noble experiment of prohibition," as President Herbert Hoover referred to it, the famous punch served at the Brighton Hotel had a renowned reputation as a refreshing and potent intoxicant. They had allowed ladies only two glasses of the concoction a day. Hearty men teetered after three, but prohibition converted the drink into the virgin sister of itself. Alcohol was no longer openly served at the boardwalk hotels, though it flowed freely in the town's speakeasies. Some felt the most ignoble element of the noble experiment was the ruination of the town's most famous cocktail.

Nonetheless, the nattily dressed older man would enjoy a single glass, *sans* alcohol, at the Brighton. The girl's mother would no doubt call for an iced lemonade, while their children sampled a wide variety of colas in the grand dining room. The father stopped three pushcart men and settled upon a price to roll them down the boards. Just then, Tony heard her name for the first time.

"Lena," her father called, "take the last cart with your sister."

Tony watched her parents and brothers settle into the first two carts, while Lena and her sister took the third that followed. As the carts passed through crowds, Tony seized his opportunity. He walked behind Lena's cart, whispered in the push man's ear, then put coins in the man's pocket to take over his job. When Lena pointed to a window display of women's apparel Tony took the opportunity to speak.

"Those dresses aren't good enough for so gorgeous a young lady."

Face beaming, Lena turned toward the cart pusher, who had made so bold an assessment.

"Look at this one," she declared to her sister. "This push man thinks he's a fashion expert," she teased. "Are you a designer?"

"I know women's fashion," he bragged. "I once worked in the textile business."

She smiled knowingly.

"Did you sweep the factory floor?"

Tony realized the young beauty could look in his eyes and know everything about him.

"Now, I'm building the Windsor Hotel," he boasted, chest filling with pride.

"So, you're an architect and a fashion expert," Lena offered playfully.

They spoke easily and arrived at the Brighton with Tony wondering.

How could so many boards on the walk have passed this quickly?

As Lena's parents disembarked from their stroller just ahead, Tony and Lena looked to each other with eyes that conveyed unspoken feelings. Tony knew he had to act quickly if he was to see her again. His words rushed.

"May I escort you to a show next Sunday?"

"Papa and Mamma will never permit it," Lena's sister interjected.

Tony held his breath, waiting for her answer.

Lena felt as if she were in a dream. She had seen the handsome boy about town but recognized the accent that declared he came from the Gargano hills. Her parents would consider him a ruffian. In America they called Italian immigrants eye-talians, dagos or worse. Ironically, from that prejudice, those who considered themselves natives of a particular town or province first became aware of their national identity as Americans. Still, regional prejudices were difficult to overcome.

From the corner of her eye, Lena saw her father tipping the pushcart men and coming toward Tony last. Time running out, Lena's desire to see the boy again overcame prudence. She spoke without considering the consequences.

"I'll meet you after mass at the Garden Pier."

Her sister blurted, "How will you ever sneak away? Papa will rap you with his belt if he learns."

Too late for reconsideration, her father approached. He placed a coin in Tony's hand without noticing the change in push men. As she and her family walked away, Lena looked over her shoulder. She and Tony kissed goodbye with eyes only. Then, when Lena entered the hotel with her family, her sister whispered in her ear and both giggled.

"What's so funny?" her father said.

"Oh, nothing Papa. Just girl talk. Can I have a large shrimp bowl?"

Lena's father nodded. "Of course, sweetheart. You may have anything you desire."

Lena wished that were true, because what she really wanted was to spend more time with Tony and next Sunday seemed so far away.

"You wops are gonna work faster or you're off this job site," the Kaiser hollered to Tony and his father. They carried bricks in wheelbarrows to upper floors of the hotel where master brick layers piled them high. The masons worked fast. As the building rose, it became more difficult to reach the upper levels with heavy materials. Tony's father appeared so tired and pale.

"Papa rest," Tony said. "To hell with the Kraut."

"Go on ahead of me," his father said. "I just need a break—only a minute, Antonio."

Tony studied his father. He stood beside a loaded wheelbarrow, dripping in sweat and wheezing to catch his breath. Still, with a wave of his hand, his father sent his son back to work. Tony lifted his load and hauled it up planks that wound around the structure to the top floors where masons waited. Tony's back muscles flexed. He moved deliberately to avoid losing his balance on the rickety incline that rose five stories high. Stopping at the top, he yelled to the brick layers.

"*Paisons*, when will you teach us your craft? These loads get too heavy as the day goes on."

"You're a young man, Antonio," one of the older masons replied. "I carried bricks and mortar for three years before they trained me. Be patient."

Tony expelled a long breath.

I'm young, he thought, *but my father isn't.*

Below, the Kaiser spotted Tony's father.

"What did I tell you?" the Kaiser roared. "Get your guinea ass moving!"

He kicked his work boot into the tired man's butt to the amusement of surrounding workers.

"Move, you lazy son of a bitch, before I boot you from one end of the boardwalk to the other."

Laughter on the ground level attracted Tony's attention five stories up. Instinctively, he reached to his pocket for his stiletto as he watched the German humiliate his much smaller father. The brick masons knew what Tony was thinking and what he grasped in his pocket. Many Italian immigrants carried sharp blades.

"Don't use that thing," an older man cautioned. "Think. Your family can't afford trouble. How will they eat? Turn your eyes, Antonio."

Tony couldn't turn away. He watched the Kaiser spit on his father's shoes and point to the building's upper stories. Then, Tony saw his father lift the load and trudge toward the planks that twisted around upward grading. Seeing Papa debased ate at his guts. He wondered what to tell him, knowing the proud man had lost face. He waited at the fourth floor so they could speak privately on the scaffolding. When his father came into view, Tony saw he was pale. He set down his load and feebly grabbed his chest.

"Why can't I breathe?" his father gasped, reaching his hand toward Tony. Then, as if in slow motion, Papa tipped over the scaffolding.

Tony lunged for his father's outstretched hand. Their fingers touched for a split-second that seemed longer yet Tony couldn't stop the fall. His father dropped into a scaffold, spun around, and sailed down headfirst.

"Papa!" Tony called before bolting down the ramp.

On the ground, he shoved through workers crowding around the broken body. When Tony pierced their ranks,

Tony eyes fixed on his father's skull—crushed like a broken flowerpot, expelling blood, brains, and life. Tony's knees buckled as he collapsed to cradle Papa in muscular arms. Grief and rage erupted as the Kaiser yelled.

"All right, back to work, all of you."

Someone brought a blanket to cover the corpse that only moments earlier had been a man.

"Shit!" the Kaiser exclaimed. "Gotta hire another guinea."

Tony reached again for his stiletto. His emotions urged him to stab the big German, but his instincts told him to wait. He followed the intuition he would learn to trust in years ahead. He would take time. *Vendetta* was something Tony knew from his homeland. At the right time and place, he would restore his father's honor.

Lena shared everything with her sister. They weighed the risks of meeting Lena's young man against the certainty of severe punishment if their parents discovered.

So, thought Lena, *time to devise a plan.*

They would return from mass with their family and remain in their Sunday clothes. Lena would say that girls from their parish school were meeting on the boardwalk, properly chaperoned of course, to spend the afternoon. They would both meet the handsome young man. The plan seemed likely to succeed, because Papa would be working. As master chef, he was privileged to enjoy only a few Sundays with his family and the girls would take advantage of their opportunity.

Lena dressed herself in each outfit she owned, from head to toe, often during the week. Nothing was special enough, so she asked her mother for permission to buy a new dress.

"Why, little princess?" her mother joked. "Think you'll meet your prince charming?"

Lena feared Mama had read her mind. Saturday night she entered bed with her sister at the usual hour. They talked until her sister could no longer keep her eyes open and Lena chided her sleepy bedmate.

"What's wrong?" she teased. "Do you like to sleep at night?"

"Leave me alone," her sister moaned, "or I'll tell Mama where you're going tomorrow."

"You wouldn't dare," Lena screeched. "You're such a cruel thing to have for a sister."

"Close your eyes, Lena. Let me be."

Lena closed her eyes, but she was too excited to sleep.

Tony's heart also raced. He drank for the courage he would need that night. He swallowed hard but saw clearly. As liquor raced down his pipes, a mean spirit filled him. Tony walked to where he'd heard he would find the Kraut, then waited in the dark. No signs or stage billings adorned the speakeasy, but mirthful sounds from Eddie Cantor's musical revue flowed into the street. The comedian, dancer, pianist, and singer specialized in the "illustrated song," singing as accompanying images painted on glass slides projected on stage. The "Apostle of Pep" also shared humorous stories, mostly of his family, filling out the popular act.

The crowd began to depart, and Tony searched intensely.

Where's the big German?

The man wasn't with them.

"Goddamn," he cursed himself. "I should have followed the Kraut from his home to make sure he hadn't changed plans."

As Tony set to leave, he heard a commotion. He turned back to see the big German drunkenly stumble from the club. Tony's heart pounded faster as the Kraut staggered down a side alley. Tony followed. Calls of intemperate merriment filled the air. So focused on what he was about to do, he didn't care if anyone was looking. Before him the Kraut bent and vomited into a large garbage can.

Now, Tony thought, *now!*

Filled with rage, his stiletto's blade slit the German's jugular vein and opened his neck from front to back.

"What's going on down there?" a woman called into the dead-end alley.

The big German fell against the can with a clatter.

"Hey! What are you doing?" a man from the street screamed.

Tony turned. An overhead alley lamp shone like a spotlight on his face.

"We see you, boy," the man called.

"Call for police," the woman shouted.

Two men rushed into the alley toward him: Tony's *paisons*, who helped stuff the Kraut's body into the garbage can headfirst. They lifted it out of the alley and into their waiting truck. The old vehicle raced through crowded streets to Gardner's Basin Pier where they loaded the Kraut filled can onboard a boat waiting with its motor running. As the small fishing vessel chugged from the docks, out of the Atlantic City Inlet and into the ocean, Tony plied the trade he had learned. He mixed a batch of cement mortar and filled the garbage can in which they had stuck the Kraut headfirst. Only the man's lower torso and legs stuck out. Tony evened off the mortar at the top with a trowel.

"Good work, Antonio," an older friend observed. "We'll make a mason of you yet. But, you know, they usually plant 'em feet first.

"That'll be my signature," Tony replied. "Sink him face down."

The cement set as their boat chugged. When they dumped the heavy can into calm ocean waters, it quickly sank to the fishes.

As they returned to shore, bright stars seemed to celebrate. He returned to the club where they'd been drinking so he could finish the evening as if nothing had happened. Tony ordered gin and the bartender studied him. When prohibition barred adults from drinking, the flourishing speakeasies served adults as well as minors. What's the difference? After all, it's all illegal. Criminalizing mundane transgressions—like imbibing spirits—lowers every standard for obedience to the law.

"Someone wants to buy you a drink in the back room," the bartender said.

Tony knew better than to go there. The Black Hand ran the place. Like many clubs in town, a straw man was designated as owner, who was really a front for the Italian crime family. In the back an illegal gaming parlor was filled with men Tony had no interest in meeting.

"No, thanks," he replied graciously. "I buy my own drinks."

Three large men came from behind him. Tony recognized them as hoods, who collected employment taxes from Italian workers on paydays. No laborer had courage to resist the men with reputations for casual violence. Stone faced, one of the collectors, whose huge lips looked like slices of raw liver, uttered words that chilled Tony.

"Someone must talk to you about a friend of ours who's missing."

They ushered Tony into a large backroom where cheering spectators filled gaming tables.

Two tomcats, chained in harnesses, descended into a miniature boxing ring. Trained to fight, the champion lacked an ear and an eye, no doubt sacrificed in prior matches. Only one animal would survive. Hundreds of dollars would change hands on wagers. The old cat's fur stood on end as its feet touched the floor. Ear-stinging howls rose from both animals as first blood spilled. Thirsty for more, the crowd's roar reverberated against clapboard walls. Tony felt a shove in the back to move him along and wondered whether he or the old cat would leave the place alive.

Chapter Seven

A Valley of Doom

ON MAY 8, 1984, REVEREND RICH LUMBERED into the courtroom head low and slow, as if he had descended to a valley of doom.

At the defense table Paul sat behind every practitioner's manual and trial handbook he could lug in his oversized briefcase. Thinking on your feet wins legal arguments in court, not tabletop research. Yet the books made Paul feel more secure. If serving no other purpose, he'd hide behind them when the judge started yelling.

Paul watched Hoss Grender wink to his trial team's newest member at the prosecution table. She adjusted her chair, pulling it away from the man, perhaps an indication of uneasiness around her boss. The strikingly tall Assistant County Prosecutor had no more experience than Paul and had introduced herself when he entered the courtroom. Her cordialness helped allay his jitters: he justifiably felt like an amateur ball player batting first time in the big leagues.

Paul watched Carol adjust her black jacket over a skirt. She had called the garb her courtroom costume. During their brief conversation, she had admitted to feeling out-of-place dressing so formally after years in college and law school wearing blue jeans. Paul admired her style and knew she would quickly become comfortable in her new attire. Carol had the makings of a first-class lawyer. She looked his way, but Judge Hastings diverted Paul's attention.

"Mister Prosecutor," the judge called out, "you may deliver your opening address to the jury."

Grender rose to speak, brimming with confidence that comes from knowing your evidence is strong and your opposition is weak. Peering from behind his book fortress, Paul wondered why he hadn't chosen a dental college instead of law school. Repairing molars seemed easier and the consequence of unintended malpractice less severe.

What's at stake, Paul thought, *is my client's liberty*.

"Ladies and gentlemen of the jury," Grender began, "the State will present evidence proving the defendant stole one-hundred thirty-five-thousand dollars from church collection plates over a period of seven years. This man," Grender said, pointing a stubby finger at the Reverend, "took his congregation's money without consent from his parishioners. You'll see indisputable evidence that this so-called man of the cloth is guilty of theft by deception. He committed a despicable crime while using the Lord's name for personal gain. The defendant broke mankind's law and God's commandments to satisfy his selfish desires."

Grender was on fire. Paul innately sensed he should have objected to the inflammatory arguments, but they don't teach that kind of thing in school. Lawyers learn from courtroom experience. He let Grender have his way and saw the result. Jurors studied the Reverend with unconcealed contempt. The jury box filled with sourpusses. Grender had them hating Paul's client before a single witness had testified. When the harm was done, Grender sat and folded his arms across his chest, a picture of pudgy smugness and contentment.

Silence enveloped the courtroom. Paul's turn had come to address the jury, but he remained seated. Judge Hastings beckoned from the bench.

"Defense counsel, don't you have something you would like to say?"

Paul looked at the Righteous Reverend Rich, then rose to tell the jury what Lee had suggested before leaving him with the nearly empty file folder.

"Folks," Paul began, speaking in a slow rhythm that allowed time to look each juror in the eye, "I've never done this before. It's my first case. Please forgive me if I make any mistakes and try not to hold it against my client."

Paul sat. Each juror looked stunned. They peered at each other. Then just as Lee had promised, they smiled understandingly. Some chuckles rippled through the courtroom. Even Judge Hastings looked bemused as he stretched his neck trying to spot Paul over the stacked books.

"Is that it, Mister Cameron?" the judge called.

"I think so, Sir. Thank you."

The state methodically called witnesses to the stand. First came the very eager deacon. Words raced from the mouth of the bitter man who'd been betrayed by his cheating wife. He testified that each week for the past seven years Reverend Rich had stood at his pulpit and beseeched his congregation to fill collection plates. The money was for the church, not the Rev. Reverend Rich received a modest salary. His lifestyle, which the deacon described in detail, was remarkably ostentatious for a humble cleric. Then, Grender called other congregation members who corroborated the deacon's testimony.

"And what kind of car did he drive?" Grender asked a witness, hammering home the point.

"A baby blue cadoo," replied a nervous young man.

"A what?"

"A light blue Cadillac with a bumper sticker that reads, 'Honk if you're holy'."

The witness peered sadly toward the Reverend. Subpoenaed to testify against his minister, like many others, he spoke hesitantly. Reverend Rich may have stolen from them, but he had cared for them for two generations, not the overbearing prosecutor. Everyone's heart has a niche for good and a cubby hole for some bad. With passage of time since their Reverend's arrest, most of his flock remembered the nobler aspects of his nature. Their reluctance to testify became evident.

Unfortunately, what they said was still damning. Every piece of the prosecution's case fit . . . and a completed puzzle is all it takes for conviction. Parishioners donated money to the church. Donations were counted and entered in a weekly journal. An elderly treasurer was the

State's key witness, who would tie the Reverend to the missing funds as the final piece in the puzzle. The courtroom hushed as he took the stand.

"Mister Higgins," Grender asked assuredly, "are you treasurer of the Holy Redeemer Baptist Church where the defendant is the minister?"

"I've served in that position for the past thirty-five years."

Grender stepped back from the box, giving the jury a full view of the silver-haired witness wearing a three-piece suit. With a gold chain across the vest for his pocket watch, the black gentleman was the pluperfect picture of a respectable banker.

"Will you tell the jurors, please, about your education and work experience?"

"I'm a graduate of Howard University with a degree in business administration. I spent my working years in the banking industry, starting nearly fifty years ago. I rose through the ranks at First Atlantic Savings Bank, starting as a teller until I became Executive Vice President. I'm now retired."

"Then, you're familiar, are you not, with the duties of a church treasurer?"

"Indeed, Sir."

Grender rolled.

"During the years you served in that position, you counted weekly donations placed in church collection plates and prepared books of account, did you not?"

"Yes, Sir."

"Are these record books," Grender said, while displaying books to the witness, "bearing the name of your church upon the cover, records you kept and maintained in the ordinary course of church business for the past seven years?"

Mister Higgins looked at the books and replied.

"Yes, Sir."

"Are these records accurately maintained?"

"Of course," Mister Higgins replied indignantly. "After fifty years in the banking industry, I know how to keep accurate record books."

"I thought so," Grender gratuitously offered, nodding to the jurors, who listened intently to the dignified gentleman.

"For the past thirty-five years, I've counted Sunday donations, posted amounts in record books, and given the money to our Reverend. He deposits it in the bank each Monday."

"And who receives the monthly bank account statements?"

"They're mailed to the church. Reverend Rich receives them."

"Who reviews the monthly bank statements?"

"Well, I reviewed them years ago, but we stopped that practice as I got a bit older. The Reverend reviews them now."

"How long ago did you stop reviewing the statements?"

"About ten years ago."

"Have you reviewed the bank account statements and compared them against your record books at my request?"

"Yes, I did."

"What did you discover?"

"I found that over the past seven years the Reverend has deposited one-hundred thirty-five-thousand dollars less into the bank than I entered in my books. The church bank account is missing one hundred thirty-five-thousand dollars that the Reverend took."

"One hundred thirty-five-thousand dollars that the Reverend *took*?" Grender bellowed. "He didn't just *take* that money. He *stole* it, didn't he?

"I suppose," the banker muttered, eyes down with apparent reluctance to label his reverend a crook.

"Then say it." Grender blasted: "Did Reverend Melvin Richards steal one-hundred thirty-five thousand dollars from your church?"

"Yes," said the man, eyes still focused toward his shoes.

"No further questions for the witness, Your Honor."

Whispers swished through the room. The judge pounded his gavel.

"I want silence in this courtroom!"

Judge Hastings checked his wristwatch.

"It's past four thirty. I'm inclined to recess for the day. Mister Prosecutor, is this your final witness?"

"Yes, your Honor."

"Very well. Tomorrow when we reconvene, Mister Cameron, you'll conduct your cross-examination. Court is adjourned."

Judge Hastings left the bench. Paul sat still with the Reverend until the crowd filed out of the courtroom. Carol Resnick looked to him sympathetically as she packed her notes away at the prosecution table. Paul tried smiling back but wasn't certain what expression he cast.

While she isn't a classic beauty, the thought flashed, *there's something undeniably attractive about anyone so confident and bright.*

Intuitively, Paul knew he shouldn't try to get lucky with her. He'd need all the luck he could muster for the morning court session.

"I'm going to jail, aren't I?" Reverend Rich muttered.

Paul considered saying, "Don't worry about bringing a toothbrush. They have them there." Instead, he promised what he could.

"I plan to rest our defense case sometime tomorrow. We'll have a verdict by the end of the day."

Reverend Rich squirmed.

"And Rev," Paul said as he yanked at his overloaded briefcase, "make sure you show up with your witnesses."

"Young man, those people don't know anything about this case."

"Just bring them, Rev. Bring them and pray."

Chapter Eight

Making Tony Quick Fish

"HAIL MARY, FULL OF GRACE, THE LORD is with thee. . .."

Young Tony whispered Hail Mary on that seventeenth day of August 1930, as the tax collectors ushered him past the gaming room to a small office where they stuffed him into a chair under a bare bulb hung from an electrical cord. He squinted under its bright glare until his eyes focused.

Then, he spied a man sitting behind the desk, wearing a silk suit with a hand-painted necktie. A pencil-thin black mustachio, waxed on the tips, arched upward at the corners of his lips. Palmade glistened in his heavily greased dark hair. The harsh light exposed pockmarks, scars recognizable as reminders from a childhood smallpox bout.

He clenched a gold toothpick between his teeth and spoke without removing it, spilling words in deliberate modulations, making the dialect of his Sicilian province all the more pronounced. Tony realized he faced Matteo Rosso, the boss of Atlantic City's Black Hand.

The small band limited their nefarious activities to the Italian immigrant community in Atlantic City but applied them more broadly southward to Baltimore. For that reason, the stronger Irish mob running the town left them alone. Indeed, Irish mob leader and elected politician Eunoch Lewis Carlson, better known as "Nucky," allowed them to function for a tribute, just as he allowed a black mob to run what were then known as the Negro parts of town. When Nucky was challenged by a New York City Italian mob family looking to move on his turf, the local Black Hand kept its word, remaining in the background and taking no sides.

"You've dealt with a man who is our friend," Rosso began."

How did they learn so soon? Tony wondered, realizing the statement required a response.

"I didn't know he was your friend. He wasn't an Italian."

Tony worried, knowing what it meant to harm the friend of the Black Hand.

"And," the man continued, "we don't appreciate business disturbances."

Tony felt the room growing smaller as the three tax collectors hovered more closely. They could kill him instantly on command of their boss.

"What did you do with our German friend?"

Tony didn't consider his response.

"He's floating with the flounders."

The tips of the man's mustachio curled higher. He used his tongue to flip the toothpick in his mouth like a baton twirler spinning a stick. His eyes darted to the three men standing precariously over Tony, then dead-centered on the young man.

"There will be no more work for you on the construction sites, but we'll give you a job to support your family."

"What of the German?" Tony said uncertainly.

"Let us just say that you spared us from correcting a shortage in tax collections. Something, fortunate for you, is it not?"

Tony couldn't answer. Whether it was fortuitous depended on what the boss said next.

"There will be a new foreman, who will learn to count better," the boss continued, "and we'll see that the police don't ask too many questions. The Kraut had many enemies . . . and well-known gambling debts. That often shortens life in this town."

The boss looked to the trio of hard-faced men standing above Tony.

"Take him to the Hotel Chanticleer. Let him live and work there as a bouncer. Franco, I entrust this young man to you. See that he learns what he must."

Tony studied the man assigned as his mentor. Franco's face, which had seemed expressionless, now awakened as he smiled at Tony, revealing brilliantly white teeth that stood out from his rich-olive complexion. Those choppers seemed large for the man's head, like pearly daggers that could light his smile or warn when he was ready to bite.

The boss grabbed back Tony's attention with a warning that came so gently Tony knew it was the kind you only heard once.

"Never again will you kill without permission from this family. *Capici*?"

Tony didn't answer, then quickly realized the boss never asked any question twice.

"*Si*."

He understood the blessing of remaining alive, his obligation to follow the centuries old code of the Black Hand, and the relief of not being indebted to these people . . . because he had just become one of them.

"*Certo, me ne rendo conto*," Tony said, reaffirming his understanding and appreciation.

He left the speakeasy, guided by Franco's smile that seemed to light the night, all the while wondering.

Can the rumors be true? They say the Hotel Chanticleer is a brothel filled with the most beautiful prostitutes in Atlantic City.

"He's not Sicilian," one of the two remaining tax collectors complained after Tony left.

The nattily attired Rosso again flipped the gold toothpick with his tongue, as if churning his thinking process, then replied.

"He's not Sicilian but I know this young man's province. He'll be loyal. He will never be a *capo* or a boss, but he'll make a good soldier. We'll keep a close eye on young Antonio DeBona. I admire his guile. He was quick to throw the Kraut to the fishes."

Rosso twisted the tips of his mustachio more tightly, then declared: "That's what we'll call this young man: 'Tony Quick Fish'."

Tony studied the trappings of the renown disorderly house that had just become home. Centered between row-house homes of working-class folks in the city's Duck Town section was the brothel where men quietly passed in the night. Neighbors knew what transpired there yet no one complained. The busy little bordello provided benefits to the community that overcame moral misgivings. Its mob owners were generous when a neighbor needed financial help due to injury or ill health and there was never crime on a block they protected.

The sun rose as Tony walked in the door and set himself down in the parlor. He would be the brothel's bouncer, bartender, and handy man. The place was home to six women who plied their trade in second floor bedrooms. Before a hooker went upstairs with a customer, Tony would collect the fee and mark her arm with his pen. When a woman had six marks, she was free to quit for the night. Many worked longer. Pay was good, especially in those difficult times.

An elderly, though amply robust Italian woman prepared and served meals, occasionally washed linens, and touched upon routine housework. Many customers were tanked full of hootch by the time they ascended rickety stairs the women called their "stairway to heaven." Tony wouldn't have to get physical with the johns often. Management had a strict reputation.

Tony arrived dead tired after the long night and he had much to drink before killing the Kraut. His tired eyes watched Franco greet Isabella, the only whore still awake. Franco brushed against her full body, stared at her round face, then whispered in her ear.

She turned to Tony. Pink nipples on milky breasts peeked at him like inquisitive eyes through her sheer nightgown. Isabella's flirtations displayed obvious approval as she surveyed the strapping youth. Her hand took Tony's and guided him up the staircase to her room.

They stood at the foot of a bed, where sheets were soiled with evidence of a busy evening. Tony ripped them off and lowered himself onto the soft mattress, as if falling upon a cushiony cloud. Sleep called. Ever so tired, he closed his eyes.

He felt Isabella strip off his shirt, then caress his face with her tender fingertips. So gently, she massaged his temples. As she pulled a hairpin from her bun, she casually tossed her head. Brunette hair cascaded down her back. Heavy breaths warmed his face. His lips reached for a kiss.

"Don't do that," she softly admonished. "We're only fucking, not making love."

She tickled his ear with her tongue as his hands grabbed her waist, triggering her to caresses his quick-rising manhood. Suddenly she trembled and peered down.

"I've never seen anything like this," she gasped. "You're huge!"

Isabella abandoned controlled sexuality and shattered the house with multiple screaming orgasms.

A smack to the head roused Tony.

"Hey! Wake up," Isabella called. "I *gotta* dress for work."

Sleep dust glued his eyes. Tony glimpsed toward a wind-up clock on the night table.

Four o'clock in the afternoon! My God, he thought, *can it be so late? Have I slept through my date with Lena?*

Tony donned the same clothes he'd worn the day before, ran downstairs, and raced through the living room where the whores already gathered for early birds. Scantily clad and variously shaped ladies stretched on couches and lounged in easy chairs. Soon, those seats would be taken by eager johns. Glasses of beer and gin would clink. Music from their Victrola phonograph, smoke, and bawdy laughter would fill the room.

A brunette, still wearing hair curlers, called after Tony as he sped out the door.

"You have to be back by seven o'clock, stud-man!"

All the women hooted and roared. Their laughter followed him up the street. Isabella had shared Tony's grandiose performance and each woman was eager to spend time with the new man of the house.

Tony sprinted to the boardwalk, then pushed through heavy summer crowds. He surveyed the Garden Pier entranceway.

She's not outside," he moaned as he paid the pier admission price, then frantically searched through attractions.

He didn't know Lena had waited hours in her new dress, leaving the boardwalk with tears flowing down her face. Tony never heard Lena's sister exclaim, "Papa was right. We shouldn't spend time with riffraff!" Nor did he hear Lena vow never to see him again.

Tony plopped on a boardwalk bench, facing the ocean with his head in his hands. Hungover and overwhelmed with emotion, he wondered how he could have missed their day together. Tony longed for divine assistance. He swore he would make the beautiful girl his bride someday. They would raise a family, full of love and happiness. He clasped his hands together.

"Never again will I disappoint her," he vowed.

The promise Tony made to God was one that came from his heart, but one he could never keep.

Chapter Nine

Banker Spanker

THAT MORNING, MAY 9, 1984, CAME with a bluster. Strong winds made the day seem more like late March as Mister Higgins returned to the witness box for questioning by defense counsel. The elderly black banker, who had charmed the jury the day before, wasn't a witness Paul could badger. Paul instinctively knew jurors would resent a young, white lawyer beating up the senior black man, who had likely risen to professional success over many odds cast against him. Nothing sets off jurors against a trial lawyer like spanking a likable witness. Moreover, Paul genuinely admired the man, too. Who wouldn't? Yet, Paul bore an obligation to defend his client, so he reached within himself, hoping to find more tact than he expected he possessed.

"Commence cross-examination, Mister Cameron," Judge Hastings called out.

Paul spoke softly, so he wouldn't sound disrespectful of the elderly man.

"Good morning, Mister Higgins," he said.

"What did you say?" came from the witness.

"Good morning," Paul repeated just as softly.

"I'm sorry, young man, you'll have to speak up. I don't hear quite like I used to. My age, I'm afraid, has taken a certain toll on my faculties."

"Of course," Paul countered with a voice that filled the room. "Sir, I would like you to perform a task for me. I'd like you to count the hundred-dollar bills I'm placing on the witness stand. Then tell me, please, how many you have counted when you're through. Count carefully."

"I always take my time, Son, and always make a perfect count."

Hoss Grender rose from the prosecutor's table for closer observation.

"That's a pile of ten," the witness said.

Grender couldn't contain his amusement. His lips had moved as he counted the bills with the banker. The demonstration was exploding in the face of an inexperienced lawyer.

"Now," Paul continued, as he handed the witness a second stack of bills, "count these for me, as well."

Mister Higgins engaged in the exercise.

"There are ten in this stack as well. I'm correct, am I not, young man?"

"Let me think," Paul responded, "the first time you counted a stack of ten and the second time you said—"

"I said ten the second time also," Mister Higgins interjected, with increasing volume. "That's what I said. That's two-thousand dollars, two piles of hundred-dollar bills, ten in each pile."

"Yes," Paul admitted, "that's what you said."

He put his head down and returned to sit at the defense counsel table.

"But Mister Higgins," Paul said softly.

"I'm sorry, young man. You'll have to speak up. I don't hear so well anymore."

Paul raised his voice to bellow.

"But, Mister Higgins, are you sure?"

"Of course, I'm sure. What do you want me to do with the two-thousand dollars?"

"I want you to give the money to the bailiff. And, I ask the Court to direct the bailiff to count the money in the presence of the jury."

Grender rose to address the judge.

"I observed the witness make the proper count, your Honor. I have no objection to the bailiff verifying that to the jury."

"Very well, but do it quickly," Judge Hastings directed.

The bailiff stood before the jury and counted both stacks.

"There are ten bills in each stack," he announced.

"So, you agree with Mister Higgins," Paul said, "that you have two-thousand dollars in hand."

Grender rose again.

"Your Honor," he complained, "how much more of this do we have to listen to?"

Equally perturbed, Judge Hastings answered curtly.

"No more at all. Move onto another area of questioning, Mister Cameron. This is going nowhere."

"Oh, I didn't say there's two-thousand dollars here," the bailiff exclaimed. "I counted two stacks of ten bills each, your Honor, just like Mister Higgins said, but there's not two-thousand dollars here. Most of the bills are hundred-dollar bills, but there are ten-dollar bills here also. No, there's a lot less than two-thousand dollars in these two stacks."

Whispers turned loud throughout the courtroom. Judge Hastings raised his gavel to obtain order, but Mister Higgins brought them quiet with his cry.

"You tricked me, young man! You can trick me in this court room. But when I counted money at the church, I had more light and more time to count. I was nervous here. This isn't the same." Mister Higgins' voice crackled with rage. "What you did isn't fair."

"Sir," Paul softly asked the elderly witness, "are your eyes, like your ears, not quite what they used to be?"

"What? I didn't hear you, young man."

"Are your eyes," Paul repeated to bring the point home again to the jury, "like your ears, not quite what they used to be?"

Mister Higgins turned beet red.

"I have trouble seeing without my eyeglasses. But, usually, I count bills correctly."

"When did you begin to have trouble counting bills, Sir?"

Mister Higgins let out an exasperated breath that resounded in the oak-paneled room.

"More than ten years ago, Son. I just don't wear eyeglasses when I should all the time, I suppose."

Hoss Grender leaped to his feet shouting.

"May we have a sidebar, Your Honor?"

Judge Hastings ran his hand over his bald scalp as if slicking down hair that was no longer there. His grunts indicated something that the lawyers took for acquiescence so they approached the bench, where Grender spoke softly to assure the jury wouldn't hear.

"Judge, I move to strike this carnival display from the record. There's absolutely no foundation for that test. There is no evidence to show the witness counted church money under the same or similar conditions as in the courtroom. Instead, the witness testified he counted bills in the church under better lighting, with more time, and without being in the presence of so many people, who made him nervous."

Hastings turned from Grender and looked at Paul. The jurist's frown bespoke how disturbed he was with defense counsel.

"What do you have to say?"

"I just have one more question for the witness, your Honor."

Judge Hastings sat still, then ruled.

"Mister Cameron, you can ask your question but I'm going to direct the jury to disregard the demonstration."

The judge looked up and addressed the jurors.

"Ladies and gentlemen, Mister Cameron has already told you this is his first trial. New members of the bar are prone to make mistakes. I'm specifically instructing you to disregard the demonstration you just saw. This wasn't a scientific test. Defense counsel improperly conducted it under circumstances that were neither identical, nor substantially similar, to the circumstances under which this witness counted money at the defendant's church. I therefore rule that evidence you've heard concerning the demonstration is inadmissible."

Paul prepared to ask his final question. He opened a large book on his desk and deliberately passed through pages until he appeared to find what he was seeking. He looked up to the judge, then back into the book as if deep in thought, all the while instinctively knowing jurors resent being told to disregard evidence. He could see the impact of the demonstration on their faces. They would never disregard it. By delaying, Paul gave them additional time to consider what had just happened.

"Sir, are you ready to proceed?" Judge Hastings called from the bench.

Paul saw he had to continue.

"Mister Higgins," he said, "this morning you rendered a good deal of testimony about the amount of money you counted in weekly church donations. Are you as certain about that testimony being correct . . . as you were certain about having properly counted two-thousand dollars for us?"

"Objection," Grender shouted.

"Sustained," came the judge's quick reply. "Mister Prosecutor, do you have any questions for the witness on redirect examination."

"No more questions."

"Do you rest the State's case?"

"The State rests, your Honor."

"Any motions, Counselors?"

No response came from either counsel table.

"Are you prepared to proceed with the defense case after the luncheon recess," the judge called to Paul.

"Your Honor, the defense has key witnesses we expected to see in the courtroom today."

"And?" Judge Hastings grumbled.

"They're not here."

"Did you subpoena them, Counselor?"

"There were problems securing service upon them," Paul admitted. Actually, the witnesses couldn't be found.

Rather than explode with an objection, Grender ambled up a higher road.

"Your Honor, the State will not object to a continuance until tomorrow morning."

Paul knew what the senior lawyer was doing. He saw a trial victory in his hands and didn't want to later lose on procedural appeal if the Rev didn't have an opportunity to deliver defense witnesses to the courtroom. Besides, what harm could they do?

"Very well, we will reconvene in the morning. Ladies and gentlemen of the jury, when we return tomorrow, the defense will begin its case."

A court officer escorted the jury from the courtroom. As they filed out, Judge Hastings cast a smirk at Paul, then rushed off the bench.

The Righteous Reverend Rich again clasped his hands in silent prayer. Paul watched then whispered.

"Your witnesses are missing. Do you know what that means?"

The Rev shook his head from side to side.

"It means you aren't praying hard enough."

That night, Paul would try tracking down the people, who were so reluctant to appear on his client's behalf. He would work late in town, something many nocturnal creatures do on Atlantic City streets.

Chapter Ten

The Night Train

ON THOSE SAME STREETS, where Paul searched for witnesses, Prell stood under lights too bright. Pacific Avenue afforded no darkened sanctuary to conceal her. She had spotted Poon Tang Train and scoured for cover.

The young black man had short cropped hair, eyes tightly set together, and a distinctively protruding overbite. What he lacked in classic good looks, he covered with slick street style. Train dressed with panache. His smooth talk enchanted, so long as he tempered his temper. When true nature flared, Train came-up short on words and someone always paid the price. Carving with his switchblade precisely as a surgeon dissects with a scalpel, Train had a rep as a blade man who enjoyed preying upon the weak. A rough pack of hoods joined as his posse when dolling punishment to the strong. They'd all grown up anywhere a kid found a street gang for a home, then drifted through Atlantic City where cruel could be cool.

Powerful young men like Train thrived on "the life." For them, a spicy young woman was a stiletto-heeled cash machine to be whored until she was discarded or dead. Prell tried to avoid pimps like him but Train owned corners of her world.

Protection was mandatory so none of the working girls really worked for themselves. A good man cared for Prell and she took pride in being a "hotel girl." Only lowlifes worked on Pacific Avenue, many jacked on crack or worse. For fifty dollars, they'd suck. For a hundred, they'd fuck. And, when a street girl hit the skids, she'd screw unprotected for twenty.

Venereal diseases were common. City health authorities estimated half to be HIV-positive or carrying the flower of AIDS in full bloom. Poon Tang Train, were one to become familiar beyond surnames, was typical of pimps, who worked those women. He craved Prell for his stable and called from his open car window as he slowed the vehicle to roll at her walking pace.

"Honey, your sweet ass is a money maker."

"I'm charmed," Prell replied, her heels clacking on pavement.

"See this fine ride," he said, tapping his steering wheel. "I'm going to own your ass like I own this BMW and I'll ride it just as hard if you make me. Why do that, Angel? Treat me like sugar and I'm so sweet. You've seen my ladies and the fine things they wear."

Prell's heels clacked faster.

"See my Rolex," he said holding out his arm. "You can't fit more diamonds on it. Here, you can have this watch. I'll let you wear it for me."

"No, thanks," Prell offered politely, scared shitless, knowing Train would soon turn even less enchanting.

"Look what I'm wearing, Honey," Train cooed, "a Versace suit. You gotta keep up your front if you want to keep makin' your game. Train's the man to do that for you."

"I have a man."

Train's tone turned sour.

"Don't think that *Nigga*, who's working you now, can help you out here. He ain't cool where it counts and won't last long. He's going down like a bitch when the Train does his *gangsta* dance on him. Then, where are you *gonna* be?"

Prell hoped the panic she felt didn't show.

"Why don't you come to my place? Let me and my girls show you how a lady deserves to be treated."

Prell ran into the side door of the Claridge Casino Hotel and placed a call to her man. She would be safe inside, while she worked, but it would be dangerous when she returned to the street to go home. And, she would rather be cut by Train than work the streets. She'd seen the drugged haze in the eyes of so many young women, who traipsed along Pacific Avenue, and knew why they were called street grannies before they turned twenty-three. Old came fast on the street, and those girls wore years on their faces.

Dark skinned, compactly built yet strong, AK was Prell's man. He took her call and knew what to do. AK searched the trunk of his car for artillery to flash. He didn't want anyone moving on Prell. They only "worked a town" for a few months. When the street turned bad or cops caught onto a girl, AK knew travel called. Working women cruised a circuit. They sailed from Atlantic City to Honolulu, breezed to Vegas, voyaged to Montreal, and drifted back to Atlantic City. The art of the game was knowing when to pack up and go.

He and Prell were young. For now, money was good, and he wouldn't work her butt until there was none left. Sometimes working girls found happy endings. AK would give her one. They cared for each other but not the way she thought. He would let her go but AK was "in the life" for life.

AK found Train just after midnight in a busy coffee shop at Pacific and Illinois Avenues. He breathed deeply for composure. He needed to match Trains' attitude and couldn't let the blade man sense any fear. Train was the real deal, absent of conscience. AK walked up to him without saying a word. As they squared off, face to face, Train's steely gaze pierced AK's eyes.

"Look at your shit," Train exploded. "You don't have no *gangsta* stroll. You're one of them buppies, aren't you? Watch yourself, my brother. I'm straight up and can take you down hard. Understand what you're being told?"

In the middle of Train's rap, AK launched a single punch that nearly knocked the pimp's bucked teeth through the other side of his head. Train lay cold. AK had been a golden glove fighter before suffering a ring injury. A blood clot on the brain ended boxing dreams but AK still packed wallop.

With the pimp floored, he calmly ordered a cup of coffee, remaining so word would travel about who had taken out Train. He savored the steaming brew, recognizing that Train would retaliate to protect his rep. Atlantic City had become too dangerous for AK and Prell . . . so the road called again.

The Claridge was hosting a convention of urologists, a bland group with a singular interest that eludes most folks. They had left families at home, and the gentlemen in their crowd arrived in Atlantic City with enormously large, roving eyes. Cocktail waitresses, who poured themselves into skimpy outfits hoisting boobs to their chins, always served as Prell's warmup act. Occasionally a drink server might turn a trick, but few were interested in a one-night stand with a married piss doctor on the prowl.

On the other hand, Prell loved conventioneers, who mostly confessed to boredom in their marital beds. Prell handled some straight dates—men with no bizarre quirks—then retired to the ladies room. Perched in a stall, she stuffed cash into the bottom of her shoes, shoved her feet back into the pumps, and returned to the bar. Amid a cluster of fast cheek kisses, she shouted to her new doctor pals: "Bye guys!"

In the wee morning hours, Prell readied to leave, as always, through rear service doors. All the game palaces on the boardwalk face the ocean. One block away, Pacific Avenue runs parallel to those boards. More than a name on a Monopoly board, Pacific Avenue is the strip where players rolled, and street girls strolled. Prell ambled onto the avenue and peered for a cab.

The nearness of dawn had chased street people to bed and Prell saw only one figure for blocks—Train. Instantly, she asked herself a question.

Why's he growing a grapefruit on his head?

Train rushed to her as she screamed and sprinted away fast as any human moves in four-inch heels.

Train smiled wide. He chugged after her and roared.

"You're mine, bitch!"

Prell knew she would rather be dead than his. High heels quick clicked against pavement, but not rapidly enough. Train's heavy footsteps grew swifter and closer. She cut around a corner onto New York Avenue, then darted into an alleyway huffing.

Goddamn, it's dark in here, Prell thought.

Her eyes tried focusing on somewhere to hide, but she was blind in the shadows—running too fast in the dark, while too scared to slow.

Chapter Eleven

The Martini Mansion

YOUNG TONY'S EYES POPPED OPEN IN HIS TEENY bedroom, which was shade-down darkened for daytime sleeping. On June 6, 1933, the Chanticleer had been his home for three years, and unexpected arousals from slumber were routine.

"Wake up," Franco beckoned.

The tough guy had become a dear friend as well as his mentor. With his bright-white teeth sparkling in faint light from the hallway, he called.

"The Martini Mansion beckons."

Tony was being shifted from nightly duties at the brothel to a temporary assignment. Another alcohol shipment was arriving, and his crew would be unloading. Offshore in international waters, a cargo ship had loading holes filled with spirits from Europe and afar. Speedboats carried liquor crates to the shores of Brigantine Island, just north of Atlantic City, to deliver in the night. Swift enough to outrun any Coast Guard vessel from the nearby harbor station, the little boats were operated by men trained to approach the beach cautiously. They had to skirt detection, while avoiding the Brigantine shoals: offshore sandbars that could catch a vessel's hull and bring it to a standstill. Speedboat operators knew those waters well and used their knowledge to an advantage. Larger Coast Guard vessels had so often scuttled on shoals that their seamen were reluctant to enter the waters after dusk.

Tony and the other men in his crime family gathered at the Martini Mansion, an oceanfront cottage that served as their short-term warehouse. A tunnel from its basement burrowed to the beach, allowing them to carry crates from the water edge to the house undetected. Afterward, trucks delivered hooch to speakeasies. They paid the town cops to be busy elsewhere whenever a shipment arrived. Besides, cops on the two-and-one half man police force, which accounted their part timer, weren't eager to enforce prohibition laws that they broke themselves. After all, who didn't want to sip some gin or chug a beer? Moreover, seashore folks depended on tourist revenue from vacationers, who viewed a refreshing intoxicant as an integral part of resort life. So, it went with prohibitionist's "noble experiment."

Federal government agents called G-men, who enforced the controversial *Volstead Act*, weren't so understanding. They fought booze-bearing mobsters in a "moral crusade," albeit one opposed by the thirsty national majority. Amid the nation's moral dilemma, fortunes were made running liquor into speakeasies.

Tony earned a generous bonus with each shipment he helped unload. Part helped support his siblings, even assisting a younger brother through college, which was the realization of the American dream for any immigrant family. He was also saving for something. After this night, Tony would have enough money to forge the grandest plan of his life, making his dream to marry Lena come true.

A dozen men, all in high spirits, greeted Tony inside their tiny mansion.

"This Sunday, Quick Fish, we want to see you," someone called.

He spotted Fat Joey behind the rest.

"Don't forget," Joey shouted. "Joanna's expecting you to join us for our youngest girl's confirmation party. You don't have to attend the mass. Just make the party afterward."

"Wouldn't miss either," Tony replied.

The heavyset bootlegger had married his match, a woman of equal proportion, who shared his passions for progeny and gluttony, as their six children and ample girth attested.

Tony had grown close to every man in his crime family, their camaraderie running deeper than ordinary coworkers. Their risky ventures couldn't be shared with outsiders, so they talked shop exclusively among themselves, trusted only each other, and relied upon one another, even with their lives.

They descended steps to the basement, then slithered like speedy weevils through the tunnel to the beach, where an opening had been cleared of sand that concealed a wooden hatch cover. While they waited for speedboats, Tony studied the sky.

"I don't like it," he said.

Franko looked puzzled.

"Don't like what?"

"Nearly full moon and too many stars. We usually do this under the cover of clouds so we can't be seen."

"Stop worrying."

"And something else," Tony continued. "Did you notice the ocean? We usually do this at low tide so coast guard boats can't slip in on us."

"Gotta do this tonight, *Paisan*o. A big storm's brewing off the Carolina coasts. Could reach us by morning. This may be the calm before the storm. Men aboard the cargo ship at sea have to unload this shipment and chart a course for calmer waters."

Tony felt uneasy but the thought of earning enough money to marry Lena fortified his resolve.

Lena had developed a womanly figure that her mother hid under restrictive garments, and that Lena displayed whenever her mother wasn't around. She was proud of her full breasts and well-defined hips. Lena had even tried makeup, then heard Mama curse for the first time.

"*Faccia di puttana!*" Face of a whore, her mother shouted. "Wash it off. Scrub!"

"Mama," Lena cried, "you never want me to attract a young man."

Even Lena knew nothing could've been further from the truth. Her parents constantly reminded her that she should find a young man from a good family.

Yet, how, Lena woefully thought, *can I do anything but dream with parents who treat me like a child*?

As the custom in many immigrant households, teenage girls were given little opportunity to date. So, she and her sister simply shared fantasies in their bed.

"Do you ever think of the young man from the boardwalk?" her sister said.

"*Si*, I've seen him, and we've talked. Now, he's so big and strong."

"Handsome as well," her sister added, "but he's a member of the Black Hand. Papa will never condone a match."

"*Mia sorella*," Lena confided, "I've dreamed we'll marry. That's been my prayer from the moment we met."

Lena paused, recalling the day he had hurt her.

"Once I was so mad at him but he's the boy for me. The Holy Father will provide a plan."

"We'll be out of this business soon," Franco offered.

Tony didn't understand.

"What do you mean?"

"Most people in this country want a constitutional amendment legalizing alcohol. Our political friends can't keep it from happening."

"Our family supports politicians who favor prohibition?"

Tony's shock proved how charming something can be: the innocence of a young man who lives in a whore house. Atlantic City is a town of paradoxes.

"My young friend," Franco explained, "we make millions on liquor shipments. When alcohol is legal again, the family will lose a large share of revenue, but don't worry. We have plans."

Engine sounds diverted their attention as speedboats came into view. Tony wasn't accustomed to seeing them so far offshore.

This night is too bright, he thought again.

Boats slowed then stopped near shore, where Tony joined men unloading, then lugged heavy crates to the tunnel. While they worked, Tony thought he saw headlights down the beach.

"Franco," he called out. "Do you see anything flashing?"

Franco set down his crate and scoured.

"Nah, I don't see anything."

Lena woke with a start, trembling.

"Why?" she asked aloud.

Something very bad was about to happen, but what? She had heard reports of a hurricane that might reach their shores yet when she peered out her window, the sky was so clear. She stared into the night, thoughts returning to her young man.

“Boats are bringing the last run,” Franco remarked. “I’ll be glad to soak my aching muscles in a hot bath tonight.”

Tony’s eyes still probed. The speedboat slowed and men waded through waves to steady and unload it. Exhausted, Tony grabbed the last crate. He was still in the water, when the first shots rang out. G-men firing guns raced up the beach in an armed assault. Tony heard popping pistol shots and submachine gun blasts. Bullets zipped into the beach, kicking up sand.

Franco scampered for his weapon by the open tunnel hatch and unlocked its safety latch. The Thompson submachine gun was weapon of choice for many rum runners. Loud and quick, it sprayed a large area with bullets until a round nailed something. That’s what most mobsters did but that wasn’t Franco’s style. Cool under fire, he took time to aim and squeeze, rather than jolt the trigger and move his weapon off target. As bullets flew in all directions, he squeezed a burst that took a down a G-man, screaming woefully.

Franco’s white teeth reflected on a bloodthirsty grin as he squeezed again. More caterwauls filled the air. Franco beamed until a bullet pierced his skull between the eyes and his head snapped backward. The steel projectile slammed him into the sand next to the bloated form of Fat Joey. Around their corpses, twenty-five heavily armed G-men overpowered the remaining bootleggers. All threw hands toward the stars, surrendering as their first step toward prison for years . . . all but Tony, who remained in the surf.

"Only one thing to do," Tony uttered, diving under a breaking wave. Saltwater filled his mouth, choking him until he spit it out, then swam into the sea.

Two G-men on the beach looked into water that sparkled under moonlight, each itching to fire at any target that didn't have hands raised. The larger man fit the stock of his double-barreled shotgun into his shoulder and aimed into the ocean.

"One of them guinea bastards swam that way," he observed, pointing his gun barrels in Tony's direction.

"Don't see anything," said the other man.

"The son of a bitch is out there. I'll rake the shoreline until he swims back. Can't stay out there forever."

An inhuman wail rose from a wounded government agent on the beach, piercing the night and filling the gun-toting G-man with a hunger for revenge.

"I'm gonna kill any swimmin' guinea, who prances out of the ocean tonight."

Tony swam south. What choice did he have? Feds would be sweeping Brigantine and they'd stop anyone trying to cross the only bridge off the island. He would have to swim nearly a mile along the shoreline to the Atlantic City Inlet, then swim across its treacherous waters to Atlantic City on the other side. Unpredictable currents, there, had snuffed life from many strong swimmers but it was his only chance.

By the time Tony reached the inlet, he was exhausted and beginning to cramp.

I'll never make it, he thought, *with these heavy, wet clothes.*

So, treading in rolling surf, he stripped naked.

"Now," Tony told himself, taking a stroke, not knowing how many more he could muster.

A vision of Lena entered his mind and he would focus on her as far as he might be able go.

Chapter Twelve

You're Not Gonna Stick that Thing in Me

SMITTY JARRED HIS PARTNER AWAKE. Their unmarked car was parked in the back of an abandoned lot. Smitty's ruddy complexion always gave him away. He blushed with excitement, making rosy cheeks radiate neon hues.

"Hey, we're going after a babe!" he exclaimed to his partner.

"What the hell are you talking about?"

"A pimp just chased a girl around the corner. Let's check it out."

"That's just the usual pimp and whore shit."

The bigger man turned to his side, tilted his head back, and spoke with finality.

"Wake me when our shift's over."

"She's so fine."

"It's three in morning. Let the pimp have her," his partner sighed. "We picked up our quota for hookers this month. They don't pay vice cops a bonus for bagging over the limit."

"*Yowsa*," Smitty agreed. "I'll get her some other night. Only a matter of time."

That night Smitty would let the pimp have his way with her. He knew the word on the hustler, who was gaining on the girl. The pimp had a reputation as a blade man, who'd served time for disfiguring a hooker to settle a score. And, Smitty knew what Poon Tang Train would do when he caught the young woman he was chasing. She was going to be a scar-faced whore.

Smitty swigged coffee from his paper cup, then dropped it out the window. He pictured the pretty package.

Seems like such a waste, he thought.

Smitty started the car's engine.

"Fuck it," he said. "Let's check this out."

Slowly, he pulled out of the lot onto Pacific Avenue, then turned the corner at New York Avenue. The street was empty.

"Where could they have gone?" Smitty said.

"That pimp's probably already sliced and diced her," his partner mused.

"What a shame."

Smitty's words were sincerely spoken. Few truly sweet faces graced the streets and he would have preferred taking her that way.

"Too late, now," he surmised. "Too goddamned late."

Prell darted down an alleyway until she smacked into a brick wall at its dead-end. Groping desperately in the shadows, she banged into something bigger and more solid than the wall. It sent her reeling. Prell lay on her back, panting hard and much too loudly. Terror clenched her chest, making each gasp for air tougher to take.

Streetlights lit Train's silhouette at the alley entranceway. Tall buildings on both sides framed his form.

Stop trying to breathe, she told herself.

But lungs ache for air. Her pounding heart and echoing breaths were all she heard until the sound Train's footsteps told her he was close. He would get her, there, where she was helpless. Eyes shut, she heard a switchblade swish open.

Train straddled the young woman with his legs and peered down. How good it felt, knowing even the sound of his springing blade chilled her. Train brought the knife to her eyes and measured where he would strike. The bitch would have her face marked to damage her pimp's goods. He'd slice an "I" up her nose and between her eyes. Then, would cross that "I" into a "T" low cut across her forehead, splitting her eyebrows. He'd brand her with his initial.

An expert with all kinds of blades, Train loved the orgasmic rush that spewed whenever he carved a woman. It empowered him over the bitch—and over anyone who ever looked at her or cared about her. He did it for play and sometimes for pay.

Omnipotence surged through every fiber of his being as he pulled the knife back to slash. Sexually charged, his organ grew firm.

It's hard like the steel in my blade, he realized.

Train touched himself and a twisted smile crossed his lips. Prell's scream heightened his ecstasy, then his hand jolted toward her like a lightning bolt.

Prell's shrill screech filled the night as the blade zipped toward her face, growing larger as it neared, then suddenly stopping dead. Another hand grasped the one holding the knife. Prell screamed again as Train's eyes, only inches from her face, widened and his nostrils flared. He turned his head. She looked up, too, and saw a large man holding Train's knife hand in his own.

Suddenly, Prell realized she must have run into the guy in the dark. She watched Train position his knife to jab into the big man's guts. Then, a startled expression on Train's face told her that Train recognized him. Her attacker lowered his head respectfully, placed the blade in his pocket, and gave Prell a stare. His menacing gaze told her something else. He intended to finish with her later. Without a word spoken, Train dashed away.

I've seen him before, she thought. *Who saved me*?

Never had she been near a man, who made her feel so instantly secure.

Headlights lit the ally as a car came into view. A blue flashing light was handheld to its roof. The big man lifted

Prell to her feet. She wrapped her arms around his neck and clung.

When the car pulled up, Smitty was the first to speak. "Good evening, Mister DeBona," he said to the man.

"You don't see me," Tony Quick Fish said.

"Understood, Sir. We're out of here."

"And drop off this young lady on your way."

"Yes, Sir," Smitty said. "Is she a friend of yours, Mister DeBona?"

Tony looked at the clinging bundle. "No," he replied. Tony Quick Fish didn't know her, but that was hardly the first time he had protected a working girl.

Prell composed herself in the back seat of the unmarked car.

"Who's the old dude?" she said.

"That, my dear," Smitty replied, "was the boss of the boardwalk."

"Let's grab more coffee," his partner called.

Smitty pulled their car up to a convenience store. His partner took the driver's seat while Smitty walked inside. When the cop returned, he had three cups, one for each of them. He sat in the back next to Prell as his partner drove. She felt him eyeball her. His flushing cheeks and hasty breaths signaled unwelcome eagerness.

"How 'bout a quickie, Sweetheart?"

Prell studied him.

"For a cup of coffee? You want a friggin' blow job for a cup of coffee?"

It had been a hell of a night and that beat all.

"You can do it as a professional courtesy for your friends at Atlantic City Vice," Smitty suggested.

"That's how you operate in this town?"

His partner remained silent as Smitty opened his zipper, cradled Prell's head in his hands, and lowered her mouth to his waiting member. Prell was fast to speak.

"That's it? That's a penis? Where's the rest of it?" she choked out between gales of laughter.

Smitty's partner started laughing, too, making Smitty blush like casino front lighting. He smacked Prell hard enough to turn half her face as red as his.

"You've just ran out of luck, Honey," he said.

Prell shouted, "You're not sticking that thing in me!"

"That does it," Smitty screamed back. "We book the bitch for prostitution. Take her in."

He would straighten out her ass. Atlantic City's courtrooms were known for their quirks. Smitty had spent enough time on the force to learn tricks they didn't teach at the police academy. He'd fix that whore good.

Smitty reached back and walloped Prell across the mouth, instantly shutting down her glee. As her lips began to swell and tears welled, Officer Smith realized how much he loved law enforcement. And, that young whore was about to experience his special brand.

Chapter Thirteen

Sometimes It's Who They Think You Know

"ALL RISE," THE BAILIFF CRIED, as Judge Hastings swept into the courtroom and seated himself behind his bench, bespeaking the jurist's businesslike mood and manner. Wasting no time on morning pleasantries, he rubbed his hand over the top of his bald scalp, twitched his bushy eyebrows, and declared for the record.

"This is the case of State versus Reverend Melvin Richards. Bailiff, bring the jury back into the courtroom."

Paul settled uneasily in his seat. Since he had arrived, a tune relentlessly pounded in his head as he wondered.

Where are the people, who promised to testify for the Reverend?

In his worried mind, Marvin Gaye pounded out the Motown classic: "Can I Get a Witness." Paul whispered to Reverend Rich, who squirmed in his seat beside Paul.

"Do you see them in the crowd?"

The Rev squinted.

"Not a blessed one."

"Mister Cameron," the judge directed, "Call your first witness."

Paul took his time.

"Your Honor," he began, "may I ask the bailiff to bring extra chairs into the courtroom? I'd like to have them set up here," pointing to the seating area closest to the defense table, "for the defendant's character witnesses."

Judge Hastings' focus darted around the courtroom as, indeed, spectators filled every seat.

In a squeaky outburst that startled the jurors, Hoss Grender leaped to his feet and chirped: "Objection!"

Just then, the courtroom doors flung open and three clergymen entered. All eyes trained on the ministers, wearing clerical collars and robes, as they strode to the defense table.

"May we have a sidebar, your Honor?" Grender said.

"Counsel, come forward," Judge Hastings called.

They again spoke on the record softly so jurors wouldn't overhear. Grender recited the basis of his objection.

"Your Honor, the defense isn't entitled to call character witnesses. The State hasn't offered evidence to impeach the defendant that would open those doors. The rules of evidence prelude character testimony for being irrelevant and inadmissible."

"Mister Cameron," Judge Hastings said, "this is just the kind of thing I don't want to see from you. Even a first-year law student knows you can't introduce character evidence in this case."

"But Judge, you threw out the evidence related to my demonstration. The defense has nothing to give the jury except character evidence."

"That's not my problem."

"Well, your Honor," Paul said slowly as he thought it through, "may I call the witnesses by name in the presence of the jury and offer to prove the good character of the defendant. The prosecutor could certainly make his objection to each as I call them?"

Judge Hastings saw through the ploy.

"No, you may not," he answered sharply.

Then, he faced the court reporter to make certain that his ruling was on the record.

"I specifically rule that defense counsel is *not* to call these witnesses to the stand in the presence of the jury."

The judge then looked at both attorneys.

"Do you both understand my instruction?"

Paul glanced at the jurors from the corners of his eyes. They were watching men of the cloth console the defendant. Paul was making his point anyway. He just had to make the jury understand Reverend Rich wasn't the scumbag Grender portrayed him to be. One minister held up a small silver crucifix that hung from a chain around his neck and kissed it.

Nice touch, thought Paul.

"If there's nothing further, counsel," Judge Hastings said, "you may return to your seats. Mister Cameron, get those witnesses out of here."

Paul turned and spoke loudly enough for everyone in the courtroom to hear.

"The character, witnesses who came here to testify for the defendant, are excused. Thank you all very much for coming. Thank you, Reverend Toland. Thank you, Reverend James. Thank you, Bishop McCullough."

"Mister Cameron!" Judge Hastings screamed. "What are you doing? I specifically instructed you not to call these witnesses to the stand in the presence of the jury."

"And I'm abiding by your Honor's direction," Paul responded with full volume. "But in this courtroom, we have three men of God, who've taken their time to come here in support of a defendant. If I can't say thank you, I simply don't know my duties as a lawyer, Sir. I am merely expressing gratitude to all these prominent holy men who've come here to lend aid to the defendant in his time of need."

"Mister Cameron, I regard your comments as an affront to this Court."

"I'm sorry your Honor regards it as an affront. It certainly isn't intended so," Paul replied while returning to his seat. "Thank you, once again, for coming, Bishop and Reverends. Thank you and God Bless you!"

Judge Hastings' face was as purple as his rage.

"Now that we can't call these good men of the Lord to testify, your Honor, the defense rests," Paul said. "Shall we present closing arguments to the jury?"

Grender squirmed, making his unreadiness conspicuous. Paul surmised his adversary expected defense testimony to consume at least the morning court session.

"Judge, may we have a recess to get organized for summation?" Grender asked.

"No, you may not," came a curt reply. "This courtroom isn't going to sit empty again and I won't allow jurors to sit idle. If there are no other witnesses and no other motions, we'll begin closing arguments, now."

"The state may wish to call another witness," Grender said, thinking aloud.

Paul leaped to his feet. "Objection," he declared.

"All right, Mister Cameron," Judge Hastings said. "You haven't made any objections throughout this entire trial. What could the basis of your objection possibly be?"

"The defense objects to the prosecutor calling any rebuttal witnesses. Due to the prosecutor's objection that kept the defense from producing even men of God as witnesses, the defense was unable to offer any testimony or evidence. Therefore, there's nothing to rebut. The rules of court preclude the State from calling rebuttal witnesses."

Judge Hastings flipped through the rule book. One assistant at the prosecution table did the same while the other, Carol Resnick, covered her grin. The young defense lawyer had scored big points.

Grender lost his patience and ripped the tome away from his assistant. As stubby fingers pushed past pages, jurors chuckled. The young lawyer, trying his first case, had stumped the judge, who appeared to have been treating the defense unfairly, as well as the seasoned prosecutor who just seemed nasty.

"Well," Judge Hastings announced, "you finally appear to be right about something, Mister Cameron. Let's get on with closing arguments."

Paul forgot what he told the jury. He might have reminded them that the prosecution's case relied upon the testimony of an elderly man who may not have properly counted the church donations over a long period. Even small errors add up to big mistakes, over fifty-two Sundays a year, for seven years. Paul might have also said that gave the jury reasonable doubt to render a verdict of not guilty. Yet, the only thing he clearly remembered saying was what Lee had suggested.

"Just be sure to remind the jury at the end of the trial that this is your first case and they shouldn't hold any mistakes you made against your client." Lee explained, "That line covers a multitude of sins. The whole point is to get jurors to like you and your client. He's been a good guy in the community for years. That makes it easier to give him the benefit of a reasonable doubt. They'll like him even if he's a little tainted—and maybe more because he is. After all, you're trying this case in Atlantic City."

Paul had wondered about admitting it was his first case.

"That line really works?" he had said.

"Hell," Lee replied, "that trick worked for me for the first two years I practiced law. I used it in every case I tried until a judge finally asked me, 'Young man, haven't I heard you say that in my courtroom before?' Just get the jury to like you, Paul. It won't be hard. Everyone likes to root for a rookie."

When the jury returned from deliberations, Paul didn't have to wait for the reading of the verdict. A juror gave him the thumbs up sign.

"Not guilty," the jury foreman declared.

The courtroom burst into applause. The Reverend's parishioners filling seats were grateful to have their fiery-preaching minister cleared.

A final pound of the gavel closed the case.

Paul was called to the bench by Judge Hastings, whose face lacked expression. His brows, like two dead caterpillars, didn't move. He uttered two words.

"Beginner's luck."

The Righteous Revered Rich was amply more vibrant and inquisitive.

"When did Reverend McCullough receive a promotion to bishop?"

"He's not a bishop?" Paul replied with a wink. "I guess he was promoted when Grender wouldn't let him take the witness stand."

Grender waddled over to Paul with a promise. He wasn't a gracious loser in a high-profile case. If he had spotted the slightest doubt about nailing a conviction, he would have turned the case over to an assistant prosecutor.

"Someday, I'm going to bury you," Hoss Grender vowed, "and I'll enjoy doing it."

Well-wishers clung to Paul like he was a high roller on a good craps roll. Only one person in the crowd stood out in his mind, though. He would never forget her or her words.

"Hey, Mister Hot Shot Lawyer," an attractive brunette shouted over courtroom buzz.

She wore a minidress and spiked heels. Heavy makeup covered, and to Paul's thinking nearly obscured, a very pretty face.

"Do you do hookers?"

"What?" The question threw Paul.

"Do you do hookers, Hun? I need a good lawyer. I've got six cases against me and I'm screwed. Vice cops set me up. Will you take my cases?"

This only happens in Atlantic City, Paul thought.

He had just finished representing a man of the cloth. Before he could close his briefcase, a high-class call girl was retaining him.

"Do you have your charge sheets?"

The young woman opened her handbag and feverishly bulldozed through clutter. From its bottom, she pulled six crumpled green sheets containing charges from her arrests. She handed them to Paul, stained with coffee spills and red lipstick imprints. He tried flattening them to read.

"I've been using them as lip blotters," the young woman offered.

Paul read what he could. Prostitution charges arose from arrests on six different dates, all signed by the same vice cop against the same defendant. Something was wrong with those allegations. How could the same cop pick up the same hooker six times? At the top of each charge sheet the defendant was named in a heading that read, "State of New Jersey vs. Queen, Victoria." Paul asked if he was reading the name correctly and the young woman cheerily replied.

"Yeah, Hun, that's my street name, Victoria Queen. It always goes on my charge sheets as Queen Victoria.

You managed to get booked under an alias?

Call me Prell, Mister Hot Shot."

Paul warmed to her instantly. She was happy-go-lucky in a contagious way. He just couldn't tell, yet, whether she was clever or just lucky in a dopey way. The one trait can so easily conceal the other.

"You're exposed to a lot of jail time on all these charges."

"That's why I hung out in courtrooms today. I'm looking for someone who's good to do me."

"Your defense is going to be pricey," Paul warned.

Prell dug through her pocketbook and pulled out crumpled cash in chunky denominations.

"I can get more. I've got a lot of work lined up this week."

Paul looked at the charge sheets, then at the dough. He knew what to do. Paul would open his own law office in Atlantic City. The seashore had always called to him. It seemed like home for some reason. The words he uttered charted his life on a course that would lead to his own arrest for murder.

Looking into the smiling face, he simply said it.

"Yes, I do hookers."

Those words spoken, the clock measuring Paul's lifetime sped faster, counting down.

Chapter Fourteen

An Allover Tan

SUNUP ON THE SEVENTH DAY OF JUNE 1933, young Tony woke naked on the sands at Atlantic City's northern tip. Still exhausted from the long swim across choppy inlet waters, he surveyed the beach. Bathers would soon fill it with blankets. Children would bring pails and shovels. And unlike Tony, who was set for an allover tan, they'd be wearing bathing suits.

Lifeguards were setting up their stand at the water's edge. A policeman twirled his billy club on the boardwalk, no more than fifty feet from him. The cop turned to look in Tony's direction just as he finished covering his bare midsection with sand. His upper body was exposed. His lower legs and feet stuck out below. He stretched, as if sunbathing, and hoped no bathing beauty walked his way. He wasn't buried deep enough to cover an erection.

With no way off the beach, Tony did the only thing he could. He sunned and reflected on his young life. Franco had been responsible for security at the bustling Paradise Supper Club, but his friend was dead so Tony could rise to the position. That was the beauty of his business: jail and shortened lives inevitably made room for advancement. A new man could take over Tony's chores at the Chanticleer. He would miss the women and casual sex, but he'd laid enough hookers.

It's time, he thought, *to take a June bride.*

Tony was ready to start a family. He could only marry Lena with the approval of her family. First, he would have to overcome their *campanilismo*—the spirit of parochialism that separated the Italian immigrants by regional prejudices of their homeland. Tony's family wouldn't be thrilled either, but Mama would welcome Lena. Since his father's death, Tony had assumed the role of financial provider and that crowned him as family figurehead in the patriarchal immigrant community. Mama would respect his decision.

As for Lena, Tony never questioned her feelings, nor she of his. Love spoke in their eyes.

Tony snapped out of daydreams when he spied opportunity. A couple, who had come to lounge next to him, ran into the ocean. While they frolicked, Tony grabbed one of their towels and wrapped it around his waist like a sarong. He left the beach and walked barefoot two miles through the streets of Atlantic City to the Chanticleer Hotel, where he opened the door to whistles and hoots from women glad to see him. Street word said Tony drowned trying to avoid arrest. Franco and Fat Joey were dead. Feds booked all the other men for bootlegging, resisting arrest, killing a federal agent, and wounding three others. The family was down a lot of manpower.

Meanwhile, surmising moonlight swims have that effect, Tony was eager to gain Lena's hand in marriage. He also needed permission from his boss to engage in the courtship. No doubt, the mustachioed head of the crime family would grant permission, but at what price? The boss always collected a tribute as part of their marriage protocol. Everyone, it seemed, demanded an accommodation. He scheduled obligatory meetings with Lena's father and his boss, only to encounter greater obstacles than expected.

"Buon giorno, Signore!" Tony greeted Lena's father, who responded less enthusiastically.

"*Salve.*"

Signor Marcello's curt response and darting eyes revealed how ill at ease the man felt. Just as Lena's father had demanded, they were meeting in a public place. They sat in the main restaurant at the Heinz 57 Pier. The famous attraction extended from the boardwalk on pilings over the ocean, presenting pristine ocean views through large windows, through which Mister Marcello peered. Tony watched man's gaze turn to the spacious dining hall, looking apprehensively, as if expecting a bogeyman was hiding behind every pillar that supported the high ceiling. Finally, when a waitress appeared, he placed an order.

"Just espresso for two," he said, "nothing else."

Neither spoke again until she served it.

"Signore," Tony began, "I seek permission to court your daughter, Lena."

Mister Marcello knew why they were meeting. Tony had let word of his intentions discretely pass to his ears through the mouths of older men. Mister Marcello was mortified. He didn't trust the young hoodlum and resented his ties to the *reatos*, the criminals who dressed in fancy suits and alligator shoes. They made a mockery of decent people who worked hard for meager wages. His daughter would never marry their kind. Grander plans awaited his Lena. She was a beautiful pearl that wouldn't adorn a whoremaster. He was only meeting the *cafone* because he feared Tony's mob ties and Mister Marcello knew how to convince the hood that Lena wasn't for him.

"Young man, any father would welcome you as a son-in-law, though, I must admit, I always hoped for a young man from our old province to wed *mia figlia*. Surely, you understand such things."

Tony nodded.

Mister Marcello spoke cautiously, trying not to stammer and hoping to conceal jittery nerves. He paused to silently pray his words would dispel the hood's conjugal notions without offending him. Wrinkles furrowed in his forehead.

"I must explain some things—things that are very difficult for a father to discuss. How does one speak frankly of a daughter, and reveal her deepest secrets?"

Tony watched Mister Marcello pause to sip from his cup.

"My young friend," he continued, "it's true that my Lena is somewhat attractive. She doesn't have the face of a goat, but she doesn't possess the beauty to which you're accustomed. You have ties to the Chanticleer Hotel, where—so they tell me—the most beautiful women in the world can be savored like the finest wines. Why imbibe cooking sherry? Surely, you have not thought this through."

Tony didn't know whether to chuckle at the man's feeble attempt or to belt the bastard. He glanced outside, where teenagers on the pier were handing out the famous Heinz pickles to boardwalkers. Time had come, he realized, to lay out his plan. He gave Lena's father a scowl that stole the steam from his espresso. The man set down his cup and shut his mouth as Tony spoke from the heart.

Lena and her sister awaited Papa. He hadn't told them where he was going but both knew from Mama, who revealed the suitor's inquiries.

"Your father and I have carefully considered this matter. Papa even discussed the young man's prospects with men who know of such things."

Lena saw her mother's eyes narrow and look down. Face drawn, Mama talked slowly as if deliberating over each syllable. Expressions spoke faster that words, letting Lena know her parents disdained even having to contemplate the match.

"They say this boy has a vicious nature that his suave demeanor conceals."

Detached from what she dreaded hearing, Lena studied her mother's bottom-heavy frame. Mama was svelte in pictures taken as a young woman but had packed on poundage. Curiously, Lena wondered: *Will I look that way someday, too*?

As her mother grabbed her hand, Lena refocused her attention.

"Never," her mother said, "will your father and I condone courtship with this boy."

Tears welled in Lena's eyes. She pulled her hand away from her mother's grasp and stood.

"Nothing is so fragile as a young heart," Momma offered sympathetically, "but you'll see how quickly a broken heart mends."

The soothing words came like sandpaper to Lena' skin. She hated her parents. Lena ran to her room and wept. Thoughts of the young man had so long filled daydreams that she could never forget him. Her body shook as she sobbed. Lena didn't even hear Papa enter the house and engage in a vigorous argument with Mama.

Her sister burst into the room and exclaimed, "Your young man!"

"*Si, mia sorella*, what of him?"

"He'll be calling on our house for dinner tonight."

Lena wondered, *Can this be true*?

"And Papa's going into the restaurant business. Your young man will be his partner."

"How? Papa's always dreamed of opening a fancy restaurant, but we don't have the money."

"Your young man's giving Papa money. They'll be partners. He's as wealthy as he is tall and handsome. You're so fortunate!"

Lena's tears turned to tears of joy.

Tony sat across from his boss, waiting for an answer. What price must he tender for permission to wed and to gain help opening the restaurant?

Matteo Rosso's name alone could easily assure that paperwork necessary for building and engaging in the food and beverage business sped through city hall for municipal approvals. An ancient Greek adage adopted by Romans, then forever embraced by Italians, proclaims: "a little corruption is a good thing." If true, a bit would be a blessing. With a price declared and agreement made that Tony could pay his boss from restaurant earnings, the deal was done.

The new restaurant would overlook the inlet Tony had swum the night he vowed to marry Lena and it would open in time for their wedding party. Mister Marcello would serve delicacies that day, showcasing entrees he planned to serve there for years.

Everything was going well, almost. Tony didn't feel comfortable about what his boss also demanded in exchange for his nuptial blessing. Tony had never refused to do a hit, but that time was different. The mustachioed man wanted him to whack a family bookmaker, who had become unlucky. Bookmakers can experience a bad run, but house odds always favor their fortune. When a bookmaker gets unlucky over the long haul, he's skimming the crime family share—and whenever that happens, the bookie's luck runs out for good.

"You know I've never refused you," Tony said, "but I can't whack this man on my wedding day."

"What's wrong with you, Tony Quick Fish?"

Rosso stuck the middle finger of one hand through the cupped fingers on his other, as he spoke.

"You gonna be in a hurry for your honeymoon to give a push of the old in and out."

He laughed heartedly, nearly spitting out his trademark gold toothpick.

"You'll have plenty of time for that later but first your family needs services of the Quick Fish. This bookmaker takes bets from cops, so they'll look into this hit. You'll have an airtight alibi. Who will think you'd leave your wedding reception to do this? You're perfect for this job, Antonio. Don't disappoint me."

Tony had reason to listen uneasily. Hill people in the Gargano region knew that to commit an evil act on the day of your wedding was to curse your first-born son. They also said that taking a life on your wedding day cursed you to bury that son. He had always scoffed when Mama told such tales. Tony knew his boss was acquainted with those deep-rooted superstitions and was testing his loyalty. Rosso focused on the curls at the tips of his thin mustachio as words sliced the air with an unspoken threat.

"Fear," the Boss counseled softly, "is just excitement in need of an attitude adjustment. That's no problem for the Quick Fish, is it?"

Chapter Fifteen

Swing Kids

PALLADIUM NIGHT ISN'T FOR THE FAINT-FOOTED.

The Saturday evening dinner dance at Resorts Hotel and Casino celebrated a duo of 1940s grand ballrooms on opposite coasts: the famous Palladium at Hollywood and Vine in Los Angeles and the equally celebrated dance club of the same name on Broadway in New York City. There, youthful dancers had punished the parquet to music of Tommy Dorsey, Harry James, and king of swing Benny Goodman. Forty plus years later, the same kids dined and danced, though a few graced the dance floor with four-prong walkers. Everyone loved the swing cover band, even Prell.

Working the senior citizen affair, she sat at a round table for twelve, explaining she was her date's daughter. Some then asked if she wasn't really his granddaughter.

"I'll pay you more," her date offered, "if you'll tell 'em I'm your stud muffin."

Normally, satisfying that kind of request was easy. So much of what she did played to one fantasy or another anyway. But, Prell had to lower her profile with an upcoming trial date. Arrested on Smitty's six manufactured prostitution charges, she was free on bail pending trial.

For a vice bust to stick, a cop must prove that a prostitute offered him, or another person in his presence, a sex act for pay. Sex *sans* payment is a good time, not a crime. Smitty had promised to "jackpot her in jail" so long she'd never stop regretting what she'd told him. And, he was en route to accomplishing his mission.

She dressed that night in a slinky black gown, slit high on both sides, and towering heels that were her trademark. Mister Myers beamed to elderly male pals sitting at their table, while their wives jutted elbows into their husbands' bellies whenever they leered in Prell's direction.

"Would you like to dance with my date?" he playfully offered a friend.

"Certainly not," barked an instant reply from the man's wife.

"Well, then," Mister Myers bellowed loudly enough for even the hard of hearing, "please excuse me and my darling. We have entertainment scheduled in our room."

Prell pulled back her date's chair and lifted his bony body, his male cronies following her movements with envious eyes.

When they arrived at his suite, Prell dimmed lights, dialed room service, and chirped.

"Daddy, do you want something?"

"Nothing for me, Sweetheart, but order anything you want."

"Can I order champagne?"

"Only if you tell them to bring the best bottle this hotel has to offer."

Prell ordered Dom Perignon and raw oysters topped with Beluga caviar, then called out: "Will you'll help me with my oysters."

"Oysters on the half shell? It's been so many years since I've had them with champagne." He turned and mused, "Brings back such memories."

Prell peered around the suite, wishing it had a dining terrace. None of the casinos offered balconies or even windows that opened in their hotel rooms. Too many losers might leap. So, a table for two nestled by a picture window offered them an ocean view as Daddy and Baby clinked glasses.

"This night was every bit as wonderful as I'd hoped," Mister Myers sighed.

"The night isn't over," Prell offered. "Isn't there something you'd like me to do?"

Mister Myers blushed.

"I'm afraid," he muttered, "the old pump doesn't crank, anymore."

Prell fondled a string of faux pearls around her neck. Red-painted fingertips descended, and a delicate hand lifted one breast from her gown, making his eyes bulge.

"Ex . . . cuse me," Mister Myers stammered as he retreated to the suite's bedroom.

Prell gave him a head start, then slipped her dress to the floor. She followed in high heels, bra, and a garter belt suspending black hose with back seams—a remembrance of 1940s style—that traced shapely contours of her calves and thighs.

Prell spotted Mister Myers at the dresser with his back to her. He pulled a photo from his wallet and kissed it, no doubt the one he'd shown her earlier: a faded wedding portrait. He had spoken of fifty happy years before his wife had died, leaving him alone.

Mister Myers closed his eyes. Prell sensed he was treasuring the memory of his wife as she lowered him onto the bed and unzipped his fly. A smile lit his face that was still there when Prell washed her hands. As she left, he told her to take cash from his wallet and turn out the lights. Mister Meyers lay so peacefully Prell prayed to God she hadn't jerked him off to death.

She ambled down a corridor to leave and froze when saw him. Smitty stood by the elevator, dangling handcuffs. He was doing it again! Prell dashed in the opposite direction. He wasn't running after her.

Something's wrong, she thought.

At the far end of the hall, two officers from the New Jersey State Police unit assigned to casino waited.

"You're not gonna beat me again," she called back to Smitty, who strolled up the corridor. She threw herself at the larger of the duo.

"Take me, handsome," she sang out. "I'm yours."

The troopers laughed good-naturedly.

Smitty, however, had long lost his sense of humor.

"Thanks, fellas," he said. "I'm booking this bitch at the Temple."

Atlantic City had converted a dilapidated Shriner's mosque into its vice lock up. Cops and street people irreverently called it the Temple . . . a busy Saturday night place, where overcrowded holding cells proved you can make prostitution illegal, but you can't make it unpopular.

Prell didn't mind the Temple; she just hated riding there with Smitty. He cuffed prostitutes, then felt them up and slapped them around when nobody was looking. If a whore complained about mistreatment, Smitty charged her with resisting arrest and claimed he used force to keep her from fleeing.

"This is the seventh time I've picked you up, your Highness. Want me to book you as Queen Victoria again? How 'bout trying your real name?"

Prell didn't answer. She just let him drag her by handcuffs out of the casino and into a waiting squad car. Smitty sat beside her in the rear seat, while a uniformed officer drove.

"*Whatcha* gonna do?" Smitty spit. "The first time you're convicted for prostitution you get a fine. Second time you can go to jail. By the third conviction, judges throw away your cell key. You're looking at convictions one through seven and guess what? I've gotten your cases scheduled so they'll all come up at the same time. How does that sound, your Highness? Seven convictions on one day before the same judge. Starting with your third conviction, you face *mandos*—mandatory jail terms the judge can't spare you even if he wants. You'll gonna rot in the can for fuckin' ever."

As the patrol car passed glittering casino lights, Prell felt tears fall. Smitty's dirty hand met her thighs.

It's not fair, she thought.

Mascara flowed in black rivers down her cheeks. She had heard about lawyers, who made quick plea bargains to turn fast bucks in Municipal Court, while selling out their clients. As Smitty's paws slid higher, Prell hoped she had found a lawyer who would fight. Paul Cameron was her only hope.

Chapter Sixteen

A Good Day for Crabs

THE INVITATIONS ANNOUNCED their wedding day, Saturday, June 9, 1934, and young Tony had to wait no longer. Lena was his bride and the service had been grand, at least what he could recollect. He had been drinking all day, his custom before a hit, lifting dark spirits that dwelled somewhere within him. The grim specter of his task weighed heavily, even when he recited "I dos."

Father Ralph was a young and meek man, voice quavering, as if afraid to delay the large groom from anything he might desire, when he earnestly intoned his final words.

"You may kiss the bride."

Lena lifted her veil and offered a smooch that sobered him, if only for the moment. Lena radiated in her white gown with the glow of a virgin bride, something Tony proudly prized. She shined brighter than the thousand blossoms around the alter. After all, mob weddings and mob funerals are the same: every florist in town works overtime.

A chauffeur-driven Bentley swept the bride and groom to the newly opened restaurant along the inlet. There, the new couple greeted wedding guests and Tony drank more. What he had to do was an offense before God and someday he'd pay dearly. It was sinful to take a life—a sin he had never faltered in committing—but this act was cursed. Spilling blood on his wedding day would taint holiness of their vows yet Tony couldn't refuse the command of his boss.

The happy crowd danced to the *Tarantella*, a lively folk dance from Italy characterized by quick steps and flirtatious behavior between partners. It was then Tony took one last swig of gin, checked his revolver, slipped off his tuxedo jacket, and vanished out the rear door to find the Shark.

Bruno the Shark was a Neapolitan, his family having come to America from the province of Benevento. So, he'd never entirely fit with the members of his crime family, who were mainly descendants of the Sicilian provinces of Messina and Palermo. Worse, he had been arrogant and aloof, perhaps thinking he was too clever to get caught skimming, and too well protected to be hit.

Close to the Atlantic City Sheriff, who regularly made book with him, he had discretely forgotten to collect bets the Chief made when the man selected the wrong horse.

That old bookmakers' ploy maintained friends in uniform. Bookies also paid promptly when a cop won. The Shark figured his law enforcement pals made him untouchable, so he skimmed deeper.

Tony was thankful Bruno was predictable. He found the heavy setter at his favorite pier. The Shark's pants rose high over his rotund belly. With shirt sleeves rolled up, he was pulling rope to lift a crab trap from the bay. It emerged with a splash. Tony watched Bruno savor his catch as if salivating over crabmeat mixed into pasta. The fat man removed the lid from a bucket at his feet, tossed in his catch, and quickly resealed the bucket so the crustaceans wouldn't escape. Then, he wiped his brow and dropped his trap back into the bay.

As the trap splashed, Tony came from behind Bruno the Shark and hammered the butt his revolver deep into the man's skull. Bruno's brains and body fell separately into the bay and sunk with the trap. Tony tipped the bucket with his left foot and watched crabs crawl off the dock and escape into the bay. The Shark's body rose to the surface and floated toward the ocean with the outgoing tide.

It was a lucky night for crabs, not so lucky for sharks.

When Tony returned to the wedding party, he took another hearty swig of gin and searched for his bride. She was gone.

"*Rubare La Stosa!*" someone called.

Groomsmen had stolen the bride. The traditional game was in full swing but laced with hooch, Tony wasn't in the mood. Male members of the wedding party had hidden

Lena and joked that the groom would have to pay a ransom to enjoy his bride's pleasures on their wedding night.

"What price will you pay?" they clamored.

A soldier from the family spotted the familiar look on Tony's face that only came when the Quick Fish had struck, a stony expression that terrified.

"Get her back in here fast," the soldier whispered to members of the bridal party, who swiftly ushered Lena into the room. Tony lifted his bride to the waiting Bentley. It sped to the same hotel where, years earlier, instead of carrying a bride, Tony had hoisted bricks.

How I've grown since those days, he thought.

While Lena prepared in the bathroom, Tony peered out the window of the bridal suite. Lights along the boardwalk glistened on infinite white caps that rushed toward him like wedding gifts from Neptune. As each wave crashed on the shore, he recognized his love for her was as timeless as the sea . . . and how eager he was to have her.

At last, Lena emerged with a demure smile. Everything for which he had ever yearned swept toward him, veiled in a nightgown. White silk flowed from high neckline to the floor. No nightdress at the Chanticleer ever covered so much. He had often sated his urge to fuck. Never had he experienced the satisfaction of making love.

They met in each other's arms before the open window and kissed deeply. Then, Lena's virginal offering came like a baptismal cleansing of his every sweat bead that had ever sullied whorehouse sheets. It came so fast . . . and then he passed out.

Lena couldn't sleep. She rose to pick her new husband's clothes from the floor. A heavy lump beneath his tuxedo piqued her curiosity. She reached under and pulled out Tony's revolver. A three-inch square of scalp with Bruno's hair was attached to the pistol butt. Blood on the scalp was still fresh, the skin supple. Lena dropped the gun in horror.

This is what I've married, she thought. *What lurks inside my husband?*

Lena went to the open window, where surf sang a lullaby. Whoever said love is blind was wrong, she now realized. Love is the only thing that lets us see clearly—then lets us keep on looking. Lena crossed her arms on the windowsill and lowered her head atop them. For the first time in her life, she would slumber without her sister's warm body next to her. And, as she drifted, she could only wonder.

What does life hold in store with the dangerous man I love?

Chapter Seventeen

Whore Court

PAUL GRIPPED PRELL'S ARM to guide her through the door of the Atlantic City Municipal Courthouse that sweltering July day in 1984. Every other Friday the building turned into what participants—meaning court staff, lawyers, cops, defendants, witnesses, knowing spectators—called "whore court." Only prostitution cases were heard until midnight to process the massive number of harlotry charges crowding city court dockets. The busy trade, mostly on the street, had presented a civic quagmire: whether to vigorously assault the crime issue or turn a blind eye to a trade that supported legalized gambling. After all, some players sought easy "sex play for pay" to enhance their gaming experience.

Las Vegans accommodated the trade by allowing it to legally flourish outside city limits in licensed brothels.

Unless Atlantic City leadership found like ingenuity, biweekly court sessions would continue to generate occupants for the overpopulated county jailhouse and state prisons.

Fearful of what was about to happen, Prell transformed from a seasoned pro into the overwhelmed teenager she really was. This time, Paul hadn't packed his briefcase with books to stack on the counsel table. Instead, he brought something he hoped to counterbalance the heavy weight of evidence against his client. He had no witnesses, only the assertions of a prostitute against the word of a veteran vice officer, which would be corroborated by testimony from the cop's brethren. Vice cops backed up each other for good reason. Most hookers knew it was time to lie as soon as they were sworn to tell the truth. If cops had to falsely swear to offset a whore's perjury, they would, under the theory that two wrongs make a right.

Paul observed a dozen cops standing in a corner of the courtroom with a man Prell pointed out as her arresting officer. Cops backslapped Officer Smith as if the State had already won. With that many ready to testify, it was clear they had.

The Municipal Prosecutor approached with annoying nonchalance. Lean and nearly pinheaded, the man told Paul he would allow Prell to plead guilty to three of the seven charges.

"Pick any three you want, Counselor. I'll recommend dismissal of the rest, but she'll do six months in jail for each of the three guilty pleas."

"We'll try the cases."

"Suit yourself," the pinhead replied. "If you don't accept the deal before the judge comes to the bench, my offer's withdrawn. Your sweet thing will serve six months on every conviction—all seven. I've already briefed my officers. Save yourself the effort and spare your client the extra years behind bars."

As Paul reviewed the plea offer with Prell, her eyes moistened as she considered the prison stretch. Hushed words crossed Prell's quivering lips.

"What . . . what should I do?"

Paul turned away. He didn't want to take the easy way out. On the other hand, the young woman had only been in overnight municipal lockups. If he lost, she would serve harder time in a state prison. He was ready to make his recommendation when he spied Officer Smith from the corner of his eye. The cop gave Prell the finger. Paul's ire rose as Smitty's arrogance made his client's eyes dart to the floor, then shut tight.

The bailiff called into the room, "Everyone be seated. The judge is on his way."

Paul walked to the Municipal Prosecutor, who knew the defense had no choice but to take the plea offer and spoke softly.

"No deal."

"All rise," the courtroom attendant cried, "for the Honorable Clarence G. Light, Judge of the Municipal Court of Atlantic City."

Judge Light's commanding presence was immediately apparent to Paul. The bearded black man had perceptive eyes and a learned look. He came to the bench when city leaders, many of whom resided in the town's black community, had searched for an African American jurist to handle a heavy case load. What they got from Clarence Light was a judge who knew how to judge. He blended justice with compassion and was rarely appealed. As the saying went in the legal community: "Judge Light is right."

The judge surveyed his case list and looked around his courtroom.

"State versus Queen Victoria," he called out. "Wait a minute," he said as he leaned toward his clerk at a small desk beside his bench. "Am I reading this name correctly? State versus Queen, Victoria."

"That's her name on the charge sheets, your Honor," replied a large female court clerk in a polka-dot dress.

"Who's here on the cases against Miz Queen?" the judge called.

Paul strode forward to the microphone. "Paul Cameron, your Honor, representing the defendant."

"Is your client here, Sir?"

"She's here, your Honor. Please come forward, Ma'am," he called to Prell.

Judge Light studied her as she walked forward to stand next to her lawyer. Dressed down for her court appearance, just as Paul had instructed, she looked like a kid—a kid with seven prostitution cases.

"Mister Prosecutor," the judge said, "are you and the arresting officer prepared to proceed with all charges?"

"Yes, Sir," came the crisp reply from a veteran of many vice cases.

"Are any other police officers here for these cases?" Judge Light called out.

A dozen officers replied in chorus, "We're all here for this one, Judge."

They laughed in the rear of the courtroom and Paul could read the expression on the judge's face. It told him that the jurist didn't like what he was seeing or hearing. He leafed through the charge sheets that were all signed by the same officer.

Perhaps, Paul thought hopefully, *the testimony of this officer troubled the judge in the past.*

"Your Honor," Paul offered, "I have a brief that I ask the Court to review at the next recess. The authority cited may assist the Court in ruling upon a defense motion I intend to make before trial."

"Very well, Mister Cameron. We'll deal with your motion after the morning recess."

Paul handed the brief to the judge's clerk and a copy to the prosecutor. The pinhead rolled his eyes at the Motion to Dismiss the cases for lack of speedy prosecution. Certainly, the charges had languished on the dockets for some reason, but municipal court judges are notoriously disinterested in arguments of constitutional magnitude. They just don't have time.

During the morning recess, Smitty walked over to Paul and Prell. He lingered menacingly as a handful of vice cops joined him chanting, "Guilty, guilty, guilty."

When Judge Light returned to the bench, he wasted no time. "State versus Queen," he called.

Paul and Prell returned to the defense table. Smitty and his friends sat behind the pinhead, looking satisfied that Prell was on her way to prison.

"Mister Cameron," Judge Light began, "I read your brief. You claim the defendant's Sixth Amendment right to a speedy trial has been violated because these cases weren't timely scheduled for trial."

"Correct, your Honor."

Judge Light continued. "The United States Supreme Court case of *Barker versus Wingo*, which you've cited in your brief, mandates dismissal of criminal charges on this ground when certain elements are established. The law even presumes there is prejudice against a defendant by unaccounted delay because witnesses may disappear or be unable to recall events accurately. What do you say about that, Mister Prosecutor?"

"I say it doesn't matter, Judge. Defense counsel never applied for a trial listing. That's a requirement under *Barker*."

"Mister Cameron," Judge Light said pointedly, "how do you respond?"

"Your Honor, our state's Appellate Division recently ruled in *State versus Marino* that there's a stronger speedy trial right in New Jersey than guaranteed by the United States Supreme Court. In our jurisdiction a defendant is no longer obligated to apply for a trial listing."

"Did you know that, Mister Prosecutor?" Judge Light said.

The Municipal Prosecutor said nothing.

"Well, I know that because I read Mister Cameron's brief. Nice job, Sir," he said to Paul.

Then, Judge Light picked up Prell's charge sheets and announced his ruling.

"I dismiss each case against Queen, Victoria. Her constitutional right to speedy trials on these charges has been violated."

He glared at Vice Officer Smith and continued when he was certain he had the man's attention.

"Violation of civil rights won't be tolerated in my courtroom."

Paul guided his client outside. She was still in shock.

"You're the best lawyer God ever made," Prell proclaimed with her smile restored.

Paul had to grin back.

"Just be sure to tell your friends."

"I'll tell, who I can, but me and AK are leaving town for a while."

Confidence resurfacing as she walked away, Prell shouted over her shoulder.

"Thanks again, Mister Hotshot Lawyer."

Paul knew that word of her courtroom outcome would quickly hit the streets through mouths of working women, who were sitting the courtroom, waiting for their own cases to be called. Between clients the Reverend Rich case generated and clientele Prell's case would deliver, he'd establish a busy Atlantic City law practice.

A burley cop sitting in court for another matter had watched with admiration. Boog Johnson kept his hair trimmed short, military style, high and tight over the ears, and buzz cut on top. Early grey streaked his sides and short sideburns. As a former athlete, the plainclothes officer wore white socks for comfort and preferred sneakers to shoes with any attire. He'd developed a slight paunch, enjoying beer while watching any team play any sport. Boog worked in the detective's division and his beat covered robbery to rape, assault to murder, essentially anything truly bad. He was a respected department veteran, living a lifelong career on A.C.P.D., like his father and his father's father.

Boog knew Smitty's game and appreciated how well Paul Cameron handled it. Deciding to make a point of meeting the young lawyer, he walked to the parking lot, where he saw Smitty poking his finger in Paul's chest.

"Someday, Counselor," Smitty ranted, "you're going to be mine. Lawyers and hookers—you're all whores to me. Remember to look over your shoulder for me and remember my name."

"How could I forget your name, Smutty?"

"Smitty's the name."

"No, your name is Smutty, all right. You're filth and I won't forget it."

Boog liked the young man's brash style but felt for him. He had no idea how long Smitty could hold a grudge or what he would do to even a score. Cops always have time on their side.

Someday, someway, Boog thought, *a determined cop in this town always gets what he's after.*

Part II

Chapter Eighteen

Bedroom Games

"SO, YOU AND YOUR WIFE LIKED to play games?"

"What are you talking about?" Paul shot back.

"Sex games. Not the cuddly kind. The rough stuff. You and your wife liked bedroom games, didn't you?"

On April 4, 1989, the questions posed to Paul were framed by a veteran homicide investigator, who had the bullish look it took to do the job. His sleeves were rolled up as if he were ready to spar with more than words. Clenching an unlit cigar between his teeth, he chomped and gave a steely gaze, letting Paul know the man didn't believe him.

So far, there had been no arrests in Sarah's homicide case. Information the Prosecutor's Office had released to the press suggested they had no suspects. Paul, as the victim's estranged spouse, recognized he topped their list—

and that he'd stay there if they didn't turn up other leads fast.

Paul had never answered questions when cops initially detained him. And, he would have declined the invitation to this informal meeting, but the murder investigation was being handled by an assistant prosecutor whom he liked and trusted. Carol Resnick had a reputation for being tough but fair. Paul came at her request but arrived well protected. Lee Gunther sat by his side. His mentor had left Philadelphia to practice law in Miami. When Paul asked why, Lee had spoken with uncustomary abruptness.

"Best you don't know," was all he said.

Lee had changed. More than just having trimmed his long hair, something happened to the man, as if he had been on his own run to Hell. Paul hoped Lee hadn't lost his touch.

He had readily accepted the senior lawyer's two conditions for him to fly into Atlantic City. First, Lee would make all decisions in the case. Second, Paul would make none. Lawyers are lousy clients and good lawyers are worse.

Paul's paralegal attended and was taking copious notes. In her late-twenties, Mickey was an integral part of his law practice. She had spent many nights, during lengthy trials, pouring through transcripts and briefs so Paul could blast away the next day in court. The paralegal had an astute business look with "mousey brown hair," as she called it, kept in a bun, wearing a brown suit and wire-framed eyeglasses. She was a chameleon, who fit wherever she went, knowing how to let her hair down when the occasion called. Theirs had always been a cordial, professional relationship but lately Paul was finding himself drawn to her sympathetic ear.

The morning meeting in the Prosecutor's Office was everything he expected. Both sides jockeyed to learn more than they were prepared to give up. Paul knew, if the State's investigation didn't turn up something fast, he'd be their only target. He also knew Carol was too professional for their acquaintanceship to interfere. Paul, Lee, and Mickey bunched on one side of the cluttered desk. Carol and her investigator huddled on the other as if barbed wire kept the two sides apart.

"I didn't get an answer, Counselor," the investigator persisted. "What kind of games did you and the decedent like to play?"

Lee intervened. "You're not getting an answer. The question's out of line."

"It's not out of line," the investigator snapped back, "but your client doesn't have to answer. We'll understand what that means."

Carol interjected, appearing tired of the positioning from both sides and firing at Paul: "What do you know about Sarah's death?"

"Only what I read in the papers."

"You know we don't release all the details," she said. "The murder scene was an ugly sight."

"I haven't been back there," replied Paul. "Your office still maintains a court order closing the house off to preserve evidence."

"How long before my client gets back in his home?" Lee demanded.

"I understood Paul wasn't living there at the time of the murder," Carol mused.

"True, but he's paying the mortgage. He's entitled to return when you clear out whatever your office needs."

"He'll get in soon enough," the investigator chimed. "Right now, we have a few more questions."

"If you want more from my client, you'll have to charge him. So far, it's evident you don't have enough to charge anyone."

Paul addressed Carol directly, "What can you tell us?'

She and her investigator exchanged glances. The man shook his head, as if to indicate "don't say anything," but Carol continued anyway.

"We know the tip to the police came from someone who's been inside the local police department, someone who had access to inside telephone numbers."

"Like a local lawyer," the investigator offered, "who's been in that police station representing his clients."

Paul didn't react. Being in a station house came with his work.

"Did you find the murder weapon?" Lee said.

Carol handed Lee a photograph from her file. In turn he handed it to Paul.

"Recognize it?" She said.

Paul studied the photograph depicting a clean kitchen knife. Nothing indicated it had been used as a murder weapon.

"I can't say so."

"It's a Ginzu knife, Counselor," the investigator chimed. "Like you see on late-night television commercials. The kind that slices and dices."

"What makes you think this was the murder weapon?" Lee interjected.

"We found that knife sparkling in the dishwashing machine. Someone had taken trouble to wipe it clean of fingerprints, put it in the dishwasher, and turn on the washer as they left. We sent it to the state police lab."

The scope of their preliminary investigation didn't impress Paul. "What else do you have?"

"We're waiting on the lab work," the investigator stated, "but maybe you would like to look at these."

He opened a manila folder holding eight by ten-inch glossy photographs. Paul looked, felt ill, and instantly looked away. Sketchy newspaper descriptions of the crime scene hadn't prepared him for the graphic depictions of Sarah's mutilated body.

"Was that necessary?" Lee pressed Carol.

She turned, then said coldly, "Counselor, if your client wants to make a deal, now is the time. Give me a straight confession and I can talk to my boss about something other than a death sentence."

Paul sensed Carol hated uttering the words, but knew she had no choice. If he wanted a plea bargain, he'd have to deal fast. If the State established firm proof, the high-profile case would be too hot for any offer less than life.

"We're out of here," Lee declared, directing Paul and Mickey toward the door. Lee followed, moving more slowly on his bum leg.

After they'd gone, Carol turned to her investigator. "What do you think?"

She counted on his instinct as a bulldog, who had been with the major crimes unit longer than any investigator on staff.

He pulled the unlit stogie from his mouth and looked at its chewed tip.

"Cameron's got obvious motive. He was in the middle of a divorce where the battle focused on big bucks. Without an alibi, he's a suspect with opportunity to commit the crime. There are no eyewitnesses to the murder so we're looking at a circumstantial evidence case with both motive and opportunity."

Annoyed at being told the obvious, Carol snapped.

"Tell me something I don't already know."

"I can't do that, Counselor, but we both know your pal is guilty."

Carol knew it could be.

"If Paul Cameron is dirty," she said on a long breath, "he'll go down."

"Oh, he's dirty and he's going down."

Carol watched the cagey veteran chomp his cigar while she reflected. Through much of their interview, she had detected a coldness in Paul's eyes she hadn't before seen. She wondered if feelings for him had interfered with objectivity. Carol had always looked forward to facing Paul in courtrooms. She was certain he felt something, too. But Paul had married the attractive woman, who had come from San Francisco, while Carol dated a procession of earnest men for whom she was never equally eager.

She peered at the spread file. Evidence was already stacking up against Paul and Carol knew what she had to do.

"I'm off the case," she said determinedly. "The boss will have to handle this one without me. I'm too damned close to the only target we've got and he's wearing a bull's eye."

"As you say."

"Anyway, Grender seems interested in handling this case."

Her investigator continued speaking but her thoughts focused on what Grender would do to hammer Paul.

Chapter Nineteen

Drawing Blood

AS PAUL WAS DODGING uncomfortable questions, Tony contemplated his own quagmire. Ongoing criminal investigations of their rackets nearly overshadowed squabbles with their the Asian gang. In the hangout that his crime family owned, the Fairmont Tavern, he contemplated the dangerous course he was charting.

"Another drink, Mister DeBona?" the bartender called.

Tony dismissed him with a wave, then walked to the backroom where his *capos* waited. Many bosses had met their men there. Decisions made within those tight walls shaped the dark history of the resort's Italian mob. It had gradually displaced the town's Irish gang, following the murder of its powerful boss Nucky Carlson.

No decision would have greater impact on the crime family than the one Tony struggled to make. He strolled into his office and sat behind a desk that disappeared in relation to his proportions and contemplated.

Should we hit the prominent public figure behind these State investigations?

Familiar faces in his family waited to deal harshly with Rolland Pepperman of the Casino Control Commission. Commissioners, such as Pepperman, serve at the leisure of the Governor to strictly regulate casino gaming. Under their purview, nut-cracking enforcement measures are designed to keep organized crime out of the industry. As a half-ass attorney, who couldn't earn a living by practicing law, the man sought Tony's assistance to attain the political appointment. The job carries a less than grand salary for a decent lawyer but feeds you and offers a modest pension after ten years' service.

Open to having a friend on the watch-dog agency, Tony exercised influence over key legislators and political hacks, who pushed Pepperman into the job, just as the dull-of-wit sometimes attain lofty positions. When Tony approached him for fair recompense, he didn't expect his friend to forget him. Hardly did Tony anticipate the newly appointed commissioner would launch a public inquiry into the organized crime ties that Pepperman had found so useful in landing the job. The guy even demanded monthly payoffs.

"Help with law enforcement comes with a price tag," he declared.

When Tony refused, Commissioner Pepperman flexed his new muscles, showing off biceps strengthened by the State Police and Office of the Attorney General. He publicly decried organized crime in the casinos and became a flea on the bull-sized ass of the local mob. The Boss of the Boardwalk prepared to scratch him off.

Tony studied his *capos*. The days ahead would test them.

Slim-faced Sammy Smoke was the best torch in the business, having seared off part of an ear getting too close to an inferno. His pronounced facial features appeared to cut the wind when he walked down a blustery street, lending the look of a pan held sideways and upright.

Bobby "the Brain" Rubino coordinated day-to-day operations. Tony increasingly delegated to his clever second-in-command, who was young to be underboss, but all their men respected him.

Carmen "Dog Face," the family hammer, lacked Bobby's intellect but was loyal as the hound he resembled. Tony could trust him to bark or kill on command.

As he studied his men, Tony reflected.

Who would've ever imagined I'd become a boss?

Because he wasn't Sicilian, less qualified soldiers rose, first to lieutenant, then to *capo*, ahead of him. As those men met untimely ends to bullets and imprisonment, Tony had endured. To keep surviving, Tony uttered the words his men expected to hear.

"Pepperman is a dead man."

Then, he surprised them.

"We go outside the family for this job."

"Should I talk to our friends in Philly or New York?" Bobby flashed.

"They won't do," replied Tony. "We'll be obvious targets in state and local murder investigations. So will our friends. This job goes to the Asians. Arrangements have already been made.

Bobby, you and your wife will take a vacation starting tomorrow. Carmen, you'll fish at your brother's lodge in upstate New York. Sammy and I will attend the Mayor's hearings on revitalizing the inlet district."

Sammy Smoke lit up. "We gonna do some urban renewal, Boss?"

Tony smiled. Sammy had been responsible for many urban and suburban renovations over the years.

"No, my old friend, but we'll all be seen places that will clear us."

"How can we go to the Asians? The blood of their pusher and our soldier hasn't dried," Bobby observed. "They'll see this as weakness and try stuffing their hands in our pockets."

Tony valued Bobby's opinion, but he had just given an order, not an invitation to discuss or debate.

"Our family must maintain distance from this business," he explained. "The Asians from the west coast and New York are new to town. Pepperman's people won't know where to look for the man who'll do the job. We'll be clean and we'll use this hit to our advantage. I can't tell you how, but hearings will no longer focus on us."

Tony studied his men. His world was fast changing, and he had to keep pace. The FBI had broken the mob code of *Omerta*, the Mafia creed of silence, while pursuing the New York crime families with electronic surveillance and forensic capabilities beyond anything he had ever imagined, when he killed the Kaiser nearly sixty years earlier. Fresh faces in organized crime fought without honor. Tony didn't know if he would survive these new times. His plan would either secure his future or terminate his life.

Acid churned in his stomach.

Probably an ulcer, Tony thought.

Applying pressure to the pain, he let out a raspy breath, trying to mask discomfort, knowing ill health is a weakness that invites opportunism from enemies—and sometimes from friends.

Chapter Twenty

A Bitter Taste

LEAVING THE INTERROGATION at the County Prosecutor's Office, Paul vomited next to his car. The vision of Sarah in the investigation photos sickened him. Now, his mouth tasted like a sewer. Mickey put her arm around Paul and ushered him to the passenger side of his car. Then, she drove, as they mused over the meeting. Foolish words came though he never intended to utter them.

"Do you think I'm their target?"

"Paul, you're so naive. Sarah was financially raping you in the divorce. Even if you didn't hate her enough to kill her, nothing else will matter if they indict you."

Her words were emphatic. Worse, he realized, they were true.

"Besides," Mickey observed, "you still haven't told them where you were when she was killed. I'll give you an alibi if you need one. All you have to do is ask."

Paul wondered what would happen if their story fell apart. Lawyers typically worry more about presenting a consistent fact pattern in court than the truth, but his personal involvement precluded him from thinking like one. He said nothing as she drove, then drove faster, then too fast for Paul.

"Hey! Slow down," he called.

Mickey laughed. "This is the only Porsche alive that never hits fifty-five."

Surely, she drove the way they built it to travel but Paul couldn't think at that speed. As she slowed, he knew what they had to do.

"We needed information off the streets," he said, "the kind a cop knows how to find. Drive us to the Boogster."

Mickey drove to the tavern that had a lighted sign eternally flashing, "Open 24 hours." Former cop, Boog Johnson, ran the beer and black eye bar. Paul had met him in a courtroom, while Boog was still on the A.C.P.D. He mentioned that he had seen and admired the way Paul handled Prell's case and they became friends.

Boog was a local phenomenon—a high school football hero, who had married his cheerleader sweetheart. He joined the police department following family footsteps, even rose to detective, then hit the skids. Police-work hours and marriage don't mix well. Disability from a roof fall chasing a robbery suspect didn't combine with marriage at all. He divorced and managed the neighborhood tappy the way it had to be run. Boog always had a story to tell, an ear to listen, and a loaded .45-caliber pistol under the counter to resolve arguments. Information Paul found there was always solid. Boog even freelanced for him as an investigator. His long ears could be counted upon to hear from reliable sources.

Paul and Mickey walked into the smoke-filled room, which was busy for mid-afternoon, and grabbed two stools. Boog brought their drinks without being asked, a beer for Mickey and scotch over rocks for Paul. Mickey removed her eyeglasses and opened buttons on her jacket.

"Mickey, it's always good to see your mounds," Boog greeted in deference to her recognized abundance.

"You'll never be mistaken for a modern man, will you?" she replied.

Paul observed the usual banter between the two as he imbibed Scotland's national product. While Boog had a kind heart, Mickey was right: he could be a good-natured Neanderthal. Paul realized how much he would be relying upon the twosome, preparing his legal defense.

"Boog, he said, I need information."

"I can help you, there, a little. My people in the Detective's Division are keeping their eyes and ears open, while I'm checking the streets. I know what you need, Buddy. You're a suspect. Where were you when Sarah was killed?"

"Can't tell you, right now."

Boog frowned. "Well, you better get that straightened out fast. You're going to need a story that stands up to a lot of scrutiny if the prosecutor's office doesn't tag anybody else.

Paul saw Mickey gaze sympathetically as she lifted the beer to her lips. A red lipstick ring coated the neck of her bottle when she set it back down on the bar. He reconsidered her offer. They could say they had spent the night together, but would their story hold up? Getting caught in a lie would burn him.

Better to have no alibi than one that can sink you, Paul surmised.

He tipped his glass back, drained it, then motioned for another.

"Boog, where do you start the investigation of this crime to find the killer?"

"Oh, no you don't. You're not dragging me into this. I'll talk to friends but I'm not snooping around. Paul, you aren't just a lawyer investigating this crime for a client. You're an obvious target in a homicide investigation. If anything goes wrong while I sleuth around for you, they could nail me for complicity in the murder charge."

"You're right." Paul took another drink and looked hard at the burly bartender. "Are you going to help me?"

Boog stared downward, then peered around. "I have a customer, who needs a refill at the other end of the bar."

He walked away, then turned back sharply and yelped, "Of course, I'll help. I'm the dumbest asshole on the planet. Who else would help you with this, Counselor?"

Paul smiled and collected his thoughts while Boog waited on construction workers, who had quit early for the day. The place was easy to fall into for a drink.

When Boog returned, Paul was quick to say, "Where do we start?"

"Same place the county investigators started. We go to the scene of the crime."

"You have a key?" Mickey interjected as she glanced from Boog to Paul.

"What do you mean? It's my house."

"Sometimes you are *so* naive," Mickey said with a smile. "The first thing a woman does when her husband moves out is change all the locks. How are you going to get inside?"

Paul turned to Boog.

"No problem," said the Boogster.

"Did you learn how to pick a lock when you were a cop?" Mickey said.

Boog shook his head from side to side.

"Did you keep locksmith pass keys when you left the Detective Division?" Paul tried.

Again, Boog shook his head from side to side.

"But the department did teach us how to get into a property when you don't have a key."

"How?" Mickey wondered.

"It's easy." Boog pulled a telephone from under the bar and slid it to Paul. "You call someone who does. There's one person in town we all know who has one."

Paul immediately understood. He dialed the number. If anyone in town had a key to that house, anyone Paul could trust, it was his former schoolmate Anthony D'Allesandro. The interior designer had spent so much time in the house at Sarah's behest, decorating and redecorating, Paul would have thought they were having an affair, if he hadn't known better.

While Sarah and Anthony enjoyed long luncheon dates, where they'd talk for hours, their conversations were akin to words shared between dear female friends. Anthony was openly gay in a long-term relationship with a man he adored. Paul reached him on the first ring, spoke to his friend, and hung up.

"Anthony will help, but I don't want him implicated if something goes wrong. Local cops are patrolling the house until the prosecutor's office has its protective Order lifted. Rather than pick up the key from his office, we'll meet him at the pageant tonight."

"What pageant?" Boog said. "Miss America is behind us."

"The other pageant," Mickey answered, "at Club Cosmo."

"Oh, brother," Boog said. "We're going to a gay club?"

Mickey looked at Boog, who was a mammoth man with a moose of a mug, then looked at her smaller boss. She made the easy observation.

"Everyone's gonna know who the bitch is in your relationship."

"I'm not going with him," Paul spurted. "Everyone goes to this pageant. Gays and straights. I'm taking you, Sweetheart," he said to Mickey. "You'll be my beard."

"You're both too homophobic," Mickey joshed, "but I'll be glad to go. I always wanted to see a drag queen beauty pageant. I hear it's judged on the same formula the Miss America pageant uses: swimsuit, talent, evening gown, and interview competitions."

“How do they tuck those things into swimsuits?” Boog wondered aloud.

“It’s a date,” Paul said to Mickey. “We’ll find Anthony for the house key and see them crown this year’s Queen of Queens.”

Sponsored by Atlantic City’s counterculture, which went back to the day the town opened its doors, the annual event collected funds for AIDS research. Paul would gladly go to collect the key. Visiting the house he had left behind was another matter. He both wondered and worried about what he might find.

Chapter Twenty-One

When Devils Meet

"YOU WANTED ME TO WAKE YOU at three o'clock, Mister DeBona," the bartender said.

Tony opened his eyes. He had napped in his office chair. Rested for what lay ahead, he rose and walked through the old bar toward the door.

Bobby came to his side, calling: "Need a ride, Boss?"

"Not for this trip, he replied.

A taxicab sped him to the Sands Casino Hotel, where he entered a rear service door. The Casino Control Commission distributed photographs of reputed crime figures with orders to keep them out of the properties as casino players or hotel guests. Tony had seen their photo logbook. It looked like a high school yearbook and his picture was prominently displayed in front, as if he were valedictorian. He couldn't enter front doors, where security personnel lurked but he waltzed into every casino on the boardwalk, proving anything can be done in Atlantic City if you know how to do it.

With the business at hand, Tony was glad to enter through the rear, anyway, observed by nobody except the trustworthy young, Vietnamese man—one of the many Nguyen cousins working as casino marketing specialists, attracting and catering to Asian high rollers.

Tony moved swiftly behind the young man, consciously lifting his heels to avoid shuffling like an old man. An elevator shot them to the penthouse level, where the younger man's door raps were answered by a Chinese man, perhaps fifty or so, making him also youthful in Tony's eyes.

"Mister DeBona," his guide said, "meet Mister Shek."

Then with a slight bow in deference to Chinese custom, the young man silently disappeared.

Tony studied Shek from ground up. The Asian crime lord wore black-velvet Versace slippers, and a black lounging robe covering silver silk pajamas. Shek was pretending to be a high rolling Hong Kong businessman, who slept late so he could play baccarat long into the night. Tony felt the man's eyes survey him as well. How different they seemed. Tony being large-framed, while his counterpart was delicate, having a near-feminine comportment, though Tony knew his counterpart was no wimp. He had the eyes of a man who, like Tony, could deliver death's calling card.

Tony entered and recognized decor, which was so garish as to be reminiscent of the Chanticleer Hotel of his youth. The suite had been designed to impress highly rated players, who dropped tens-of-thousands and sometimes millions of dollars on a visit. For some reason, Tony observed, decorators took it for granted that high rollers favored cat-house decor: velvet-swirl wallpaper, an oversized black leather bar with pink marble top, and enough mirrors to please any narcissist.

"Your Mister Nguyen has been most accommodating," Shek said. "He's well-spoken in four languages . . . and I find him most interesting."

"He's that and more. He'll treat you well for the casino and discreetly to benefit our endeavor."

Shek seemed eager for business.

"Are you prepared," he instantly began, "to forget our differences?"

Tony didn't answer until his counterpart squirmed.

"If you deliver what you've promised," he said, "my reciprocation is assured."

The corners of Shek's mouth twisted upward.

"Will you allow my family to share the spoils of this town? After all, you've fought to keep us out."

Tony spoke in a monotone that concealed his emotion.

"For many years the Irish ran this town with room for other modest interests. Now, I see no reason my family cannot make room for yours."

"True," Shek acknowledged. "But you've always confined us to the Asian communities. If we do what you ask, can I believe you'll be more generous?"

"Mister Shek, we're businessmen, prepared to grant considerations, but we must always have a *quid pro quo.*"

Shek's lips curled into a full smile. Tony wondered if the man kept his emotions better concealed at the playing tables downstairs. He knew what Shek was thinking. He'd make a deal to stick his family's foot further in the door, then stomp on Tony, when the time was right.

"My interests are modest," Shek said smoothly. "You control labor through the union halls. Every convention that hits this town fills your pockets. Tradesmen charge fifty dollars to change a light bulb in the convention center, and your family receives a gratuity from each twist. Your affiliations afford influence, as you call it, at every major construction site."

"We have an interest in labor," Tony conceded, "but it's shared with families from New York."

"You're modest."

Shek's coyness was surfacing.

"We're not interested in the trades," he professed. "We simply wish to expand our modest endeavors past the Asian communities. You've stymied our bookmakers and kept us from casino support industries. The black cowboys can run whores, but we want to open a gentleman's massage parlor and an oriental escort service without interference from your people. And, we'll respect limits in drug trafficking. Together we shall be like Sears and Roebuck, shall we not?"

Tony momentarily wondered, *Whatever happened to Mister Roebuck anyway*?

"You have our blessing," he said smoothly, "if you're prepared to pay the price."

A long pause followed. That time the duration was calculated by the Asian crime lord. Tony couldn't tell what

Shek was thinking. Perhaps, his counterpart wasn't so easily read.

Finally, Shek responded. "We've engaged a very special man, who will do the deed within seventy-two hours."

"Who?"

"He who has no name. He'll do the job swiftly and leave no trace of your family's involvement."

Tony studied Shek a final time before shaking hands to seal their pact. He was about to deal with Lucifer. A delicate hand reached to meet his. One devil took the hand of the other without so much as a puff of burning brimstone.

Shek found French champagne behind the well-stocked bar. He popped a bottle and poured two crystal glasses to the rims. With Tony gone, the door to an adjoining suite opened and a Chinese man entered. He was a brawnier version of Shek with the same nefarious eyes. Shek handed a goblet to his second-in-command. They raised the crystals to their lips and sipped.

"The old man is dangling by a single silk thread," Shek said. "It's going to be easier than we expected. Commissioner Pepperman treaded heavily on the Italian family, and the old man betrayed how deeply they've been hurt."

If Shek could feel compassion, perhaps he would have felt it then.

"The old man's a beaten dog," he continued. "Time to put him out of misery."

"Perhaps," his associate suggested, "we shouldn't take out the commissioner. Let him weaken the old family further, then move into Atlantic City more swiftly with impunity."

"No. Better that the commissioner dies. Pepperman would come after us next, anyway. Have patience, as the proverb says: 'grass will be milk soon enough'."

His associate nodded.

"We've paid Commissioner Pepperman long enough to exert influence over these dagoes," Shek commented. "Time to trim our payroll. Our assassin will move in three days' time. That shall start the end of the old man's reign."

They clinked glasses, then savored fine champagne, just as they savored the certainty of an abundant future.

Chapter Twenty-Two

Here She Comes . . .
Miss Americock

LIQUOR FLOWED. TRACES OF COCAINE under the nose of the hostess didn't blend with her beard-covering makeup any better than Paul initially melded into the crowd. The scene was high camp. That's what you called it if you knew. If you were straight, you might call it something else. Literally speaking, it was a damned lot of fun in jam packed Club Cosmopolitan.

Paul and Mickey dressed for the affair as Anthony had suggested. The simple chicness of Paul's Armani tuxedo came in contrast to Mickey's low-cut floral gown that revealed the reasons some might call her "Mickey Mounds."

"I'm wearing it," she told Paul, so no one mistakes me for a drag queen."

She paused to grab Paul's arm, then added: "and so no one mistakes you for not being straight."

Still, Paul caught more furtive glances from unattached men than Mickey as they searched for Anthony and his longtime partner Emile.

The pageant was amid an intermezzo, while participants changed from gowns for the bathing suit event. The Silly Girls entertained on a platform to the side of the main stage. The drag band sang a medley of Village People hits. Paul found himself enjoying their rendition of "Macho Man," which the lead singer sang in a deep bass voice and backup vocalists twirled high stacked wigs around in circles imitating a Tina Turner review. He understood Donna Summer hits also made their play card and, from time to time, they would break into a familiar refrain belting: "Here she comes, Miss Americock. . .."

They found the couple in a corner booth for four, Anthony and Emile sitting close. As fast as his welcoming smile, Anthony stuck his hand out to greet Paul. When their hands shook, Paul felt the key go into his palm. Anthony was a man of his word.

Though he and Paul were the same age, Anthony appeared older than his years. His hairline had receded, and early grey streaked the sides, lending a dignified look. Emile was slightly built with deep-set eyes from which nonchalant glances seemed to have deeper meaning.

Both men were well educated and highly respected in their professional communities. Emile was a clinical psychologist, who regularly published articles and study results in professional journals. They were a dashing couple in their formal wear and Paul never brought himself to consider who was pitching and who was catching in their relationship.

They chatted over the noise and enjoyed the evening. When time came for the talent phase of the show, Mickey pulled eyeglasses from her purse for a clearer view. Contestants consumed bananas to determine who'd perform the task most erotically. The crowd cheered and urged on their favorites. Mickey convulsed with laughter.

"How come," she asked, "the darkest banana is the biggest?"

"Honey," Emile suggested, "don't think. Just take notes."

She studied their techniques. Her lips stretched. Her fingertips covered them as if measuring. Deliberately uttered words sought scientific certainty.

"Is my mouth big enough?"

Paul smiled, then excused himself to use the men's room. Anthony joined and as they reached a quiet corner, Paul stopped to speak from his heart.

"I owe you, Buddy."

Simple words conveyed a world of meaning. Since Sarah's murder, too many eyes no longer met his when he turned to associates and avowed friends. Paul had learned two things with stone certainty: suspicion is ugly as guilt—and nearly no one stands close to a lost cause.

"You don't owe me anything," Anthony said, speaking as if he only recollected their good times

Paul reflected. When Sarah had insisted that a decorator assist her in furnishing their home, Paul could think of no one other than Anthony, knowing his traditional inclinations might tame Sarah's garish tastes. He didn't want a living room that guests might mistake for a casino lobby. So, Sarah controlled all decorating decisions, somewhat tamed by Anthony's notions, while Paul's contribution was writing checks to cover them. Along the way, Sarah and Anthony had become friends, spending time over long lunches amid endless decorating and redecorating that contributed to Sarah and Paul drifting apart.

"Anthony," Paul asked, speaking softly, "what can you tell me about Sarah that might help me find her killer?"

"I know Sarah was seeing someone before she was murdered," he said. "The relationship was going badly. She even talked about breaking it off."

"Did Sarah mention his name?" Paul pressed.

"Never." Anthony cast his eyes down, as if ashamed he hadn't told his friend earlier. "She just said their sex was terrific, but it wasn't enough. We talked, but . . . well, you know Sarah. She never dwelled on details the way many women do. She always had a side she wouldn't let you see. I never knew anything at all of what she had done before your marriage."

"Sarah lived for the moment," Paul reflected, "so intently she never savored the past."

"Did she have family?"

"No one close. Her father deserted her mother when she was a toddler and her mom died shortly after we married. We were both 'only children,' raised by single parents. That was probably the one thing we shared in common."

"I always found it strange she didn't speak more of her days in California. It was as if she had run from her past."

Maybe she had, Paul thought. He had married a mystery yarn with no final chapter. Some things about Sarah, he sensed, he'd never learn.

They entered the men's room together. Paul opened the door to a stall, where two men inside exchanged tongues in a passionate embrace. Paul leaped back as Anthony laughed.

"You've never been in a gay club before, have you?"

Lines at urinals were so long that a shorter one formed to pee into a trash can. But the mood was amiable, even jovial, as everyone burst into song, "Here she comes. . .."

When they returned to their table, Paul said goodnight to Mickey, who was so fascinated by the affair that she elected to stay for crowning of the winner.

"I'll be fine," she assured Paul. "Anthony and Emile will take me home."

Knowing she was in safe in their hands, Paul left to find Boog. He was anxious to enter the beach house, hoping to find a clue that would point the Prosecutor's Office to another suspect. The trick would be to enter, search, then leave without being spotted. Patrol cars would pass. While the house was subject to a Court Order sealing it off, Boog had warned, it would be on the police patrol sheet.

Paul's pulse pounded more quickly as a car valet handed him keys and he drove away. Boog was waiting at the other end of Pacific Avenue. Paul studied the endless stream of strollers on the casino strip. Street girls strutted their wares, waving to carloads of men. Paul recognized some women as clients, then came to a stop for Boog to jump in the car. The big man was uncharacteristically quiet as they drove.

"Paul," he finally said, "I know you have a lot on your mind, but I may need your help."

"You've got it."

"We can talk more about this later. I don't think it's all that serious, but Francine called me."

"I thought you weren't speaking with your ex."

"Barely," Boog said sharply.

Paul felt the edge in his friend's voice. He sensed Boog never fully recovered from his broken marriage.

"We just talk about our teenage daughter, actually. I don't hear much from either of them. The kid's gotten into trouble again, though, and may need representation. It's a minor problem but I'd feel better, if you handle it."

"Bring her to the office tomorrow," Paul said, "and don't worry about it again."

Boog glanced out the window.

"Full moon," he observed. "Maybe we should do this on a darker night."

"Don't have time to wait."

Still, a nagging premonition stung Paul as they raced over the Brigantine bridge. He drove faster than usual, too quickly to think clearly. Breaking and entering was reason enough to be nervous but he had an unsettling feeling, one he couldn't articulate, akin to déjà vu.

Maybe, he thought, *it has something to do with the brightness of a nearly full moon over Brigantine Island.*

Paul listened to their tires spin over pavement. All the while, he wondered if they would find anything to help catch the demon, who had carved Sarah.

Chapter Twenty-Three

He Who Has No Name

THE DEVIL'S WORK WAS KNOWN to certain elements of organized crime in need of special services. He came from another land and time—and was as much a part of the living as the dead. How he killed was his trademark.

On January 27, 1975, during the final days of the Vietnam War, Lance Corporal McDonnell was first in his squad to spy it on a morning patrol. United States Marines forged through dense thickets into the clearing where they came to a village. Morning mist, still rising from the ground, dissipated in languid air. Temperatures would reach 120 degrees by noon. For the past few clicks, each being one-thousand meters, he'd taken point, walking ahead of his eight-man squad. They had left An Hoa combat base expecting a routine patrol. The day belonged to friendlies while night was owned by the Viet Cong in the valley.

When he saw them, he froze: Vietnamese peasants—a woman and a man—tied to trees outside a tiny hamlet. Wire wound so tightly around their wrists, it cut through their flesh and into their bones. Both had tongues sliced out and placed in a slop bucket for feeding pigs, next to their eyeballs.

The squad pulled up behind the lance corporal and he directed a private.

"Fetch the oldest man in the village."

The interpreter from the Army of the Republic of South Vietnam, who had been assigned to their patrol, would question him. The old man came at gunpoint, trembling.

"Tell him," McDonnel directed the ARVN, "we're his friends."

As the interpreter spoke, the man balled up on the ground.

"Tell him we're here to protect him from the Viet Cong, who did this to the people of his village."

More gook gibberish followed.

"What did he say?"

"The old man said the Viet Cong didn't do this. He claims a Vietnamese man who works for Americans did."

"Tell that lying son of a bitch I'll personally blow his balls off with my M-sixteen if he repeats that lie."

"He not lying," the ARVN said.

McDonnel jolted. He turned from the ARVN to the old man.

"Tell me what you said is a Goddamned lie," he screamed. He grabbed the old man's hair and lifted him, so their faces met, inches apart, as the Marine hollered again.

"Tell me that's a lie, *ông bà*!"

The man, whom he addressed as grandfather, defecated and the lance corporal set him down. He had seen terror dance in those old eyes. The Viet Cong didn't commit the atrocity and the Marine wondered.

Who could do this?

They didn't have to ask the locals. The ARVN already knew.

"This is the work of he who has no name," he said. "American Special Forces send him out to interrogate and strike fear into the hearts of the villagers in suspected Viet Cong strongholds. He travels alone by night. Villagers don't know his name and wouldn't dare speak it if they did. All that's known of this man is he's a Vietnamese of Chinese extraction.

"It's said when he was a young boy, VC entered his hamlet and randomly selected his family to serve as a warning to those who might sympathize with our forces. Their soldiers beat him nearly to death, then raped his sisters in a village square and killed his parents before his eyes. The Viet Cong left him with no soul."

McDonnell peered at the human remains bound to the trees and wept. His country's Special Forces had employed a psychopath to fight for them. With the war winding down, Americans would be going home soon. Troops from the furthest reaches of Vietnam were already packing. There was no need for those people to meet death, and not even an animal should die that way. Someone had exercised violence for its own sake.

Where will this monster go after the war? The lance corporal wondered. *We're handing South Vietnam to the North Vietnamese and that kind of man will face execution under the new regime.*

Yet, McDonnell also knew Special Forces took pride in caring for their own. Indubitably, they'd bring the madman out of the country with thousands of decent South Vietnamese, who were seeking asylum. That man would be sent to America.

My God, he thought.

The lance corporal pointed to the eyeless and tongue less corpses and ordered his men.

"Bury the sorry bastards."

It had been what Commissioner Pepperman liked calling a "Peppy day." On June 12, 1989, arduous preparations for the morrow exhilarated him but time had come to go home. The Arcade Building, where the Casino Control Commission maintained its offices, was nearly empty so late at night. Only the combative commissioner remained with janitorial staff.

Before leaving, Pepperman primped in a public rest room. He peered into a mirror above the lavatory sink, combing over greased hair from a low part, scarcely concealing his expansive bald spot. Eyes behind thick spectacles clung to oversized ears on an elongated head. The man looked like one of the Pep Boys. He could take a job standing as signage at the auto parts stores, if Manny,

Moe, or Jack ever retired. He dislodged a food particle stuck between teeth and admired his reflection.

Rolland, he thought with a chuckle, *are you more attractive on the inside or out?*

Pepperman felt more alive than he had in years. He had personally spearheaded the investigation into organized crime. Hearings would reconvene in the morning after a two-week recess. Two lawyers from the Attorney General's Office would call witnesses to the stand under the Commission's subpoena power. The two Deputy Attorney Generals specially assigned to his staff were ruthless. The eager young man and woman both sought career advancement that would be theirs in the casino industry private sector after they brought down Antonio DeBona, sending the old mob boss on a journey through the legal system that would end in prison for life.

Perhaps, Pepperman thought, *I'll be eyed as gubernatorial prospect in the coming primaries*.

He had no fear of mob retribution. As a Commissioner, he was untouchable. His death would bring heat from every law enforcement agency with jurisdiction over Atlantic City. He knew it. More importantly, he knew the mob knew it.

Pepperman walked into the hearing room where it would take place in the morning. Commissioners would sit behind the long bench up front. The press would fill the room. The chairwoman would sit in the center, flanked on both sides by the other commission members.

How long, he wondered, *will it be before I sit at center stage*?

Nobody had ever taken on the local mob so voraciously and Pepperman was rapidly making a name for himself. Ironic, he realized, the old dago he was targeting had made the investigation possible by seeing to his appointment.

He should've paid me, Pepperman thought indignantly.

When DeBona refused his demands for cash, Pepperman found the Asians hoodlums, who sought to expand their operations in the resort city.

Yellow money is as good as guinea gold, he reflected.

Kickbacks began filling his offshore bank account in the Cayman Islands. That vacation spot was the Switzerland of the Caribbean, where banking laws forbade disclosure of deposits to governmental authorities. For the present, he would live modestly from commission wages, while squeezing local crime figureheads, until retiring a wealthy man.

Pepperman stored evidence on two 3-1/4-inch floppy computer disks that remained in his coat pocket, always. Only the pair existed, and each disc had been encrypted with a protective code. A self-infecting virus would destroy the information if duplication or unauthorized use were attempted. He trusted no one with the material.

In the morning, those two disks would shoot sparks from his laptop to zap the old dago and his crime family. Even Pepperman's Deputy Attorney Generals hadn't seen all the evidence, some of which the Asian mob had contributed, unaware they'd be next on his hit list if they dallied on payoffs.

He strolled out the front door of the Arcade Building onto the boardwalk and stared into the night. The old building housed the Miss America Pageant Headquarters on the lower level and the Commission above. Pepperman always fantasized about meeting a pageant contestant, there, late on a night such as this, and taking her on the spot. For a moment, he studied the high-rise casinos, north and south along the boards.

Funny that I attained this position, he reflected. *I so rarely enter the gaming houses and never much care for people they attract.*

Pepperman walked down the Tennessee Avenue ramp toward his car. Urban renewal hadn't reached that blighted section nestling between grand casinos. Casually, he strolled to the parking lot where he kept his old Dodge, unlocked its door, and climbed behind the wheel. He tapped his coat pocket to feel the computer disks and watched a car in the parking space in front of him back out abruptly.

"You're backing right into my car!" Pepperman shouted.

The bump from the impact disoriented him but Pepperman quickly recovered. He straightened his eyeglasses, leaped out like a spastic leprechaun to inspect his damage, and vented.

"You just cost me a grand of trade-in value! Show me your driver's license and insurance card."

Pepperman was so angry when he approached the driver, he didn't see his face or the look in his eyes. He never saw the knife zip from the man's pocket, and he felt nothing as the blade entered his gut and twisted forcefully, shredding intestines. Pepperman was still stunned as the knife carved a canyon in his throat. It was only then, in his last ever glance, he caught the empty, thousand-yard stare on his killer's face.

He who had no name didn't see what he was doing. When he killed man or woman, he never focused on his victim. Instead, he saw his sisters raped by soldiers wearing black-pajama fatigues. The girls would forever be whores in the eyes of villagers and unworthy as brides. He saw his mother and father, being forced to watch their daughters being taken repeatedly. Then, he eyed his parents' suffering until they drew last breaths. Always before him was the grinning Viet Cong officer in command of the atrocities. And, it was always that officer he maimed and killed before disappearing without remorse.

The hired assassin took the disks from the dead man's pocket, assuring that Pepperman's investigation recessed forever. They were to be turned over the Italian mob boss but instead they would go to Mister Shek to use against DeBona's family when time was ripe. Tony hadn't received a pardon so much as a temporary reprieve.

Those disks revealed the name of every man in Tony's organization and detailed accounts of their criminal activities. The information came from someone inside Tony's family. Shek would pay dearly for it, money well spent to bring down the old Italian boss. But first the assassin had his own use for it.

Chapter Twenty-Four

A House is Not a Home

THEY DROVE INTO BRIGANTINE ISLAND'S darkest alley and rolled to a stop. Paul looked at Boog. What they were about to do was stupid.

"What do you say, Counselor?" Boog said. "We can still drive back over the bridge to Atlantic City."

Paul let out a deep breath, then jumped out of the car and they started walking. Surf roared as if rendering an easily decipherable warning turn back. Yet, they hiked to the beach, then along the ocean side of the dunes to Paul's house.

As they came to it, Paul stopped and slipped off a shoe. He poured sand from it, then did the same with the other, as they studied the large masonry structure with wide glass expanses to take advantage of ocean views.

Every morning, when Paul had lived there, he wakened to a different vista—like rising to a portrait in a constant flux. One day the ocean was calm as if it had forgotten to wake with him. The next, savage gales blew surf and spray over shimmering white caps. After he separated from Sarah, Paul found a high-rise apartment on the Atlantic City boardwalk. It wasn't so plush, but it offered the view that always brought solace.

He and Boog walked to the rear door. Paul pulled out the key Anthony had given him and placed it in the lock. Suddenly, it occurred to him.

Can I turn off the alarm system once we enter? Sarah had surely changed the code numbers on the entry pad since he had left. He looked at Boog.

"Would the police have set the burglary alarm?"

"Doubtful."

"What's that mean?" Paul said. "Doubtful they did or doubtful they didn't activate it."

"Doubtful that I really know."

Paul grimaced. He had come that far; he'd go all the way. They entered the house and Paul scurried to the alarm box in the ground floor laundry room. If they had triggered it, there would be a 120-second delay before the interior siren sounded and a call alerted the local police department.

"Alarm on?" called Boog.

"No. We're free to roam."

Boog pulled two small flashlights from his jacket and handed one to Paul.

"Try to keep the house lights off," he suggested.

Paul searched the first floor while Boog started at the upper level on his own. Having seen police photographs of the crime scene, Paul didn't want to go upstairs unless there was a compelling reason. They looked for any clue that would lead to the identity of Sarah's boyfriend, any odd telephone number in an address book, anything out of the ordinary. It was a craps shoot.

Boog called from upstairs.

"You have to come up here, Paul. You'll have a better idea of what's out of place or might be helpful to us."

Paul knew Boog was right. He ascended the stairs with trepidation. When he rounded the final turn in the winding staircase, he saw Boog at the fireplace, checking a framed photograph on the mantlepiece.

"Anyone in this picture look interesting to you?" Boog said.

Paul came close and stared: Himself and Sarah.

"I thought I'd been taken off that mantlepiece a long time ago," Paul reflected. "Sarah was in a constant state of metamorphosis. Even things she liked didn't last long."

"And, she married the man who never tries anything new," Boog wryly observed. "Way to match up, Counselor."

Paul continued to study the picture.

"It's strange there aren't new photographs here. This mantle was like an art gallery that always had new work on display. There should be more recent snapshots somewhere."

They searched but found none. Paul recognized that as being unlike the Sarah he knew. He was hoping to find a photograph of the new love in Sarah's life—even a memento.

"Boog," he said, as their eyes scoured, "where would you go to discover who a woman was seeing romantically?"

"Her hairdresser. Did she have her nails done by a manicurist? Ask the nail technician. Hairdressers and nail girls know everything about a woman."

Perhaps, Paul thought, *but she was a loner*.

Sarah kept things to herself as Anthony had observed. It was worth trying, though.

"I'll send Mickey out to Sarah's hair and nail salons," he said. "Let her go in as a customer to learn what she can."

"Where did Sarah like to dine? If she had some favorite restaurants, we can eat and snoop around at 'em."

Paul didn't have to think twice about favorites. There was only one. It was one of the few casino restaurants with a water view. Every casino in the town could have created an elegant dining room with a view of the ocean or bay, but few did. Casinos wined and dined their players, but not over long, leisurely meals. They designed everything to place players back at the gaming tables quickly as possible. Sarah's favorite restaurant served northern Italian cuisine and overlooked a picturesque harbor.

"I can check with Ky," said Paul.

"Ky?"

"Ky Nguyen at Trump's Castle. He's the casino's top gaming executive. Sarah had him line up a table from time to time."

"You two didn't gamble enough to rate that service. What'd you do? Get friendly with Donald and Ivana?"

Paul chuckled.

"No, you moron. But I've known Ky a while. Got him out of trouble years ago. You know the Vietnamese.

They're very loyal. Ky would find us a table when the town was crowded. He knows a lot about AC. Has to in his position. I'll pay him a visit."

They ambled through the upper floor of the house together, flashlight beams darting like mini search lights. As Paul perused kitchen cabinets, Boog pulled a beer from the refrigerator, unscrewed the cap, and swigged. They were walking into the dining room before it occurred to Paul.

"Sarah never drank beer," he said.

Boog took another sip and looked at the label.

"Domestic," he observed. "That doesn't help us much. I serve this stuff all day. If it was imported or a microbrew, maybe it would tell us something about whoever was drinking it."

"It tells me something. That beer wasn't for Sarah. Too declassee for her tastes. She'd never drink it. Ordinarily, she wouldn't even serve it. We're talking about a woman who seriously asked a plumber to install sparkling spring water on tap in the kitchen. Her tastes ran to imported champagne, not domestic brewskis."

Boog finished the bottle and placed it in a kitchen trash container. He sorted through the rubbish but found nothing of interest. Paul remained in the dining room while Boog entered the master bedroom suite. He called after a quick walk-through.

"The bedroom's clean. No evidence of a struggle. Why don't you check it while I spend time in the master bathroom? You won't want to head there."

Paul entered slowly, feeling as if Sarah's ghost would appear from thin air to redecorate the place. She had redone the bedroom since he'd left. The bed was in its familiar position, but he didn't recognize draperies, matching bed cover, and throw pillows. He separated the drapes to peer out a window that faced the street. Headlights shined from a car traveling up the beach block. As the vehicle came into view, he called out.

"It's a patrol car."

Boog rushed to the window. His big hands carefully pulled back the drapes further for a better view. They watched the patrol car stop. A lone officer in the car eyeballed the house, then picked up the handset to his radio and made a call.

"What's he doing?" Paul said.

"Logging in, it looks like. This place is on his patrol sheet."

They backed away from the window slowly and waited for the squad car to leave. It didn't. The car remained parked then headlights from another car shone. A second squad car delivered two more officers, one in uniform, the other wearing plainclothes. Both leaped out to join the first officer.

"Backup," Boog said. "The first cop must have called for backup. They're coming in the house."

"Will they have a key?"

"Probably. This place was closed as a crime scene. Someone may have given the cops a key to keep an eye on it. How do we get out of here?"

They walked to the living room. Boog started to descend the stairs until Paul grabbed him.

"Can't leave the way we came in," Paul warned. "There's only one staircase to the first floor and that'll take us past the front doors."

Boog's head turned toward the glass double-front doors.

"Anyone approaching will see into the house and spot us, if we walk down, there, he said."

"There's only one thing we can do," Paul declared. "We'll go out the kitchen window onto the pitched roof above the garage, and cling to the shingles. It's too high to drop down, but we can hang there until the cops leave, then climb back inside."

Boog froze. His eyes darted to the window and his words came fast.

"The last time I was on a roof I fell off and nearly killed myself. No rooftops for me, Pal. I've seen them in my past and I definitely don't see them in my future."

Paul studied his friend, who seemed so obtuse . . . and well, so Boog.

"Oh, you see them in your future," Paul related, "and that future is now. Get yourself the hell out there or these cops will book us for breaking and entering, violating a court order that protects a crime scene, and whatever other charge they dream up to implicate us in a murder rap."

Boog's sigh bespoke resignation. He pulled another beer from the refrigerator, then opened the kitchen window. Paul climbed through first.

A key turned in the front door lock as Boog stood frozen. Police officers entered the house with guns drawn. Their footsteps sounded on the winding staircase. Boog took a hearty swig from his bottle.

"I hate rooftops," he groaned before disappearing into the night.

Outside, they clung to the steeply slanted roof. Paul looked below. If he lost his grip, it would be a breakneck forty-foot drop. The full moon and star-filled sky lit up the night. He realized they would be visible to anyone who looked up from the ground.

Paul was certain nobody had ever done anything so stupid. He was almost right. Then again, he hadn't seen Sammy Smoke in action five years earlier, celebrating the day after Labor Day

Chapter Twenty-Five

Cooking with Gas

THE DAY AFTER LABOR DAY, September 3, 1984, Sammy Smoke played with fire. He poured gasoline over the kitchen stoves and throughout the restaurant dining room. Then, he returned to the kitchen and tipped a can of grease atop a lighted stove burner. A careless cook must have left the burner partially lit when he left, fire officials would surmise when they declared it a grease fire.

Sammy turned his slim face in one direction, then the other to marvel at his handiwork. The old wooden structure was a half block from the boardwalk in a lonely part of town. Initially, nobody would see smoke rise from the building. Nobody would call the fire department until it was too late, and Sammy would score full payment on the insurance loss.

He pulled a wooden match from his pocket and struck it against false teeth. It lit before leaving his lips. Casually, he tossed it, watched flames leap, then watched them spread. Sammy felt his blood pressure rise as nostrils whiffed black smoke that announced departure time. Sammy strolled to the rear door and savored a final glance.

God, he thought, while observing the conflagration, *this joint is torching fast.*

Sammy turned the doorknob and pushed the old steel door. But it was locked—and he needed a way out fast. His eyes darted to kitchen windows.

"God damn," he declared, "this dump's burglar-proofed with iron bars!"

He'd entered by the front door but the access way from the kitchen to main room was ablaze. The dining room was crackling with its ceiling smoldering and caving, letting Sammy know—just as Chicken Little proclaimed—the sky is falling. He jammed his weight into the door, then hocked a loogie before pushing the immovable object with all his might.

"Holy shit, this thing is solid!"

Heat broiled facial flesh, flames set eyebrows afire, and his ears felt like they were melting. Sammy became lightheaded as fire sucked oxygen from the room. With his last breath Sammy flung himself against the door and bounced off it like a ricocheting bullet.

Did the door budge, he wondered, *or was that just my imagination*?

Flames torched his pants seat, rousing his scream, and causing his head to lower like a battering ram. He charged the door headfirst. The impact caused stars to flash. The old door flung off rusty hinges and Sammy careened into the night, flames following, but turning upward to the sky.

Sammy lay on the ground while his clothes smoldered. It was one hell of a way to end the beach season. Sammy Smoke was smoking, and his fire would introduce Tony DeBona to Paul Cameron.

A need for renovation came with changing times. Resorts International Hotel and Casino was the first legal casino in Atlantic City, opening its doors in 1978, followed by eleven more glitter domes. Donald Trump, whose moniker was his brand, sired three—Trump's Plaza, Trump's Castle, and Trump's Taj Mahal Casino Resort. The game palaces attracted players from New Jersey, as well as from neighboring states that forbade the evil specter of wagering. More bus passengers arrived in the small town than any city in the world. Players and show goers also drove there themselves or flew into an airport that was forced to expand.

Often folks sought libations and feasting outside the bustling casinos, so they sampled local haunts, many being broken down beer and gin joints that Tony's crime family controlled. Though mob figures were never owners on paper, due to State-regulated liquor licensing, straw men fronted for them. These legitimate businesses also laundered cash from mob illicit activities. With legit business down, Tony had their money man talk to his capos in their Fairmont Tavern haunt.

Ira Wolf was a financial wizard of sorts. The bookish little man had graduated from the esteemed Wharton

Business School at the University of Pennsylvania and dressed to let you know he was an Ivy Leaguer in his blue blazer, tan slacks, and penny loafers, something his small audience that morning never noticed. He scratched his nose, then stuck it into their fiscal woes.

"Your problem," the Wolf explained, "is the rundown condition of these businesses makes them unprofitable. Not enough customers are patronizing the places to justify income we're showing on the books.

His audience appeared nonplussed.

"Gentlemen, you launder cash from illegal activities through restaurants and bars. That makes sense . . . when your legit businesses have steady cash flow. But those operations are losing money. It's impossible to justify all the cash you're running thru them. You own a bar that served less than a six-pack last week and it deposited seventy-five thousand dollars in cash into the bank. This can't continue without bringing heat and I won't be able to stand behind the books."

"So, we get another Jew to do our books," Dog Face said.

"That isn't the answer," sighed Mister Wolf.

"Ira," Tony interjected, "what do you suggest?"

"Do what businesspeople have always done when their businesses are no longer profitable: reinvest or liquidate. You can renovate to attract customers . . . or you can sell the businesses and reinvest in enterprises showing greater cash flow to launder funds."

"So," Dog Face said, "we're supposed to dish out cash to rebuild these joints or else sell bars and restaurants that have no customers. Who's going to buy them?"

"Gentlemen, I'm only here to explain the problem."

"We understand," Tony said, dismissing the accountant with a wave.

As the Wolf packed his briefcase, Tony sensed their accountant surmised his pragmatic plan. Only when the accountant closed the door behind him, did Tony reveal it to his men.

"Torch these places," he dead panned. "Then, we rebuild with insurance money or sell off the ground with the ashes. "We've got insurance up the wazoo.

"Bobby, your brother-in-law is our insurance agent. Make sure policies covering our joints are issued by different companies. I don't want all our owners showing up with their hands out to the same insurer. A lot of money shows on the books of these businesses. Be certain that every property has coverage for lost business income, when they sizzle to the ground, so we recover more than property values."

Tony turned to Sammy Smoke.

"My dear friend, you're back in business. After Bobby verifies our insurance, you'll do the rest."

Tony didn't need to say more to Sammy. His jobs were untraceable and rarely detected as possible arson. Sammy Smoke was sure-fire.

Sammy was still smoking. He'd passed out behind the inferno and woke to blaring sirens. Fire engines and police vehicles, racing through the night, grew nigh. He lifted himself to sit. Blood streamed from the top of his head into his eyes. His hair and clothes were still smoldering. He had to get away quickly to avoid a twenty-year arson rap, which would trace the job back to his crime family and place his pals behind bars.

Sammy rose to one knee, then tried standing and collapsed.

"I'm too damned dizzy and weak to rise," he wheezed.

Then, he peered at flames rising two-hundred feet. With heat blistering his flesh like pig skin on a grilling spit, he called out.

"God, that's fuckin' marvelous!"

Spirit lifted, Sammy Smoke rose and dashed.

Tony's people cashed insurance checks all over town. Only one claim didn't pay: Sammy's day after Labor Day inferno. City fire inspectors discovered that somebody had broken out the back door of the burning building. Looking at the huge dent midway down the steel door, one opined emphatically.

"Whoever did this used a sledgehammer."

Insurance representatives sent their own pyro-experts, who concurred. Clearly, someone had used a sledgehammer to bang their way out of the burning building—indubitability after setting the blaze at the behest of the business owner. So, the insurer refused to pay and a million-and-a-half dollars hung in the balance.

Tony roared indignantly.

"They can't keep *my* fucking money!"

He needed a lawyer to sue for their business proprietor and looked to his men.

"We need an *avvocato* to bust *testicolos*."

"Why not hire our usual lawyers, Boss?" Dog Face said.

"We need a fresh face, someone with no ties to organized crime. The cops and insurance company will be looking to see which attorney sues. If we use one of our lawyers, the fire will be traced to us. We hire an outsider."

"Use the kid," Bobby suggested.

Tony's eyes arched inquisitively.

"What kid?"

"The kid who defended that preacher. He's clean. Nobody will associate him with organized crime. And, no one will ever think of him as a *paisano*: no vowel at the end of his name.

"Who? Tony shot.

"Paul Cameron."

"Cameron," Tony said, stroking his chin as if distracted. All right, I'll call upon this young man to see what he's made of."

Chapter Twenty-Six

Intimate Advice

AN EFFICIENT WOMAN, WHOSE FORM MADE HIM momentarily reflect upon the Chanticleer, escorted Tony from the law office reception area to the *avvocato*'s office.

"Mister Cameron will be with you shortly," she said, "He's finishing with a client in our conference room."

Tony watched her depart, then examined framed certificates and artwork hangings. The boardwalk office, unlike his own, was large and bright. He turned to the window, and watched a seagull circle above the shoreline, then dive into the ocean to rise with a small fish in its beak.

When the female staff member returned with the lawyer, Tony thought he spied something unexpected in her eyes, but let it pass.

"Thank you, Mickey," the lawyer called, after she had made introductions, then turned to leave them alone.

The younger man sat behind his desk while Tony took a chair across from him, neither parting words.

So, this is him, Paul thought, *the Boss of the Boardwalk.*

For a moment, they seemed to study each other over the desktop. Sensing the mob boss would appreciate a direct approach, Paul began bluntly.

"I know why you're here. What I don't know is why you did it the day after Labor Day."

"Young man, don't speculate about what I've done or why I'm here. I've only come to help a dear friend who owns a restaurant."

Paul concealed skepticism that would serve no purpose to unmask. Besides, he had already learned, in this gambling town you never show all the cards in your hand.

"The place that you've come to discuss burned down the day after Labor Day," Paul continued. "No wonder the insurer refused to pay. Somebody milked that cash cow for the summer, then torched it the day after tourist season ended. That timely coincidence alone would be enough for the insurance company to question the origin of the fire. On top of that, someone smashed out the backdoor after the fire started. Your friend will have to answer difficult questions. Where is he?"

"Unfortunately, a family member's illness summoned him to Sicily. He's asked me to find a lawyer for his case."

"Your friend is more fortunate than he may think. If he had remained in this country, police may have arrested him for arson."

Paul paused to allow his words to sink in.

"Mister DeBona, your friend will have trouble collecting payment. There's apparent arson. If I speak with the insurance claim adjusters, they'll ask me why my client had a fire. What can I tell them? My client had a fire because he couldn't start a flood."

Both fell silent. Tony rose and stretched his limbs by the window, then settled back into a chair that was too small for his frame, and uttered words that carried all his weight.

"There's a considerable insurance policy at stake. It shall be your job to collect it and my friend would not expect you to champion his cause without fair compensation."

Paul reflected.

"I'll need costs paid in advance," he said, "to hire the best fire investigator in the business: someone with impeccable credentials to convincingly testify that the fire arose from an accidental source."

"You will receive your funds, but you'll guarantee a favorable result."

"Mister DeBona, surely you know that Attorney Ethics Rules prohibit lawyers from guaranteeing any courtroom outcome."

"Yes, I understand that to be true. I also understand it is said anything can happen in a court of law. But you'll guarantee a favorable result in all our dealings or we shall have none."

Paul studied the mob boss. The hood was dangerous enough to have him slain if he lost. Yet, for reasons he didn't understand, Paul felt compelled to shake the outstretched hand of Antonio DeBona, the Boss of the Boardwalk.

The old man looked in his eyes with a gaze that penetrated.

"You have no pictures of children in your office," the mob boss said.

Not knowing why he acknowledged it, Paul's words seemed to flow.

"My wife and I have no children, Mister DeBona."

"No children," repeated the older man. "Then you have no marriage, only a living arrangement. Family is everything, my young counselor."

"My wife and I don't—"

Paul stopped himself, unprepared to disclose intimacies.

"Speak to your wife plainly about this," the older man counseled.

"Plainly as you're speaking?"

"Only two kinds of people can speak without inhibitions: strangers and lovers. Everyone in between is negotiating. And, we are mere strangers setting boundaries for business dealings, are we not?"

The mob boss turned to silently stare at the sea.

Perhaps like me, Paul reflected, *this old man feels drawn to it for reasons he doesn't comprehend.*

Paul reflected on the older man's marital advice. In their uncommon cosmos, where good embraced evil and sinners lay with innocents, a man like DeBona sought to teach his lawyer how to love. Yet, what of love could a killer truly understand?

Chapter Twenty-Seven

Girls Just Want To Have Fun

WITH THE CRACK OF DAWN, on January 25, 1950, bugles blared the sound of charge. Armed forces of Communist North Korea smashed across the 38th parallel of latitude invading the Republic of South Korea. The smaller and ill-equipped army in the southern republic was unable to defend its border. The United Nations sent a force from sixteen nations to push the communists back. Armies from Communist China and the Soviet Union joined the North Koreans. They bitterly fought the South Koreans and the multinational forces that supported them.

Thompson, who went by Tommy, was a Second Lieutenant, who joined the American Divisions assigned to the U.N. army three years later. Peace talks in Panmunjom were grinding on without success. The Korean War became a standoff with opposing forces entrenched along hard-fought battle lines. The lieutenant preferred to spend his time in the trenches rather than on patrol. Under a star-filled winter night sky, Tommy sat in a foxhole thinking of the bride he had just kissed goodbye in the States.

Amanda was petite with a blond pixie cut, and a trim yet athletic figure. Her sophisticated deportment came naturally from being raised in a family of "Hillers," in the Chestnut Hill section of Philadelphia. She came from old money. Amanda's family never bought jewelry. They had it, just as they had and took for granted so much.

Tommy planned to join his father's manufacturing firm upon graduation and spend his working years at the helm of the family business. Who would've known that a bugle call in Korea would sweep him away?

A flare went up along the American line and slowly drifted down. Someone saw movement on the hilly peaks that North Koreans occupied just two-hundred yards away. Both sides were well dug into their positions, but each side tested the other for weakness. Intermittent skirmishes raged between infantry patrols along the border. Occasionally, full scale assaults erupted. While trench lines weren't impregnable, assaults from either side were more often politically motivated than strategically significant. Opposing forces fought to keep their military postures strong while peace talks ensued

Devotion, like he had never known, grew for Amanda as time passed in that forsaken place. Thompson thought of her back at the Harcum College campus. She remained in her sorority house after they married because he'd packed off so fast.

She had written that she caught a flu. Feeling a glow in his heart that warmed the winter night, he wondered if she was feeling better.

Amanda had a rockin' pneumonia and a boogie woogie fever. The girls of Alpha Phi Omega were on a road trip to Atlantic City and Amanda was five beers happy and hankering for more. Saturday night started at the 500 Club, where they listened to the sophisticated sounds of amply ancient Sophie Tucker.

"Boring," was all Amanda could say.

By midnight, they found the Rocket Club that featured a new band called the Comets. They had no idea the lead guitarist, Bill Halley, would keep them rockin' around the clock. Her head was swimming from dancing and drinking.

"One o'clock, two o'clock, three o'clock, rock. Four o'clock, five o'clock, six o'clock, rock. We're gonna rock around the clock. . .." Bill Haley was singing it again.

Doesn't this band know another song? she wondered. *Who cares? This song is cookin'.*

Amanda grabbed the hand of the nearest unattached man and hit the dance floor again.

Tony watched from across the room. He ran a string of clubs for the family and traveled between them. As he eyed the room, he admired the little number decked in red, a blond Audrey Hepburn with a carefree manner that radiated across the room. She was slim, unlike his Lena who had put on weight after bearing three daughters. Tony observed the young woman accept another beer, perhaps one too many, but it wasn't his job to slow consumption. He was tasked to see that customers stayed happy and he could see the young woman was beaming.

Tony had seen cheerier days himself. At thirty-eight years of age, he was in his prime: handsome, fit, and strong. His children were scattered in age. The oldest was nearly as old as the tomato in the red dress. He and Lena remained devoted in their way to one another. She knew little of his business, other than it kept him from home so many nights. Perhaps that's why their bed had grown cold. To keep the fire in his loins burning, he occasionally visited the Chanticleer. Working women in the old hotel afforded a sexual outlet without social commitment. A whore never asked if you would respect her in the morning.

Amanda's head spun. It occurred to her that she hadn't seen her girlfriends in the club for a while.

"What time is it?" she said to the burly man who had been her partner for the last few dances.

Suddenly, she recognized that she was dancing with a guy who looked like he should be named Joe Palooka.

"What's wrong, Honey? You got an urge to go home with me?"

"No, I have an urge for another beer," Amanda replied.

Joe Palooka went for her drink and Amanda took the opportunity to escape. She dashed to the ladies room and checked herself in the mirror.

"Amanda, you're going to need a lot of powder on that nose," she told her reflection.

Unfortunately powder from her purse kit wasn't cooperating. The powder pad kept missing her nose.

Missed again," she giggled, until she was forcefully swung around.

"Joe Palooka!" she gasped to the hulk of man, who had gripped her shoulders. "What are you doing in here?"

She looked around the ladies' room for the first time. It was empty except for the two of them.

She wondered, *How late is it, anyway*?

The big man brought her close and placed elephantine lips atop hers. His thick tongue pushed past her lips and mingled with hers.

His breath, she thought. *As drunk as I am, I can tell he has horrid breath . . . and his tongue feels like it's fur coated.*

She bit down hard on the invasive organ and sent her knee into his groin. He groaned and fell to the floor.

Amanda felt tipsy but knew she had to get out of the bathroom fast or he'd rape her. The shock woke her senses. She scurried toward the door, then felt a tug on her shoulders. Joe Palooka spun her around like a top and smashed her face with his fist, reeling her to the floor.

As Amanda tried rising to her knees, she heard the swish of a switchblade opening. He grabbed a handful of blond locks and raised her head to fly level. He unzipped and reached in his pants with one hand and held the knife to her throat with the other.

"You're going to kiss something else now, Sweetheart. And if you bite again, I'll knock your teeth out. Pucker up, Princess."

Amanda stared as tears welled in her eyes. His grip tugged her hair from the roots as he pulled her closer to his trousers. Amanda said a final silent prayer and God answered.

Tony burst into the rest room and slugged Joe Palooka with a solid uppercut that sent him reeling across the bathroom where he bounced off the wall and onto the floor. Tony looked down at Amanda. Her lipstick was smeared, and tears stained her cheeks. Already, a swollen shiner was rising.

Joe Palooka sprang from the floor and charged Tony with knife in hand. Tony sidestepped him and held the man's knife hand with his left hand while bringing all his force down on the man's arm with a chop of his right hand. The sound of lower arm bones cracking filled the room. The Palooka cried out as two of Tony's men rushed in and held the guy down.

"No cops," Tony told them. "Get him out of here and see that he doesn't come back."

Those words signaled that the big man would be leaving by the rear alleyway, where his other arm would be broken, too.

Amanda cried from relief and wrapped her arms around her handsome knight in shining armor.

Tony looked down at the slender blond and thought: *This is so much like the old days at the Chanticleer.*

"Please take me out of here," Amanda said. "I want to leave."

"Of course," Tony replied.

Chivalry wasn't dead. In Atlantic City, the ancient ideals of bravery, honor, and gallantry sometimes come alive. That was one such moment.

"Where do you want to go?"

Amanda still felt the liquor and answered without hesitation.

"I want to go home."

"Of course," Tony replied.

"With you," Amanda added.

Tony looked into her eyes, realizing the first thing a classy dame dropped, when she had too much to drink, was her moral standards. So, Tony did what came naturally. After all, a knight in shiny armor isn't a saint.

In the morning Amanda woke with a start. Room service at the President Hotel on the Boardwalk had delivered a feast for two. Through still focusing her eyes, Amanda spied platters of fresh baked pastries, fluffy omelets, a pitcher of squeezed orange juice, and piping hot coffee. Then, she realized she had to puke.

A door looked as if it led to the bathroom. Amanda dashed through it and into a closet. She emerged sheepishly, grinning at Tony, who sat with an open newspaper at the table set for two. He pointed to another door to her right, where she scurried just in time. Amanda nursed the mother of all hangovers.

She took a cool washcloth to her face, then noticed that someone had left open bottles of aspirin and Alka Seltzer for her relief. Amanda popped both and looked at her hands. Her rings were missing! The wedding band and three-karat engagement ring were gone. She sprang into the bedroom and tore sheets apart.

Where are they? she frantically thought. *They can't fall off. They need resizing because they're too tight.*

"I put your jewelry on the dresser," Tony offered. "Last night you weren't feeling well enough to secure them yourself."

Amanda ran to the dresser and slid both rings on her fingers fast.

"Thank you," she said.

She looked around the room, again feeling secure with the handsome stranger.

"Who are you?" Amanda inquired.

She remembered why she was with him but had no idea of his name. His broad smile and the rococo decor of the stately suite made her feel like she was Scarlet O'Hara. Was she in a pre-Civil War fantasy before that good life was *Gone with the Wind*?

"They call me Tony Quick Fish," he replied.

Amanda fell to earth. She wasn't at Tara, but she found comfort in her handsome stranger, whether he was Captain Rhett Butler of the Confederate Army or Tony Quick Fish of Atlantic City.

Rich fragrance drew her to coffee. Amanda sat at the mahogany table as Tony poured her steaming java. She searched for something to settle her queasy stomach and polished off three Danish pastries.

Tony watched with a bemused smile.

"You're a hoodlum, aren't you?" Amanda said nonchalantly, "You're my hoodlum."

"And, you're a beautiful young woman."

He ran a mental check list of comparisons. She and Lena differed in so many ways. Lena was olive complected and ethnic in appearance, while the fair-skinned WASP appeared to have ancestors, who were pilgrims at Plymouth Rock. The wealthy blueblood had just tumbled in the hay with a proud first generation, Italian immigrant who had brought himself up by his own bootstraps. They were from different worlds that collided by fate in a bar bathroom. The Daughters of the American Revolution rolled in the hay with the Sons of Italy.

Truly, Tony thought, *this country is a melting pot*.

When she finished breakfast, her eyes glanced at the bed, then turned to his conveying an invitation.

His eyes replied more meaningfully than lips whisper.

At nightfall, Tony took her to the train station. She boarded the train that would deliver her to 30th Street Station in Philadelphia. Amanda returned to the cozy comfort of her sorority house, while Tony returned to a world so different.

Tony entered his home sheepishly that night. He looked at his Lena who had matured gracefully. After bearing children, she had developed a classic Mediterranean bottom that gave her a pear-shaped figure he still craved. Her full hips called to his loins. Olive skin and dark eyes gave Lena the exotic look that always enticed him.

Without a word spoken Tony realized she knew. He poured himself straight whiskey, drank heartily, then poured more. Neither would say anything until she was ready. By then, Tony would be deadly drunk. He rarely drank except to ready himself to kill. After all the years, drinking and killing seemed to go hand in hand. He drained the bottle's last drop, then stumbled to bed, where Lena already cuddled under sheets. He reached for the warmth of her body, but she held him off. He used drunken strength to pull the covers away and was ready to mount her when she screamed.

"I never complained when you fucked the *puttanas*, but now you've slept with a college girl half your age—and returned to this bed. Out!" she screamed. "You won't sleep with me again!"

Tony was shocked that she had so quickly discovered his indiscretion and more shocked she uttered such language.

Lena smacked him across the face. When that didn't hurt him, she rose from bed, strode to her dresser, and returned with a vase. Tony's head nestled in a downy pillow, his snores already ripping through the room. Lena did what she had to do. She smashed the vase over his head and shouted again.

"Out of my bed and never return!"

Tony's large hand massaged his skull. Blood seeped through his fingers. He was too drunk to hurt or to reason. He rose and snarled at Lena, who stood before him, shaking with rage in her night gown. He ripped the gown from her body and tossed Lena onto the bed to have his way with her. Resting atop her with all his weight, his large member grew firm. She cooed into his ear gently as only she could. Just as he readied as to enter her, she gnashed her teeth, severing his ear cartilage. Suddenly, it was Tony who screamed as he leaped from bed.

"You'll never have your way with me again," Lena vowed, standing naked and panting, a kitchen knife in her hand that she had placed by the bed.

Tony picked up the pistol he kept under his pillow with one hand and held his bleeding ear with the other. He was still too drunk to comprehend what he was about to do.

"Get in the car. I'm going to kill you . . . and I don't wanna wake the kids."

"*Va Fanculo*," she shouted back, fuck you.

He dragged her by her hair as she kicked and hollered. Their children must have heard and kept clear. When they reached the front door, she screamed.

"I'm not going into the cold naked, you monster."

Tony pulled the fur coat he had purchased for her birthday from the closet. He allowed her to put it on, then dragged her barefoot into the street and forced her at gunpoint into the trunk of their car. Lena could scream but who would hear? He drove southward until they reached an empty beach in the quiet nearby town of Margate.

Tony opened the trunk, pulled out his frantic victim, and dragged her to the beach, where he laid her in the sands. No one was around. The safety lock on his pistol was unlatched. He extended the gun at full arm's length to plug her full of holes. She seemed to be swimming beneath him though she wasn't moving at all. Liquor impaired his senses to the point that he had trouble aiming at a target three feet from the gun barrel. Tony blinked his eyes, then saw what had to be done before he killed her.

"Take off the fuckin' fur coat," he screamed. "I just paid for it."

Lena looked terrified but remained defiant.

"No way, you bastard. You're going to have to shoot me in it. If I die, I'm goin' in silver fox."

Tony was too drunk to reason it through.

"Take it off," he pleaded. "Goddamn it, I wanna kill you."

"*Va Fanculo!*" she screamed.

Lena wouldn't remove the coat. She knew her husband well enough to know he would never pull the trigger so long as she was wrapped in it.

Upon the impasse, Tony looked upward into the cold, clear night sky. A thousand stars shone down to lay witness to his reprehensible act.

"My God," he cried. "What am I doing? What have I done?" Tony dropped the gun by his feet, fell to the sand, and wept.

Lena had never seen the big man cry and realized he had come to senses. She lay beside him as his huge frame shook with grief, then opened the coat, displaying her lush figure for a singular purpose. At once, neither felt the chill of the night.

"*Mi amore*," she called to him. "Join me, here, under the stars."

Tony peered at the only woman he would ever love and vowed before each star in God's heaven that he would never be unfaithful again, a vow he would keep to the extent of natural limitations. Lena was loved to sleep, comforted by powerful arms that carried her home.

Lena pledged to keep the coat until the day she died. Their children would complain that fur from its pelts was falling out with age, but she'd never discard it. On special nights, when Lena and Tony were alone, she would don her silver fox coat and they would join as they had under heavenly stars.

Amanda puked in the bathroom of her sorority house as she had for the past two weeks. She had taken a pregnancy test from a local physician and awaited words she didn't want to hear. A newly accepted sorority pledge entered the room.

"Someone's downstairs for you, Amanda," the young woman said.

Amanda expected bad news but was surprised that someone from the doctor's office was personally delivering the test result.

I must be pretty friggin' pregnant to rate this treatment, she thought.

She pulled her head from the toilet and brushed her teeth. She would probably have to leave college when she began to show. She could move back into her parent's home, but it was all so annoying. She rewrapped her bathrobe, pushed her feet into furry slippers, then descended the main staircase to meet her doctor's assistant. When she rounded the final bend in the stairway, she found someone else. A man in uniform delivered different news.

"Missus Cameron," the soldier began, "I regret to inform you that your husband was killed in action at zero one hundred hours, on the twenty-sixth day of February, nineteen fifty-three, while fighting in the service of our county."

He said more but Amanda heard nothing else, indeed nothing for days.

When her doctor phoned to confirm her pregnancy, she did what she had to do. She called Thompson's parents, who months later joined her bedside at the Chestnut Hill Hospital. Resting in the maternity wing, she was cradling her newborn.

"What have you decided to name the baby? her mother-in-law said.

Amanda looked up to the woman and her father-in-law, then replied: "Paul Thompson Cameron."

The tribute to their son drew proud smiles on the new grandparents.

"We'll see that our grandchild lacks for nothing," they promised.

Amanda knew the father of her baby, though the final military leave of her husband and the tryst with her hoodlum were merely days apart. Of the only men in her life, one was dead and the other would never learn of the child.

As she kissed her baby's forehead, Amanda knew no one would ever question the paternity of Paul Cameron.

Chapter Twenty-Eight

Humpty Dumpty

"I HATE ROOFTOPS," Boog said for the hundredth time.

It was a consensus. Paul did, too. They had been hanging onto the steeply sloped roof for twenty minutes.

Why are three police officers inside the house? Paul wondered.

It wasn't a routine patrol to make certain the house was secure. The cops were looking for something in the middle of the night. Rough edges of cedar shingles scraped his hands. Paul's fingers were raw, his muscles straining. He couldn't hang much longer. A nursery rhyme played endlessly in his head: "All the king's horses and all the king's men couldn't put Humpty together again."

Boog had climbed higher and hung to the roof's peak directly above him. Paul waited just above the kitchen window.

He tried making sense of what had happened in the past few days. There was no mistaking the direction of the Prosecutor's murder investigation and Paul's alibi was further up in the air than he was.

With suspicious eyes focused on him, he counted on Mickey to learn whatever Sarah's hairdresser and manicurist had to offer. She was a good amateur sleuth, having worked with Boog on cases in Paul's law practice. Mickey could get people to give up details they didn't even know they had by using a ruse. She delighted in the role playing that was so often necessary for effective private investigation. Paul knew he was fortunate to have a paralegal, who effectively handled a wide range of responsibilities. In a small firm every member must do it all and Mickey did everything pretty well.

Boog's pals had furnished little news. City streets were busy with something astir: a power struggle between the old Italian crime family and an Asian gang that was eyeing the gambling Mecca. Already, blood had spilled. That crime war stymied tongues on usually talkative sources, who were now afraid to talk about anything.

While Boog did what he could, Paul would tap his own resources. Ky Nguyen would probably help. Some of his cousins knew members of the Asian gang. And, Tony Quick Fish knew everything that happened in town.

Tony had once been a friend, Paul thought, *but will he help, now*?

Paul would also check with his clients, some of whom lived on the streets and dwelled in the gutters. He'd lean on many friends in low places.

Paul wished Carol Resnick had given him more information. He sensed she had told him pretty much everything her office knew about the case. Carol was a straight shooter. Just before Sarah's murder, he had considered calling her for dinner. She had a boyfriend, but Carol always had a boyfriend. Since he had separated from his wife, Paul had grown weary of trying to catch her between them. Perhaps he hadn't acted sooner because he'd been reluctant to start a relationship between courtroom advocates who were so accustomed to shouting "objection" at each other. Certainly, now, with all that was happening, he couldn't think of her amorously.

Paul gazed at the stars and listened to waves pounding the shore. A storm raged far out at sea. Somewhere past the clear skies, angry waters were sending six-foot white caps toward the island. He turned toward Atlantic City's lighted casino skyline. From afar it was the Emerald City. Suddenly, clamor came from above. Boog lost his grip and slid downward, feet first, toward Paul's head.

"I hate friggin' roofs!" the Boogster cried.

Paul lost his grip as the larger man cascaded into him. All that separated them from the forty-foot drop was trim to the kitchen's window frame. Paul reached for it with his left hand and missed. He slid more, and stuck out his right hand, grabbing with all his might. Paul caught something—the window bottom ledge—and clung tight. Boog slipped further still but managed to snag one of Paul's ankles. There, they hung, Paul from a window frame and the

Boogster from his ankle. Their eyes shot upward as the kitchen window popped open. A uniformed police officer and a cop in plainclothes peered out.

"I heard something outside," the uniformed officer said.

"I don't see anything," the other man replied.

Paul recognized the latter voice.

What's Smutty doing here? he wondered.

The police officers peered into the night while Paul and Boog hung directly beneath.

Thank God, Paul thought. *They aren't looking down*.

The window closed. Paul sighed from relief. If they had caught him, suspicious prosecutors would claim that he was attempting to tamper with evidence to cover his involvement in the murder and his arrest could have led to serious charges. Then, it happened. Boog sneezed long and loud. It reverberated like a 737-airliner takeoff. The kitchen window flung open. Both police officers looked down and Smitty was the first to speak.

"Well, good evening, counselor," he said. "Interesting to find you hanging around, isn't it? Who are you hanging out with these days? Why, isn't that my old friend, former police officer Boog Johnson? Good to see you, Boog."

"Fuck you," Boog replied.

"I haven't seen the Boogster since he fell off a rooftop and left police work," Smitty said to the uniformed patrolman. "Boog, you should really try to keep your feet on the ground."

"What are you doing here, Smitty?" Boog asked. "Aren't you out of your jurisdiction?"

"Not at all. I had a chance to apply for county detective time helping the Prosecutor's Office in this murder investigation. How could I pass up an opportunity to make overtime, while investigating the murder of the counselor's wife? That just seemed too good to be true. I didn't think life could get any better until now. Guess why. I get to book you and the Counselor, that grand master of malarkey. Let's see, the charges should be breaking and entering, violating a court order that protects this crime scene, and about a dozen other offenses. I bet this makes you a sure thing for a "murder one" indictment, Counselor. Life's sure grand, ain't it?"

"Just get us off this roof before we fall and kill ourselves," Boog called up.

"All in good time. First, we have a little formality to observe. Gentlemen—and Counselor, for sake of these formalities, you're in that group—you have the right to remain silent. Anything you say, can and will be used against you in a court of law. You have the right to an attorney. . .."

Smitty took his time reading the *Miranda* card. All police officers carried them, but no officer had ever shown more joy reading one. Paul's muscles ached. He couldn't hold on much longer. If someone didn't pull them into the house fast, he would lose his grip and they would both tumble.

Smitty finished reading and turned to the uniformed officer, who stood beside him with a pistol trained on Paul and Boog.

"Oh, nuts," he exclaimed in mock disappointment. "I think I missed something."

"If we don't get them inside, they're going to break their necks," the uniformed officer said.

"I sure hope not," Smitty sighed, "but I can't deprive these gentlemen of their constitutional rights. We all know how important it is not to violate a defendant's rights, don't we, Counselor? There's only one way to be certain."

Smitty paused, then more slowly read the card again.

"You have the right to remain silent. . .."

Paul grunted. He wondered what the charges would be. He knew what they would face initially, but how far would it go? If the incident was catalyst for a murder indictment, they might not allow him post bail. He'd be off the street, unable to find Sarah's elusive boyfriend. Whatever the arrest led to; it could only be bad.

Chapter Twenty-Nine

Unsolicited Proposals

PROPOSALS CAN ARRIVE IN THE NIGHTTIME without invitation. Exhausted, Paul had nodded off early—likely around eight thirty in the evening he figured. That had become his custom after being charged with disorderly conduct from his rooftop arrest. Just after midnight he was roused by the telephone. His office line was transferred to a second home phone in the evenings. Clients in a criminal practice need to reach their lawyer when they need their lawyer: often fast on a schedule that isn't nine to five. So, when the call came, he staggered with drowsy eyes to exchange hellos.

"Yes," Paul muttered. "I know your name by rep. But we've never dealt before."

"This is my number one. I need her out, man."

Paul understood. When a business manager, as pimps are known in the trade, learn that their goods have been arrested, they need them free fast: both to keep a reputation as a protector and to maintain business cash flow.

"Your lady is in the city vice cop lock up. Bring your retainer to my office in forty minutes and I'll run there to spring her."

"No can do, Counselor. I'm out of town and you gotta spring her now."

"Sir. Unfortunately, that makes it my turn to say no can do. You must know how this works. It's the Cardinal rule in criminal law: 'payment up front'."

"She'll have your fee."

Paul knew better. "The cops strip arrestees of their pocketbooks, wallets, and cash," he said. "They'll book her, then send her out to the county jail pending a bail hearing."

"She's got the money on her. I swear on my Momma."

What the hell, Paul thought. *I'm up anyway.*

Carol knew she should feel great. Instead, she just felt full.

"This ring can be the start of a new life for both of us, Sweetheart," Barry said.

She sat at the table for two, surrounded by anxious violinists and waiters. Carol had expected their waiter to deliver dessert. Instead, he brought a diamond engagement ring on a silver serving tray. The ring was still in its open box and an anxious violinist and serving staff awaited her answer, while a hundred diners in the jammed restaurant turned to face her. Barry had arranged the surprise.

"Will you accept this engagement ring and make me the happiest man who ever sold a used car?" Barry Kane, Car King, as his well-known ads proclaimed, beamed.

She studied the ring.

Could it be all the wine I had with dinner? It's a crystal walnut, she thought. *Must have cost a bundle.*

Barry was wealthy enough to afford it. With jet-black hair and a deep tan from fishing on his pleasure craft, he was also mildly attractive. She could never quite get over the tick in his eye, though, which made his left lid flutter when excitement grabbed him at just such moments.

"Come on," Barry chimed. "What's it going to be?"

The violinist held her instrument under her chin, waiting for Carol's answer to play. Waiters stood ready to pop open champagne, and diners with mouths ready to chomp their next bite awaited her response.

"Give me your answer, now!" Grender screamed at the Boogster."

Boog looked around the small room in the County Prosecutor's Office. After he had been released from his rooftop arrest, he came when the prosecutor called. They wanted to see him after regular business hours. That let Boog know their business would be less than regular. When he arrived, Grender offered to dismiss the single charge against him but Boog knew there would be a catch.

"Testify against Cameron," the prosecutor pressed. "Cooperate and the State will drop the charge against you."

"All you have against me is a disorderly conduct offense for violating a court order."

"Maybe," Grender said, "maybe not." He picked up a file folder from the desk. "I see your daughter was picked up for shoplifting. I think my juvenile unit will have some interest in the case."

"Shoplifting. Are you're telling me that you're going to come down hard on my kid for a shoplifting bust?"

"No. I won't tell you that. I'll tell you something else my staff and I found interesting. Apparently, this teenager was picked up, once before, for joyriding with friends in a stolen car. The charges vanished, somehow. Someone in the Atlantic City Detective Division lost the file. How do you think that might have happened?"

Boog looked away.

"I think we have a juvie, who needs to enter a reformatory, and a parent who may get convicted of obstructing justice. That's serious enough to put you in the can, and maybe strip your pension. This is your last chance to make a deal. Think about it. Just give us what we want on Cameron. I'll make the charges against you and your kid disappear."

"All I have to do is sign a statement?"

Grender warmed.

"It's no big deal," he wheezed. "We just want you to say Cameron was trying to toss out evidence at the house. You don't have to implicate yourself. Say you were there for legitimate private investigation—and only learned what the guy was up to after you arrived. It's all in the statement my people prepared."

"Let me see it."

Grender handed him the affidavit.

"Should I call in a notary?"

"I have to use the bathroom," Boog replied. "Can I take this thing with me?"

Grender nodded.

"Good, I'll wipe with it."

Boog was sticking by his friend.

Cops and lawyers called it the Temple. Paul always hated its stench. The city had purchased a former Shriner's temple to process their vast array of nightly street lock ups. Toilets in the place regularly backed up and every room reeked of urine. Paul found his potential new client with her hands cuffed behind her. The handcuffs were latched around a steel rod attached to the back of the steel bench where cops had seated her. Paul knew how to start.

"I've been sent to spring you."

"Yeah. Well, it's about time. This place is givin' me itches."

Paul studied the woman. Even seated, she appeared tall with strikingly frizzy red hair.

"I'm told that you have your retainer," he said, "but you don't have a purse."

"Take off my left shoe," the woman barked.

"What?"

"Take off my left shoe."

"Keep your voice down," Paul counselled.

He lowered himself to his knees and studied footwear that, by size, bore more than slight resemblance to the row boats used by city lifeguards. He pulled off the left golden gondola and peered inside.

"Down in the toe," she whispered.

Paul reached in and pulled them out: two well folded and toe-moistened thousand-dollar bills.

"I'm not sure this will cover your fee," he explained.

The big woman barked.

"I got two feets, fool!"

A chorus of cheers rose. Embarrassed under so many watchful eyes, Carol accepted the ring. With the musician playing her violin, the champagne cork popping, and so many people clapping, no one noticed that Carol kept the ring in its box. She hadn't put it on her finger, yet.

Chapter Thirty

Salon Treatments

A HONEYMOONER ON AN OCEAN CRUISE, that's what she felt like. Mickey peered out the windows of the long stretch limousine. She was only riding a few blocks but Paul had reserved her the biggest limo in town so she could arrive in style. The first stop was Sarah's nail salon.

"You can have me paged when you're ready to be picked up, Missus Rockwell," the driver said with a courteous nod.

Mickey enjoyed using ruses while investigating cases for Paul. She could have walked into the shop, told them who she really was, and just asked questions. Yet a direct approach wouldn't generate what Paul so badly needed to know. People clammed up when they thought they might be dragged into a legal proceeding as a witness. They hedged on what they knew. Paul needed information fast, and not only facts. He desperately needed gossip, rumors, and innuendo that might lead to something useful for his defense.

Comfortable in her false identity, Mickey pretended to be the wife of a cardiologist. Her doctor husband was in town to play at the casinos. She was on the prowl, while her husband gambled. In Atlantic City, that scenario was common as seaweed washing up on shorelines. The limo took her from the Sands Casino to the nail salon, where her driver helped her out of the car, and opened the shop door. She entered with all the fanfare expected.

This is the good life, Mickey realized.

She knew of Sarah's extravagant tastes and the salon didn't disappoint her. Hefty prices matched expensive decor and lush appointments.

"Can I help you?"

The receptionist asked with one ear waiting for an answer, while her other pressed into a telephone. The shop was a busy place.

"I have an appointment with Sally to do my nails."

The young woman checked her log.

"Of course, Missus Rockwell. Please, take a seat. Sally will be with you in a minute. She's finishing her three o'clock."

Mickey sat on a black leather sofa that overlooked the nail stations. Her customarily subdued appearance gave way for panache. Her hair was down. Paul had bought her a Jean-Paul Gaultier prêt-à-porter dress that bespoke the eponymous fashion label. As she leafed through an issue of "Town and Country," Mickey observed that every word spoken at the nail stations was heard throughout the room.

She mentally prepared by closing her eyes and reflecting upon a cherished Zen mantra:

> Those who hear truth even once
> And listen with a grateful heart,
> Treasuring it, revering it,
> Gain blessings without end.

"You can go back, now," the receptionist called. "It's the first station on the right."

Mickey breathed deeply and strode to the manicure desk.

"Hi, Missus Rockwell," Sally greeted.

Mickey quickly surveyed the woman's teased blond hair, jaws clacking gum, and silver stretch slacks.

Be cultured yet cordial with her, Mickey reminded herself.

"Please, call me Michelle," Mickey said.

The two women smiled at each other as Mickey sat. Sally blew a pink gum bubble, popped it, and chatted between chomps.

"Are you staying in town?"

"Just for a quick trip. My husband is playing at the Sands, but we have to return home tonight. He's scheduled to perform surgery in the morning."

"Where does he practice?"

"Manhattan. He operates from Mount Sinai Hospital."

Mickey knew she sounded as if she had struck the motherload with a high rolling surgeon husband. She also perceived what Sally was thinking. When a high roller's wife came into a nail shop, everyone was well tipped.

"What brings you here?"

"Oh, I never care for salons in the casinos. You know how they can be—crowded, filled with too many *yentas* with time on their hands, while their husbands are glued to game tables. A girlfriend from college told me about your place a long time ago. I always said I'd try it, when I came to town."

The woman's warm expression let Mickey know the customer's referral flattered her.

"Who's your friend?"

Mickey paused. Then, she spoke loudly enough for all to hear: "Sarah Cameron."

Every head turned to look at her. Sally looked flustered, just the way Mickey wanted her.

"I guess," Sally said tentatively, "you know about Sarah's murder."

"Yes, I heard. I don't know much about it. Never even met her husband. We were good friends in college, but you know how it is. We drifted apart after we married. She came here and I was in New York. We talked after she separated from her husband. She told me something about having a boyfriend but that's about all I know."

Sally and the other women, who had first stiffened when hearing Sarah's name, relaxed their postures. Mickey didn't want to sound so attached to Sarah's memory that they would conceal their feelings. She suspected that the murder had been the talk of the shop for weeks. Anxiously, she waited for their prospective. Sally bit the bait.

"We think her husband did it. Sarah was getting ready to take him for a bundle in their divorce. That's all she talked about whenever she came in here."

"He must've killed her," one of the other nail technicians snapped.

"I still say he was awfully good looking and too rich to care about what he would lose in a divorce," chimed in the third.

"He's good looking enough," Sally expressed pensively, "but you're never too rich not to care about losing money. We all want to see him fry."

Her comments typified some, not all local sentiments.

"Maybe her boyfriend had something to do with it," Mickey suggested, attempting to sway the conversation in a different direction.

"Him?" Sally said. "No way. She only fought with her husband and he was the one who had something to gain by her death."

"What do you know about her boyfriend?"

"Sarah never said much about him. Never even referred to him by his name."

"She must have called him by some name when she spoke about him."

"No," Sally sighed. "She just called him her mystery lover. Sarah liked the intrigue, I think. All she ever said about the relationship was that her love life had never been better."

"This guy knew how to push all her buttons," another woman chimed.

All three nail technicians laughed knowingly with their customers. Just then, a commotion at the front door distracted Mickey.

"I need an appointment pronto," an enormous woman called. "My dogs are barking. They've been walking these streets in high heels every night this week. Whooie! They hurt. Tonight, I got me a big spender, who appreciates pretty feet. You better find me a time slot because I need corns and callouses scraped to the bone."

The receptionist appeared sympathetic. Women who worked Pacific Avenue in their high heeled shoes had what prostitutes referred to as "working girl feet" and what nail girls called "hooker hoofs." They came into the shop, unabashedly complaining of their occupational malady, then soaked their tootsies in a special footbath to soften and sanitize them. Afterwards, a technician filed away dead skin and callouses. They did it the same way a blacksmith files down hoofs on a horse.

Manicurists loved the working women, even if they were notoriously poor tippers. Hookers dished good dirt. They always knew whose husband was paying for sex-on-the-side and nail shops thrive on that kind of blather.

Mickey looked at the loud woman, then turned away fast. At six feet tall with a mop of flaming red hair, so frizzy it looked as if she styled it by sticking her finger into an electric socket, the woman was impossible to forget. She was one of Paul's clients. If she recognized Mickey, the ruse would be blown.

Sally was ready to dry Mickey's freshly painted fingernails under a cool-air blower. Mickey turned her face to a wall. She sensed she was near discovering everything the women knew about Sarah's lover. She would have to ask direct questions, and escape without being recognized by the whining Godzilla of prostitution they called "Whorezilla" in the law office.

"I'll give this guy a toe job, maybe smack him around a little as a warmup," the woman was explaining.

Mickey sneaked another glimpse of Whorezilla.

Truly, she thought, *there's a rat for every hole*.

"Then, I'll overcharge him. Masochists love being overcharged!"

Mickey turned back to her nail technician.

"What did Sarah's boyfriend look like?"

Sally blew another gum bubble that hid her lower face. When it popped, she continued.

"Nobody in here knows. Sarah never said anything about his looks. She was always kind of funny about that. All she ever talked about was how much she enjoyed the sex."

"I need an appointment, now, Honey," Whorezilla boisterously demanded. "Am I gonna get one or not?"

Sally took the receptionist off the hook.

"I'll be with you in a couple of minutes," she shouted to the front of the shop. "Soon as I'm done, here."

"Thank goodness," the big woman sighed.

She plopped onto the sofa, rested her tired feet on top of the coffee table, then yanked off her shoes. Mickey was close enough to catch a whiff. Gambling that the hooker wouldn't recognize her voice, she called out loudly, hoping someone in the shop would offer a clue.

"You mean nobody knows what Sarah's boyfriend looks like or what he does for a living?"

"Long hair," someone called from other side of the room.

"What do you mean?" Mickey probed.

"Sarah complained a couple of times about getting hair in her mouth when they made love. Sounded like he had long hair."

"What else?"

"Well," Sally said, "whoever he was, he must've known a lot about divorce cases. Sarah relied on his advice. She said she wouldn't have had half as strong a case against her husband, if it hadn't been for her boyfriend."

"Maybe he was a lawyer," Mickey offered.

"No. Sarah claimed she would never touch another lawyer. One was too many for her. She wanted a clean break."

"Was he a local guy?"

"Could've been. Hard to tell. But, toward the end she complained about seeing too much of him. He was coming over at the drop of a hat and getting pretty demanding."

"From the looks of things, she may have liked someone who was demanding," another woman added.

They all laughed. Sally blushed embarrassedly, as if they were getting too familiar around one of Sarah's old friends. Mickey tried to put her at ease.

"That's okay," she said. "Sarah was quirky. I'm not offended. I'd like to find her boyfriend though. Is there anything you could tell me that would help?"

Sally just shook her head from side to side.

"Hey, when are you gonna do my dogs?" Whorezilla called from the sofa. "I've been airing them out and they're gettin' chilly."

Sally looked over to her next customer, then back to Mickey.

"We're just about done with your nails," she said. "Would you like me to call for your limo?"

Mickey nodded then wondered.

How do I leave without being recognized by that hooker?

She knew she had to be careful. Boog might want her return to the shop later.

Finally, she said, "Which way is your ladies' room?"

Sally pointed to a door in the back of the shop. Mickey pulled out two hundred-dollar bills to satisfy her tab in high roller fashion, then whisked toward the rear of the shop. She waited there, out of sight, for her driver. When she cautiously emerged, her chauffeur was outside, holding the limousine door open. Whorezilla was soaking her feet in tubs of the salon's famous foot bath.

"Woof!" Whorezilla barked. "My dogs are feeling relief."

Sally pulled out the tools of the trade, a scraping instrument that looked like a carpenter's plane, a grinding file, and a pumice stone. The size thirteens she was setting to engage belonged on a pro basketball player. Corns topped bunions. Dime-sized calluses covered each foot from heel to scraggy toes. Sally moaned, then reached for a larger file. The job demanded more than her usual instruments. It required carpentry tools.

"Woof, woof," Mickey heard, as she hustled toward the limo, off to Sarah's hairdresser.

Mister Michael ran an exclusive Atlantic City hair salon that also catered to high roller trade. Other women came in limousines, but Mickey knew the hairdressers would greet her with greater aplomb. Thanks to Paul, her limo was longer. That denoted swank in a town where garishness so often measures respectability, causing courtesy to flow. She played her role, but Mister Michael looked at her uncertainly.

"Dearie," he said, "who's been doing this to you?" Mister Michael held dead ends of her hair and observed the obvious. "You look like you've been streaking . . . this . . . this hair . . . with a home bleaching kit."

Mickey always touched up her own hair, something few high rollers' wives would do.

"Oh, Sweetie," the stylist flustered, "you haven't been very good to yourself, have you?"

Cracking information from Mister Michael was tough but he did offer something that would keep Boog busy. The last time Sarah had gone to the shop, she had mentioned buying her boyfriend a gift, a fancy cigarette lighter. She wanted something special, but not too special all at the same time. She didn't want her boyfriend to read more into the gift than he should.

Mickey sat under a hair dryer and fumed. She didn't like the way the hairdresser checked her out. The guy wasn't like Anthony and Emile.

He's over the top, she thought.

Mickey was liberal minded, but his cool glances told her that he was looking down at her. She was glad to retreat to her limousine and direct her driver to Boog's bar. The chauffeur's eyes brows arched when the high roller's wife gave the address.

Fuck him, too, she thought. She liked the place. Besides, Paul would be there with Boog for a rundown.

Paul was glad to catch Mickey's smile. She moved close and planted a kiss on his cheek. It came without warning. Before he could even show surprise, she was sitting in the booth with him and Boog, telling them what she had learned. It didn't sound like much until Boog put it in prospective.

"Criminal investigation," he said, "is a matter of sifting through known facts to establish the unknown."

Then, he laid it out simply.

We can discover the identity of Sarah's boyfriend by creating a profile based on our leads. Look at what they tell us. Our suspect has long hair. He's a stud. That puts his age somewhere between twenty and forty-five.

"Narrow that age down more," Paul suggested. Sarah was thirty-five years old. Keep the age closer to hers.

"But, Micky offered, you told me she was sexually adventurous. Sarah may have experimented with a man much younger or older.

Paul mused, while the Boogster rolled.

"The guy's knowledge of divorce law suggests he knows his way around the legal process by profession or experience in his own familial proceeding."

They sat silently until Boog tossed in a notion.

"My buddies at the Detective Division owe me a couple favors. I'll run this past them and squeeze 'em for their thoughts.

Paul looked down wearily.

"My glass seems to have sprung a leak," he said.

Boog called out.

"Another round for three!"

Mickey cuddled up to Paul and tried relieving his stress by massaging his temples.

"I'm sorry they didn't tell me more," she apologized, "but look how good my hair and nails came out." She beamed as she tilted her head and displayed ten talons.

Paul chuckled, the first genuine laugh he'd had in a while. After Smitty had arrested him on the roof with Boog, prosecutors charged him with entering the crime scene in violation of the court order. They quickly released him without bail on his own recognizance. A murder indictment would have come swiftly in view of Grender's feelings toward Paul but came even faster as women's groups fumed with indignation.

"A wife killer shouldn't be walking the streets," was their battle cry.

Grender delighted in bowing to public pressure. He formally charged Paul. Also cognizant of popular sentiment, the arraignment judge set high bail and the case was moving toward trial too quickly.

Paul leaned on his former boss, Lee Gunther, hoping the lawyer he recalled as a toughened legal wizard could still conjure courtroom magic.

What, he wondered, *happened to Lee? Does he still have it in him to pull this off?*

Grender was holding the minor charge against Boog in abeyance. The juvenile charge against his daughter also languished at the prosecutor's direction. Grender threatened to use them as hammers against the former cop but Boog was steadfast. He trusted Paul to save him and his daughter from trouble—so long as Paul could save himself first.

As for Paul, he wondered what was wrong on the street. Boog couldn't get the kind of information he customarily found so quickly. Street people shouted the general opinion that the lawyer had killed his wife, but no one even whispered information the defense could use.

It's unnatural, thought Paul, *on streets that always hear evil, see evil, and speak evil.*

Something was happening in Atlantic City, but what? Paul looked up as the bartender summoned him to the telephone. He wondered who knew to reach him there.

"Paul," the caller said.

That was all he needed to hear to recognize his high school chum.

"Yes, Anthony," he responded.

His old friend's voice was so good to hear. Anthony and his partner, Emile, had taken keen interest in the case. Emile was developing a psychological portrait of the killer that Boog could use in his investigation. Forensic psychology wasn't Emile's specialty, but he knew how to enlist well-qualified assistance. He traded professional courtesies with colleagues, who knew him by affiliation and reputation. He was also probing top practitioners at a criminology convention he was attending in Washington.

"Emile may have information important to your case," Anthony said. "He'll meet you tomorrow night when he gets back into town. He wants to talk to you, face to face. I think he's onto something big."

"Anthony, if he can help me, I need to know now. Time's running out."

"Emile never jumps to conclusions, Paul. He's a very cautious man. Meet him at our apartment at eight sharp. I'm going to be working on a residential design job in Philly. I'll leave a key under our doormat in case he's a little late getting back."

Paul returned to their table and planned the next day ahead. He and Mickey would be at the courthouse while Boog checked jewelry stores to see if anyone knew anything about the gift Sarah wanted for her boyfriend. That was a longshot, but they were grasping for anything.

Paul contemplated the call from his decorator friend, sipping his drink, perplexed, wondering what Emile may have learned at a convention of criminologists.

Why, he thought, *is the information so sensitive that Emile feels compelled tell me face to face*?

Chapter Thirty-One

A Loose Tongued Auntie

TONY PULLED HIS BLACK LINCOLN TO THE REAR of the dilapidated Fairmont Tavern. Before he could open his car door, a rapping on the passenger-side window startled him. The old boss looked to see the Oriental man who was well known to him. Tony had made a point of finding Shek's hired killer to make private arrangements with the deadly assassin. He who had no name lived by a mercenary code with allegiance to himself alone. Instinctively, Tony reached under his seat for the loaded revolver always kept near his side.

The man put him at ease by opening his hands to show Tony that he wasn't carrying a weapon. He looked clean and made a motion for Tony to lower his car window so they could speak. Tony cautiously complied, his pistol in hand and out of view.

"I have something," the man said in English lightly accented by Vietnamese, "something of value to your people for a price."

"Get in the car," Tony said. He wanted the menacing figure in full view as they spoke. Their dealings had been in death, never in merchandise so Tony's curiosity piqued.

"What I offer warrants a heavy price."

Tony didn't like being squeezed. "Not interested," he simply said.

"You'll speak to me now, Mister DeBona, or you'll pay a much higher price to someone else later."

Why is the hired killer here? Tony wondered. *What did he have to sell*?

Tony studied him. Of average build and ocher complected, the man stood out in no way, save one. He displayed no emotion as if he had none to offer, never a trace of a smile or frown. Tony sensed the man was incapable of expressing joy—or for that matter anguish. The mob boss always studied eyes. He could read all that a being was within them. Yet, Tony saw none of the signs that unveiled a killer, let alone a psychopathic butcher. Those vacant eyes declared only that there was no life story he would ever tell.

The man pulled one of Commissioner Pepperman's disks from his breast pocket. Computers weren't Tony's forte. He had no idea of what dangled in his face, nor the significance of what it contained.

"This is a computer disk," the man began, "containing telling tales. It can't be duplicated and the data on it cannot be printed. You can only see the information on a computer programed with its companion disk to decipher the encryption code. The two disks are called the dago Brothers. One is no good without the other."

"You're wasting your time," Tony said. "I know nothing of computers."

"You'll have an interest in learning what tales these disks tell."

"If I was interested, my car horn would summon associates, who'd nab it free of charge."

"Surely that's true. But I've warned you that the two disks only work in concert with one another. The disk in my hand contains information that no one can see without the encryption disk that's in safekeeping. You could take this one from me. Yet, without its brother, you would never learn who made it. That someone could disseminate the same information again. Do you know what that means?

Tony didn't answer.

It means you have a loose tongued auntie in your house, who gossips shamelessly."

"What?"

"Your bookmaking take for the first eight weeks of the year are these figures, are they not?"

The man held figures before Tony on a handwritten scrap of paper.

"I don't know what you're talking about," Tony replied.

"The people who banked that book are the men on this second list, correct?"

Tony was mortified. No one could obtain that information outside his family. He stared at the disk with keener interest.

"I'll talk to someone who knows about these things," he said. "I must be assured the data you wish to sell can't be regenerated, if matters of confidence are involved. You must also give me greater taste of the information to appreciate its value."

"I'll open the data on a computer where we both feel secure. When you pay my price, you'll discover your rat by learning what secrets these discs tell. But, don't delay, Mister DeBona. Other buyers are in the market for computer wares."

Suddenly, he knew Shek's game from the start. Someone in Tony's crime family had funneled the data to Commissioner Pepperman. A flea like Pepperman could never have climbed under his skin without inside help.

Pepperman would use the data to and advance his career at Commission hearings or it could be sold to Shek, who'd want it to rid the town of opposition by turning its information over to the County Prosecutor's Office or the FBI. Tony needed to handle Shek irrevocably and had to learn the identity of the "loose tongued auntie" in his family. Tony would pay for the disks, then his enemies would pay him back.

The hired assassin left the car and disappeared around a corner. Tony followed his catlike movements.

This one too dangerous, he thought. *In time, he must be eliminated as well.*

Tony grabbed his newspaper from the rear seat of his car and glanced at a local headline he had helped manufacture. The trial of the young lawyer, who had betrayed him, was about to begin. When it did, that small headline would grow large. The *avvocato* was going down.

When he had crossed Tony, the lawyer tripped himself without even knowing. Soon, a jury would convict him.

Tony had seen to it by having his people feed information to the prosecutor. Years of experience had taught Tony many cagey tricks and he would employ them for his *vendetta*: Paul Cameron would be quick to the fish.

Chapter Thirty-Two

Court is Now in Session

THE HONORABLE EDWIN C. HASTINGS, Judge of the Superior Court of New Jersey, was presiding over the trial that would cast Paul's fate. Either side could have rejected the jurist, before whom Paul had tried the case of Reverend Rich. But, Grender was glad to have Paul back before Hastings . . . this time as a defendant. As for the defense point of view, Paul had gleaned respect from the judge, during and after the Rev's trial that rendered the bald jurist—who remained string-bean lean, humorless, and stone faced—a more palatable option that any "conflict judge." Even a change of venue, moving the case to another county, was an option rejected by the defense because Paul had made friends in the community, and had garnered a reputation as lawyer who won tough cases for good folks.

Paul joined Lee at the counsel table. Mickey and Boog sat behind on the front row of spectator seats, ready to help. The jury had been selected the day before, and Paul had remained true to his word. Lee put them in the box without interference from his client. Even after the jury selection process was complete, Paul kept his dissatisfaction pretty much under wraps.

"Juror number one, Mister Premmington," he had said to Lee.

"What about him?"

"He scowls. The guy's too surly to find for a defendant."

"The danger of removing him with our last peremptory challenge was someone worse could have replaced him. You have a tough case and we have as good a jury as you can hope to snag."

"Juror number four?" Paul looked at his yellow legal pad for the name of the crone that he had circled. "Patricia Menster-Stoham. He showed Lee his note reading, "self-proclaimed *extreme* feminist."

"Just means hairy legged and man-less," Lee offered.

Paul underlined her initials: P.M.S. That seemed to say it all.

"Let your lawyer worry for you, Pal." Lee said. "I'll tackle what's going on inside the courtroom. You handle what's happening on those streets you know so well. Give me what I need to feed this jury. They're hungry for the truth and we have to deliver it . . . even if it comes without exactitude. Find a suspect fast. We don't have to prove he actually killed your wife. We just need to generate a reasonable doubt by offering a plausible alternative."

Paul knew how much they needed that.

"And Paul," Lee said softly, "reconsider your decision not to take the stand with an alibi. You have nothing else to offer as a defense. The prosecution's proofs are damned good for a circumstantial evidence case."

Paul had time to think about the advice that morning as Horace Grender gave his opening address to the jury. Grender blustered like the pompous windbag he was. He screamed unholy Hades, while pointing his "finger of shame" at Paul as the "killer who thought he was above the law because he knew the law." Grender delivered fiery rhetoric in his falsetto voice. Paul would have suspected the guy was a eunuch, if hadn't known about the man's sexual proclivity.

"I like sodomy. How odd of me," Grender had callously joked to Carol Resnick after too many drinks at an office Christmas party.

Carol had confided the incident to Paul long ago. It appalled her to the extent she wished there was a venue to report workplace harassment. Paul had also heard of Grender's sexual preference from hookers he represented, who said they declined the man, who wanted "a girl to pop in the pooper."

With trial underway, Horace Grender the Rear Ender was steam rolling. He promised to call witnesses to the stand who would prove Paul had motive to murder his wife.

"The State will produce the victim's divorce lawyer. She'll testify that the matrimonial case would have cost this defendant hundreds-of-thousands of dollars now and much more in alimony over years to come. Financial experts will show how the divorce was his million-dollar nightmare.

What's more, insurance representatives will prove that he maintained a substantial policy on his victim's life. The defendant's motive is obvious: greed and avarice.

"We will also prove the defendant had no love for the victim of his murderous scheme. He hadn't lived with her for more than a year. All that time, he paid for the expensive house she occupied, and for her lavish lifestyle.

"In his twisted mind, the defendant had plenty of reasons to murder Sarah Cameron. He also had the opportunity. There's no explanation of his whereabouts on the night of the murder because he *is* the murderer."

Paul listened to bits and pieces. Grender observed that Paul's fingerprints were throughout the house. Later, when Lee addressed the jury, he would remind everyone that Paul had once lived there. Naturally, his prints were inside. Still, Grender planted seeds of suspicion that could bloom into guilt. The pudgy prosecutor spoke for most of the morning. Judge Hastings was mindful of the hour when Grender concluded and waddled to his seat.

"Mister Gunther," the judge cried down from the bench to Lee.

"It is now eleven forty-five, Counselor. Would you prefer the Court to take an early luncheon recess before you present your opening address?"

Paul saw that Grender had snared the defense in a little trap. If Lee insisted upon opening just then, the jurors would be annoyed that the defense was keeping them from lunch. That was a horrible way to start a trial. On the other hand, no lawyer wants to address a jury immediately following the luncheon recess. While digesting, jurors tend to nod off and miss a lot. Experienced counsel generally reserve the hour following lunch to place a weak witness on the stand while jurors pay less attention. Grender had droned to put Lee in that position and the trial lawyer had to make a tactical decision.

"Your Honor," Lee said, "unlike the prosecutor, I will be to the point. My comments won't keep us from the customary noontime break."

Paul also knew Lee would be brief because he couldn't say much. The defense hinged on claiming Sarah had a boyfriend who killed her. Yet, if the defense couldn't produce a suspect, Lee would never convince the jury that their theory was credible.

As Lee rose to speak, Mickey discretely delivered Paul a note. Reverend Rich wanted to meet him, right away. Paul reflected and grimaced. The last time the Reverend had summoned him that way, events triggered that put Paul at odds against Tony DeBona.

The Righteous Reverend had assumed a holier than thou persona following his acquittal. He had convinced Paul to ride a moral high road and that's always bumpy. The holier-than-thou Rev had been infinitely easier to deal with when he was simply hornier-than-thou. Yet, it left Paul wondering.

What does Reverend Rich want?

Paul whispered into Mickey's ear.

"I'll meet the Rev tonight on my way to see Emile. Call Anthony. Have him get a message to Emile that I may be a few minutes late."

Mickey hurried out of the courtroom to make the arrangements as Lee calmly addressed the jury. Paul listened, while wondering whether Boog was having any luck.

As the Boogster pounded his old beat, hitting jewelry stores all over town, he learned Sarah had stopped into all of them. Her tastes ran extravagant, even on small purchases. Every casino had its own jewelry shop to relieve a lucky gambler of winnings on an impulsive purchase. Outside the casinos, jewelry shops dotted the town's corners. Sarah even shopped in pawn shops that collected diamond rings for gas money home from gamblers who had lost everything in their wallets and on their credit lines.

The familiar turf was where Boog felt most at home. He had investigated robberies there when he was a member of the Detective Division. Faces he crossed were friendly. Jewelers and pawn brokers told him what they could. A couple remembered the free-spending decedent as a former customer. Unfortunately, nobody knew about the cigarette lighter. Boog was ready to quit for the day when he stopped into Jay's Jewels on the boardwalk.

Jagan had learned the business in India before immigrating to a better life by the boards. The skinny jeweler dressed like a casino dealer so gamblers would feel comfortable with him. A black vest covered his white shirt and red garters adorned his sleeves. Mutton-chop sideburns flared wide enough to make up for a paucity of top coverage.

His store opened and closed late. When gamblers first cashed their chips, they viewed winnings as the casino's cash, and were quick to spend. By morning, they were tighter with money they now regarded as their own.

Jagan remembered Sarah well.

"Boog, I still have the lighter," he lamented. "She wanted the initial letter of her boyfriend's last name engraved on it. Normally I'm paid upfront for something like this, but she was a reliable customer. She put half the purchase price down to have it monogrammed. Then, she got herself tied up and killed. I'm stuck with it. How am I going to sell a personalized piece?"

Jagan shook his head and handed Boog the lighter.

Boog looked at the "M" boldly engraved in 24-carat gold across the front and declared: "Ring it up!"

He took the lighter as possible evidence and placed a fast telephone call to Lee's office. Lee would have to add Jagan to their witness list, which the defense is obligated to provide the Prosecutor's Office. Rules of Court require disclosure of all potential witnesses or the judge can exclude their testimony.

Afterward, Boog tediously scoured local telephone directories for every "M" in the books. He also cross-referenced the profile they were developing with motor vehicle records accessed by his friends at the Detective Division. He was a busy Boogster.

He would track down someone else, too. Her name had been placed on the defense witness list even though they hadn't found her yet to discover what she knew. Paul had a hunch the woman would know something, so he had Lee identify her as a precaution. Prell was back in town. She always checked into Paul's office before she and her "business manager," AK, checked into a hotel. Prell had a lawyer on retainer in every town she worked. She'd been around long enough to know that if she was arrested, she wanted counsel to sweep her out of lock-up fast. So, she always had money on account with Paul as her insurance policy.

Boog would find Prell and have her talk to her friends. Hookers, who survived the town for any length of time, shared a loose camaraderie from facing common dangers. Prell had endured long enough to be called a "street granny." If the defense was to break the silence on the streets, she was as reliable a link in the network as they'd find.

He knew one way to find her fast. Boog called her service and made a date. He chuckled when the answering service clerk announced: "Miz Prell is now accepting MasterCard."

Back in the courtroom Judge Hastings called out, "That's all for the day. We'll reconvene in the morning."

Lee would spend the night preparing for the next court session, while Paul whisked away for two pressing engagements.

Chapter Thirty-Three

Settling Old Scores

TONY STOOD BESIDE LENA AND SPOKE SOFTLY so only she would hear. A night mist covered her grave, seven years having passed since her death. He had fresh flowers delivered weekly—sweet bouquets that had always lit her smile. And that night, he delivered words reaffirming devotion to her memory, then told her what he suspected: "I may join you soon, *Amore Mio*."

What if I meet death? Tony pondered.

In a kaleidoscopic vision, he recalled faces he had cherished and death masks that bore his mark. He had devoured life's passions yet retained a voracious appetite for more.

No, he realized, *it's not time to die.*

Tony refused to leave lose ends behind. A strong believer in the concept of an eye for an eye, Tony still had some to poke out. He also sensed a notion of benevolence only time would allow him to bestow.

If he was to survive, he would have to settle all old scores quickly, some to keep his house in order and others for sake of vendetta. And, until Tony discovered the rat in his family, he could trust no one.

A drizzle fell upon the cemetery, landing quietly as a man approached Tony from behind. When he turned, their faces were inches apart. If the man had intended to harm him, Tony knew he would already be laying on the grave site where he would someday rest next to Lena. The man was no threat that night; he came to deal. He who had no name was first to speak.

"Are you prepared to pay my price?"

"Yes," Tony replied. "Your discs have value, but I'm not wise in the workings of computers. You'll meet someone on my behalf who has such skills. He'll examine them and tender payment for delivery."

"Then, we will deal with your loose tongued auntie."

"That shall also be part of our bargain. Your skills will settle that score, when time is right. And, I'll apply your talent, now, to reconcile another account."

The two men continued to talk. Tony saw the man's nose twitch, perhaps smelling the blood he'd draw. It would be a busy night for the killer, and for others as well.

Smitty stared at Poon Tang Train. The bucked tooth pimp with the nasty rep as a blade man was bopping down Pacific Avenue.

"*Yowl-sa!*" he blurted. "Yes Sir, indeed. Time to bring him down."

Smitty and his partner moved across the rain-slick street with guns drawn. The veteran cops knew how to make a fast arrest. The scumbag wouldn't get an opportunity to pull the knife he used so skillfully. If Train reached to his pockets, they'd shoot, rather than risk their lives.

The two plainclothes officers nabbed the pimp from behind, shoved him against a wall with his lips pressed into a storefront, and clasped his hands atop his head. Smitty kicked Train's feet apart to keep him off balance, then patted him down. His partner kept a pistol cocked and jammed it into the back of Train's skull.

"One move, numb nuts, and I'll blow your brains onto the pavement," Smitty's partner warned.

"Found it," said Smitty, as he pulled Train's switch blade from his jacket pocket.

"Goddamn," his partner wheezed. "That's at least a nine-inch blade."

"And what have we here?" Smitty continued, pulling his hand from another pocket. "A bag of white powder. You are one unlucky son of a bitch."

Smitty stuck a finger in the bag then tasted the dust with the tip of his tongue.

"Field tested positive for cocaine. My, oh my. You're a sorry pimp, tonight."

"What the fuck are you talking about, man?" Train screamed. "This ain't my jacket. I picked this thing up in a bar down the street. Borrowed it from a man. I don't know nothin' about this shit."

"Did you hear that?" Smitty said to his partner. "This gentleman is a victim of circumstances. Let's put him in the car."

He cuffed Train's hands behind his back and dragged him to their unmarked car. As he shoved Train in the back, Smitty was careful to knock the pimp's head into the steel door trim. He liked bringing them in with their heads spinning. Smitty relaxed up front, while his partner drove. Windshield wipers clapped and their police radio squelched.

"What are you taking me in for?" Train demanded to know. "That bust was bogus, man. You can't make a warrantless search without seeing me commit a crime."

"Listen to this!" Smitty exclaimed. "This man knows the law. I'm impressed."

"You made a search without even reading me my rights. That won't stand up in court," Train said. "You might as well drop me off, here."

"Where the hell do you think you are, Shithead? This is for real!" Smitty shouted red-faced. "You ain't in the movies."

Smitty turned to his partner.

"Didn't we see this guy buy a bag of cocaine from a suspected drug source before we arrested him?"

"Looked that way to me."

"Didn't I read his rights from my *Miranda* card?"

"Yep. Looks like a good bust to me."

Smitty glanced back at Train, "How's it looking to you, now, dirt bag?"

They didn't drive toward the Temple where vice cops processed arrests. Smitty knew Train would see they were heading in the wrong direction. It gave him a warm glow to watch the pimp squirm, wondering where they were taking him.

Chapter Thirty-Four

Find Me an Angel

COLD STARES DELIVER ICY GREETINGS. Aside from pious figures on stained glass windows, who rendered those glances, the place seemed damned empty. Paul readied to leave the nearly dark church when he spotted the Righteous Reverend Rich knelling at the altar. Paul approached from behind, placed his hand on the minister's shoulder, and expected him to rise. Yet the Rev remained transfixed: silent, motionless. Then without turning to face Paul, his low tones resonated.

"Counselor, I want to thank you for everything you've done—not only for me but for members of my congregation, who have come to you over the years."

Paul nodded halfheartedly. He had come for more than an expression of gratitude, no matter how well intended. His ears hungered for more than they were hearing.

"You changed my life," the Rev continued. Now, I pray that I can help you. Wait in the rectory. I've asked someone to join us and wish to be alone until she arrives."

Paul knew the way. He had met Reverend Rich and other members of his large flock there in the past. Paul entered the office chamber and closed the door behind him. Dark wood-paneled walls and burgundy carpet matched the church décor. A portrait of Jesus, face pointed to the heavens, hung above the Rev's mahogany desk.

It's been so long since I looked there, he thought.

His mother had raised him in followings of the Episcopalian church. She strictly adhered to its tenets and accepted religion as she saw life: treasuring purity of the soul over warmth of the heart. As if possessing the tenacity of a reformed sinner, she had tried instilling pious virtues in her son while protecting him from life's passions.

The Rev's clerical robe, which perched on a coat rack, refocused Paul's thinking. It reminded him of the black garb worn near sinisterly by Judge Hastings. At least that's how it seemed to him as a defendant. Paul knew the cue-ball headed and bushy browed judge would sentence him to die if something didn't break in the murder case. Paul was desperate for help and wondered what the Rev planned.

He remembered all too well the last time the Reverend had brought him into the rectory. The invitation had come as Paul was preparing Tony DeBona's fire insurance case for trial. It came years after the Boss of the Boardwalk had retained him for "a friend." Both men understood that the burned-out restaurant was mob owned.

Paul initially attempted to settle the case with the fire insurance company. Its counsel had vowed to fight. The woman believed that the fire was an arson committed by organized crime figures who were the true business owners. Paul couldn't dissuade her.

"Mr. Cameron," she had sighed. "We know your reputation for nailing civil verdicts. I've even factored that into my evaluation, but this isn't a case you can win. My company only has to prove one of the two elements: either the fire wasn't accidental, or the business had undisclosed principals associated with organized crime. Either way, my insurer isn't obligated to pay.

Paul knew she was correct on the law, but he was prepared to meet her argument.

"If your company intends to try this case without an eyewitness, you'll have to rely on expert testimony to establish arson. A jury will weigh the word of your specialist against the findings of my client's expert who wrote the book on pyrotechnic losses. My guy has better credentials and will be more credible."

"We don't know how you got the top man in the field to disavow arson evidence that the city fire inspector found."

Paul knew. His client had paid their expert handsomely.

"But," his adversary continued, "we aren't concerned over a battle of experts."

"Are you telling me that you have an eyewitness?"

"All I'm authorized to tell you is that my insurance company won't voluntarily pay on the claim."

That told Paul they had an eyewitness. Undeterred, he sued. DeBona's associates complained to Paul about how long it took the case to reach trial. He was patient with men he recognized as dangerous.

"Yes. It's a long time in the life of a geranium," he explained. "It's average in the life of a lawsuit with Atlantic County's backlogged civil dockets."

Paul planned for what always bothered him about a two-week trial: rotating suits and ties he'd be wearing before the same twelve jurors. Then, days before the trial started, he wrestled with a greater concern. How would he handle the insurer's eyewitness?

He was working in his conference room when Mickey entered. Papers were stacked high and books were strewn across the table, open to case law on point.

"Paul," she called, "Mister DeBona is here."

"Does he have an appointment?"

"He never makes appointments. You know that."

Paul nodded. DeBona had arrived the same way when they first met. The mob boss uncannily knew when Paul would be available. Mickey brought the older man into the conference room, where he and Paul sat at the table and studied each other. Finally, DeBona broke silence with his customary economy of words.

"I understand my *avvocato* has a concern."

Paul expelled a long breath then took it from the top.

"During pretrial discovery," he began, "I served interrogatories requiring the insurer to produce statements that their investigators took from witnesses. They took one from a woman who will testify that she saw something detrimental to our case. She claims a man crashed out of the building while it was in flames. He stumbled to the ground and she ran to see if he was alive. She took a good look at him while he laid unconscious, then left to call the fire department. Police had her check mug shots when they became suspicious of the fire origin. She positively identified a photo of a torch with a prison record. Reputedly, he's connected to your family."

Paul looked for DeBona's reaction, but the man was unreadable.

"Authorities never pursued arson charges," he continued, "but they may if the woman testifies in this case. If a jury buys what she says, the judge will be obligated to refer the matter to the County Prosecutor's Office for probable prosecution."

"We have a friend there," DeBona offered casually.

Paul knew the mob boss held power with those kinds of friendships but that didn't matter at the civil trial.

"Her testimony will be pivotal," he continued. "Frankly, what this woman has to say will cost us the case."

"Can the insurance company use her written statement if she doesn't appear at the trial."

Paul lifted a pen and twirled it.

"No," he reflected. "The insurer's lawyers screwed up. They never took her deposition. And, they're so convinced of the woman's cooperation that they never subpoenaed her to appear. If the insurer can't prove she's dead, the written statement isn't admissible as evidence and what she said to the insurance investigator isn't admissible as hearsay."

Paul set down his pen and looked DeBona in the eyes.

"The woman will be in court, though. She's a bonafide pain-in-the-ass do-gooder."

"When will she be called to testify?"

That question comes too easily, Paul thought. To his surprise so did his own answer.

"Our case will take a week. Then, we can expect her to be called as the insurer's first witness."

"Don't concern yourself," DeBona offered casually. "She won't testify."

"Mister DeBona, opposing counsel says their witness will appear. There's a fifty-thousand-dollar settlement offer on the table. Consider taking it."

"Apparently you didn't hear me. This is still a million-dollar case."

Paul opened his mouth, but the older man's raised hand impaled his words before they crossed his tongue. He watched the old eyes roll back as if a thought was coming from the dregs of long passed memories.

"Fear," the mob boss offered softly, "is just excitement in need of an attitude adjustment. That's no problem for my *avvocato* is it?"

Eerily, Paul felt his blood flow halt. He knew stories about the man sitting across from him. That woman's body wouldn't be found. If she was dead, the Rules of Evidence would allow the insurance company to read her damning statement into evidence. If she simply could not be found, the insurer would have to proceed without its star witness and without her statement. DeBona's meaning was clear and Paul knew where Tony Quick Fish would dump her remains.

Goddamn, her thought, *I have to get out of this case.*

As DeBona rose to leave, Paul called: "Mister DeBona."

Paul never uttered another word. The mobster's icy stare let Paul know there was no way out.

"I'm leaving for the night," Mickey called into the room.

DeBona left as well. As Paul packed for the day, he received a call from Reverend Rich that sent him to the church rectory, where the Rev introduced Paul to a trembling woman who'd had the misfortune of seeing Sammy Smoke smoking.

She wore no makeup. Grey hair was clasped in a ponytail. Paul noticed her simple wedding band on a hand that was raw from ravages of physical labor, as if she was a cleaning woman or toiled in some other hard way. Fear danced in her eyes: she knew killers were targeting her.

Paul turned to the clergyman, whose face was covered by veil of compassion.

"Since you spared me from prison, I have sent many members of my congregation to you. I've done so because you're a skilled lawyer. And though you may not be aware, you're a moral man.

Paul winced, but not enough to deter the Rev.

"Once, you restored my faith. Now I'll help you find your soul. This woman will testify against your client. You must know that men want to kill her. Paul, you can't let her die to collect money from an insurance company."

Paul ushered the woman from the room. When the door closed, his eyes met the Rev's.

"They'll kill me," he said, "quickly as her."

"Can you live with yourself if they murder that grey head?"

As the Rev pushed, Paul wondered how much he could explain.

"I don't control these men," he said.

"Look how low you've sunk. Have you become one of them?"

"Preacher, save your fire and brimstone for the pulpit."

"Counsellor. Save your rebuttals for the courtroom. Articulate tongues always offer excuses. Don't reach for wisdom; find heart. That's generally found somewhere between your brain and your behind."

Words deserted Paul, not the Rev.

"I've been where you are. Remember? I know what it's like to sink low. Others may help you fall into that hole, but *you* have to dig yourself out."

Paul wondered if his conscience had deserted him. He badly needed the contingency fee while separated from Sarah. Maintaining the beach house he had vacated, combined with temporary alimony and the cost of his own apartment was burdensome. He hadn't thought twice about what he was doing for the mob. Perhaps he had too eagerly corrupted himself, hiding behind ethics of a profession that tended to venerate zealous advocacy over virtue.

"We can sink to no depth too deep for God to find us," Rev intoned, "if we seek salvation."

Perhaps, Paul reflected, *but DeBona will have me killed if he discovers my hand in this*.

Paul peered again into the Rev's eyes and wondered if there was sagacity in them or just blind faith. Sometimes it's hard to tell one from the other. Then he turned to the portrait above the Rev's desk, and let words flow.

"Oh, Jesus Christ. Hide her in my apartment. They'll never think to look for her there."

If souls have a door, Paul thought, *the fucking hinges on mine are creaking.*

"And, Rev, if this gets out, keep my funeral service short."

"I preach and pray as long as it takes."

So, Paul took the fire case to trial. As the old woman approached the witness stand, Paul followed his client's instructions: "If she shows, settle." The mob boss accepted fifty-thousand dollars from the insurance company rather than risk consequences of her testimony.

The woman had been hidden at Paul's apartment on the boardwalk, fearful even to answer the door. She was there, alone with Paul, on the night of Sarah's murder. Paul could never reveal her as his alibi witness without signing his own death warrant. Being slain by Tony Quick Fish was more certain than a death sentence before Judge Hastings. Paul elected to take his chances in the courtroom rather than on the streets.

"Tell me what I can do to help you." the old woman said as she entered the rectory with the Rev.

Paul studied the twosome. One thought he had saved her life and the other imagined he had saved his soul. Neither could help. Already stories circulated on the streets that the mob boss suspected Paul had somehow betrayed him. If the woman testified at his murder trial, DeBona would have him killed him just to save face.

Paul left the rectory, hoping for better luck with Emile. He called over his shoulder, "Pray for God to find me a guardian angel," unaware that Boog was already with one.

Chapter Thirty-Five

Brief Encounters

THEY MET IN ADEQUATE HOSTELRY. Boog had booked the cheapest room of the Comfort Inn by the boardwalk, when he scheduled their date just to find her. After explaining his relationship to Paul, Prell offered a discount. The Boogster didn't expect sex but the trade is bound by ironclad rules.

"Look, Hon'," Prell explained, "I've got a professional obligation to charge you. Paul always collects a fee when he walks into a courtroom and I always charge when I walk into a bedroom."

Boog looked uncertain until Prell flashed her smile, stuck out her hand, and snapped her fingers.

"*Gimme, gimme*," she said.

Boog smiled back and stuffed her palm with cash. Prell neatly folded the dough and stuffed it in her left shoe. As they sat on the side of the bed, she pulled down the elastic band around the top of her dress. Breasts exposed, they discussed Paul's plight until Boog sighed.

"You must be the only person in town that didn't know about the murder charges against Paul."

"Just arrived here from working in Honolulu," Prell replied. She clacked her gum and promised: "But I'll do what I can."

As they spoke, Boog's appreciation of her charms saluted.

"Paul's always taken good care of me," she continued. "I'll talk to the ladies on Pacific Avenue before AK takes me home tonight. And, I'll keep at it until the streets talk."

As a former cop, Boog knew how much street talk can sometimes reveal. He reflected on it as Prell flew out the door, leaving him alone with a lap full of her memory.

Emile hurried to his door at the first knock. The information he had could save Paul's life. What Boog had deduced from investigating, combined with Emile's psychological profile of Sarah's killer, generated explosive results. Just as the psychologist had suspected, the conference in Washington provided a sounding board for his theories. He spoke to criminologists, who had instant access to forensic facilities. If Emile didn't know the identity of Sarah's actual killer, at least he had identified a someone, who would serve as a convincing suspect. At last, Lee could establish the reasonable doubt so important to the defense.

Emile had also learned what was happening on the streets of Atlantic City. An FBI agent from the Bureau's organized crime unit had been following the struggle between the old Italian family and the new Asian gang. No one knew all the details, but the something big was afoot. No wonder people were afraid to speak. Anything they said that revealed a secret of either crime family could bring their final breath.

He had much to tell Paul and swung open the door eager to spill it all out at once. Instead, blood spilled from a knife shoved into his groin. As Emile grabbed his crotch, he saw his fingers turn crimson. The knife struck again in the same place, piercing his fingers and causing him to pull his hands away. Then, the knife dug deeper between his legs.

A gasp rushed from his throat. He panicked with realization he had been discovered. Retreating from the doorway—dazed like a wounded deer—Emile wobbled across the living room until he fell to the floor. There was no escaping the killing machine that came for him. The knife ripped his groin again and again, until something jammed his mouth, gagging his groans.

Paul arrived at the apartment late, finding the door locked. He grabbed the key Anthony had promised to place under the mat and entered. Knowing his friend's place well, he turned on lights, and lifted a bottle of Chivas Regal from the liquor cabinet. If he had to wait, at least he'd be comfortable.

Anthony's residence was a show case. Often, he sold accessories displayed there to clients, sometimes making as much money hawking tchotchkes as selling larger furniture pieces. He had a talent for finding unusual knickknacks and Paul always enjoyed finding them, while touring the apartment.

He strolled until saw feet sticking from behind a Queen Anne sofa. Paul rushed to Emile's warm body. Blood dripped down Emile's chin, but not from a mouth wound. Emile's penis had been shoved between his teeth; his throat slit.

Paul dropped his drink and staggered. He was alone at a fresh murder scene, while amid a trial for allegedly committing an equally brutal slaying. Paul staggered to the phone, started to dial police, then set the handset back in the receiver.

Instead, he picked up the Chivas, and tilted the bottle for a major swig. He wiped his lips with his sleeve, drank hard again, and wondered.

What the hell should I do?

Chapter Thirty-Six

It's a Beautiful Day in the Neighborhood

THEY THREW POON TANG TRAIN into an interrogation room. Cuffs still locked his hands behind his back. Smitty shoved him into a chair.

"Why ain't I at the Temple?" he demanded to know. "What the fuck's goin' on? You bitches can't book me here."

Horace Grender smiled as he watched. Smitty and his partner had delivered Train to the County Prosecutor's Office just as he ordered. Smitty was still putting in county detective time and his special assignment to the prosecutor would continue through the remainder of the Cameron murder trial. Grender had taken a shine to the cop as they worked together on the case. He admired the weasel's dedication to the job and his attitude that was undeterred by any nagging sense of right or wrong. Smitty had no moral dilemmas. The man just loved doing what he did on the street with impunity his badge afforded. Grender had immediately recognized that Smitty's pocket shield was more than a symbol of the little cop's authority: when he pulled it out, he was displaying his manhood.

Grender spoke to the pimp.

"My name is Horace Grender."

"You're one fat fuck," Train replied.

"I'm this county's Chief Prosecutor, and I—"

"I know who you are, you squeaky bastard. What I don't know is why your bitches are doggin' me."

Grender sat back. He wanted Cameron's conviction badly enough to accept abuse from the pimp, just then. Later, Grender would remember Train's words, when he would bust him under the pimping statute. He had seen the man's rap sheet and knew what he was.

"Poon Tang Train is your name, I understand," Grender calmly conferred. "How'd you get that name? My mother looked at me when I was born and named me Horace. Your mother must have peeked at you and said, 'This one looks like poon tang'."

"I've got a retarded pit bull that looks better than you!"

"Mister Train, I'm going to leave the room. When I return, we'll start this conversation over."

Grender's heavy form rose from his chair. He nodded to Smitty and the cop's partner. When the door closed behind Grender, the cops swung. Four fists used Train's head for a punching bag until it snapped back and forth on his shoulders as if his neck were a slinky toy.

Grender returned with two cups of coffee. He sipped from one and placed the other in front of starry-eyed Poon Tang Train.

"Take off his cuffs," he told Smitty.

The gesture was less generous than it appeared. Grender knew the pimp was in no condition to threaten. Moreover, Smitty and his partner stood directly behind Train, ready to pounce again, if he so much as sneezed in the prosecutor's direction. Grender pointed to the coffee in front of the pimp.

"I put extra sugar in yours."

The prosecutor paused to sip, then offered more pleasantries.

"You look like you prefer sweet things. Shall we resume our discussion?"

Train didn't say a word. He put the Styrofoam cup to swelling lips and grimaced at the touch of the steamy brew.

"Mister Train, we could book you tonight for promoting prostitution. You know what kind of time that charge brings a man with your record, don't you? How were things in detention the last time you went away? You remember the pen, don't you? A grey bus drives you there. The first things you see when you arrive are those big gun towers on top of the walls. My records say you got jumped and hurt pretty badly, there, on your last stint. A nasty group of boys danced on your head.

"And, you know," Grender continued, "my investigators learned something else that's interesting. We have an outstanding warrant for a young man who fits your description. Seems he jumped bail a few years back, using an alias. Does the name Damon Monroe sound familiar?

The guy committed a crime with a weapon—a knife. My records show you weren't incarcerated at the time. You were on the streets. Suppose I ask you a few questions about that."

Grender checked his wristwatch.

"Oh, goodness," he snapped, "look at the time. Maybe we should cut this conversation short and just send you to the can. What do you think, Mister Train?"

"What do you want from me, Man?"

Grender smiled to his officers, aware he had made his point.

"I want you to be my friend. Just like neighbors. Please," Grender said—mimicking the beloved host of a children's television show, who so adored wearing cardigan sweaters knit by his mother: "won't you be my neighbor?"

"So, now you're Mister Rogers?"

Train tilted his head from one side to the other as if loosening up from taking punches.

"You know," he offered, "there never was a girl or boy, who thought Mister Rogers would pull shit in their neighborhood. I'm not so sure about you."

"Are you ready to be my friend?" The prosecutor persisted.

"I'm ready to be your bitch. What do you want?"

Grender slid a police mug shot of a young woman across the desk to Train.

"It's important that my office finds this prostitute. She works the hotels. My men haven't seen her on the street. She's been identified as a potential witness in a case. I want to interview her and put her, shall we say, in safe keeping during the remainder of the trial. She's been difficult for our vice officers to find . . . but you and your associates may have better luck. If you do, we can remain friends."

Train looked at the mug shot. The name on it read, "Gardner, April, a/k/a Queen, Victoria." He took his hand to his busted lips, gently massaged them, and mused.

"She sure takes a pretty picture, don't she? Do you mind if I deliver the goods slightly damaged?"

Grender looked away.

"Deliver her, fast."

Poon Tang Train was back on Pacific Avenue, strutting his *gangsta* stroll, a man on a mission. He knew Prell wouldn't be easy to find, so he would need help from his posse. The pimp liked having a new friend in a position of power, and his boys would help solidify his new relationship.

"Yes, Sir," he said aloud. "It's a beautiful day in the hood. Atlantic City's gonna be a friendlier town to the Train."

He felt good allover: his head was swollen but he sensed no pain. He was off to catch a whore for his new bud. Knowing by street reputation what the man liked, he would also see that she performed to his satisfaction. Train was chuggin' down the tracks.

"Wherever you are, bitch," he promised, "I'll find you."

Prell set down her comb, brushed her teeth, then reapplied lipstick. Her oversized handbag was like a suitcase, holding everything from pleasure toys to toiletries, and she had just finished with both. As she left the hotel room, her date slipped her a little extra cash.

"Thanks, Hon'," Prell said, before hitting the streets for Paul to learn whatever she could.

Paul sipped another Chivas at Viva's Lounge in the Castle Casino. As the late-night band pounded out dance hits, Paul pounded down scotch. He should have been drunk, but visions of Emile's mutilated body so overwhelmed his senses that alcohol lost its punch. A young woman at the VIP services desk was paging Ky Nguyen to meet him at the bar.

While he waited, he also thought of the telephone call he had placed to Anthony before leaving the apartment. He had found his decorator friend through Anthony's answering service and broke the news of Emile's death as gently as he could. Anthony wept, but remained cool enough to warn Paul to get out of the apartment. Anthony would return home to report the murder.

Paul spotted the casino marketing exec as he approached. Ky was immaculately attired from tailored suit to wingtips. Armed with charm, as a professional greeter and accommodator, the young man shook Paul's hand firmly and wrapped his other arm around him.

"What can I do for you, my friend?" Ky said in lightly accented English.

Paul set his drink on the bar.

"Tell me what's going on in this town."

"What do you mean?"

"Help me put pieces together. Something's happening. I'm not sure what it is. Somehow, I'm caught up in it."

Ky looked toward the band. As a raspy-voiced blond belted out a cover of "Love Shack," she jiggled her head, making long hair extensions twirl.

Paul grabbed Ky's elbow to re-engage him.

"You owe me, Pal. When the Casino Control Commission came after you for delivering prostitutes to high rollers, I defended the charges and saved your casino license. You're drawing two-hundred thousand a year plus perquisites because I helped you keep that ticket. If I hadn't pulled every string I had to get you off the hook, you'd be packing grocery bags at your family's Seven-Eleven."

"I've never forgotten, Paul. You spared me from jail and saved my family from losing face."

He sensed Ky had something to say and let him take time.

"War may wage," Ky cautiously conveyed, "between the old crime forces in this town and the Asian gangs that come from New York and the West Coast.

Paul's mind clicked. The thought of a mob war gave hope. DeBona would be a prime target for his rivals. If he got whacked, Paul would be free to give his alibi.

"My cousins and I know many faces in the Asian gangs," continued Key. "Often, they're comped in the casinos as high rollers. A dangerous man is among them. He came from my country at the end of the war when so many of us fled. Find him if you can. He's a hired killer my people feared for years in Vietnam, and now fear here."

Ky paused. He looked around as if afraid to speak.

"The gruesome way that he kills is his signature. If you cross his path, you're marked for death in a way that will torment your soul. Sarah's murder bears the signature of he who has no name."

"What are you talking about?"

Ky started to order his friend another drink before he answered but Paul stopped him with a wave of the hand. He wanted to be certain he heard whatever Ky had to say with a clear head.

In another part of town Poon Tang Train worked to clear his noggin. Still groggy from his beating, Train stopped in the Illinois Avenue coffee shop he used as an office for street business. Black coffee was what he needed for the long night. His posse was already loose.

Train tried smiling through swollen lips as he thought about the girl he had been after so long. His posse was after the bitch to rope her right. Train fretted, thinking the hotel hooker would be difficult to find . . . not knowing Boog had unwittingly placed Prell in their path.

Chapter Thirty-Seven

Standing in Sleaze Up to Your Knees

TONY FELT HIMSELF LOSING GRIP. The price he'd paid for the computer discs proved their worth. Only one person in his family had access to all the information so neatly transcribed: the loose tongued auntie was a trusted *capo*. Tony would deal with the rat—if he had time—as well as Shek, who was making moves Tony had to counter.

"These accounts," he said to himself, "can only reconcile with spilled blood."

He stood in the quiet graveyard with Bobby the Brain protecting his back. Tony lifted a freshly cut flower, the fragrance reviving recollections of Lena's essence before he'd taken her. Yet, the hand holding the stem belonged to an elderly man, who had no time to contemplate. He knew he must keep moving.

Slow down, Tony recognized, *and everything you're chasing will catch you.*

Judge Hastings released the jurors for the day. As they left, Paul sat sullenly with Lee. Grender addressed the judge and the eagerness in his voice told Paul things were about to worsen.

"Your Honor," the prosecutor wheezed, "the State has an application to make."

Six police officers entered the courtroom, all moving toward Paul. One fidgeted with his holster. Behind them, Paul recognized two local news reporters, who should have been filing their stories.

"The state is making an arrest for the murder of Doctor Emile Ricardo," Grender announced. "I'm prepared to read the defendant his rights in the presence of his counsel. I ask the Court to revoke Mister Cameron's bail."

"What's this all about?" Judge Hastings muttered, sounding as perplexed as the defense.

"Your Honor, my office has sufficient information to arrest and charge Mister Cameron with another murder. The manner of Doctor Ricardo's murder is frighteningly similar to the case at bar. The State asks the Court to place the defendant in custody pending full disposition of his charges."

"Mister Gunther, what do you have to say?"

"I have no information leading me to believe my client is connected to the doctor's murder. In fact, we were relying on the him to conduct research that would've benefitted the defense."

"Perhaps, Sir," Grender said addressing Lee, "your client was unhappy with the doctor's findings."

Turning to the bench, he continued.

"Judge, my office has information we are prepared to release. It establishes that the defendant went to the doctor's home on the evening of the murder. Fingerprints are throughout the crime scene, even on a drinking glass that was partially full. We positively matched those prints against the defendant's fingerprints taken at the scene of his wife's murder and against the full set he gave upon arrest. The weapon used to kill Doctor Ricardo is similar to the weapon that killed Sarah Cameron. In both slayings, sexual organs were mutilated. Your Honor, we have to imprison this defendant to protect the community."

Judge Hastings looked down with scorn.

"Mister Gunther, can you think of any reason why I shouldn't revoke your client's bail?"

"Your Honor, a presumption of innocence cloaks my client until proven guilty. So far, the State hasn't proven him guilty of anything."

"Yes, yes, yes," Judge Hastings spewed. "I don't want to hear platitudes so late in the day."

The judge acted swiftly in the presence of reporters eager for a story.

"The defendant will rise," he called to Paul. "I'm revoking your bail and remanding you to the Sheriff's custody. You'll be incarcerated in the county jail pending further disposition."

Paul shook as he considered the consequences. He turned to face Mickey who was, as always, on the front row of spectator seats. He would have to count on her and Boog to be his eyes and his ears while he spent time outside the courtroom in a cell. Mickey looked back plaintively. Paul understood the unspoken meaning of her expression. A tear rolled down her cheek as they handcuffed him. He watched her as Grender read his rights.

Where's my guardian angel now? Paul wondered.

Prell half skipped down the street. Not every woman can accomplish feat that in high heels. But, Prell had a passion for pumps and there wasn't much she couldn't do in them. She had news for the Boogster and was on her way to his bar where he was finishing the day shift.

She had taken a date, arranged through one of the Nguyen cousins, with an oriental high roller. Ky Nguyen thought the man might reveal something helpful, given proper prodding, and he'd been right. Eager to impress Prell with his importance in the new force taking over the town, the man had uttered words she was anxious to share with Boog.

She had tried phoning his bar, but he couldn't hear her over a blaring juke box and loud talk. AK would pick her up to drive there, just as the sun set and Pacific Avenue prepared for its nightly rebirth.

AK didn't like picking up Prell in town. Prostitution in Atlantic City carries a maximum jail term of six months, while promoting prostitution carries a term up to seven years. "Business managers" had to steer clear of the city to avoid the major offense. Only flakes flaunted themselves like super-flies. He parked their beat-up Beemer in Bally's Grand self-park garage. Prell was late but he wasn't worried. His lady just had no conception of time.

As AK lit a cigarette, five men stealthily approached, using parked vehicles for cover. Suddenly, both front doors flung open. Fast-moving hands pulled AK from the car, wrestled him to the ground and beat him. Train walked into view and slowly raised his hand. Following his command, Train's posse backed away.

"You *shoulda* killed me when you had the chance," Train said to the motionless form at his feet. He peered around the garage, then directed his men.

"Put him back in his car. Slump the chump over his steering wheel like he's catching some zees. If he wakes up, put him back to sleep. Now, spread out and lay low. The bitch will come for him. Then, she's ours."

Mickey raced to Boog's bar from the courthouse. Frantically, she told him about the arrest. Boog poured her a stiff Rock 'n' Rye to settle nerves.

"It's my grandmother's recipe for curing all that ails," he told her. "Drink up."

Mickey sat as if in a trance, understanding for the first time that Paul wouldn't get himself out of the mess. He had always been lucky in courtrooms representing clients and she'd always been a part of it. Until then, it had been beyond comprehension that the defender could be found guilty. Boog interrupted her thoughts.

"I'm waiting for Prell," he said. "I couldn't make out what she was trying to say on the phone, but she has something for us."

Mickey was hopeful yet felt a jealous pang, thinking that perhaps a woman from the streets would be the one to save Paul.

"Maybe I should go look for her," Boog suggested. "She should've been here thirty minutes ago."

"Don't worry," Mickey said knowingly. "Prell never makes it on time for an appointment."

Prell saw AK sleeping with his head on the steering wheel. Glad to see her man, she opened the passenger's side door and shouted.

"Get up, sleepy head!"

He said nothing as she slid into the front seat and planted a kiss on his cheek. It was wet from something. As her eyes adjusted to darkness inside the vehicle, she saw blood streaming down AK's broken face, his nose twisted and right cheek sunken.

She screamed loudly but two strong hands grabbed her mouth from behind to muffle her. She bit down and heard a yelp from a man in the back seat. Prell leaped from the car and sprinted in loud-clacking heels toward the nearest garage exit. Men came at her from all directions and one horribly familiar face blocked the exit: Poon Tang Train. She knew the chase was over and stopped in her tracks.

Men closed in like a wolf pack on prey, all the while Train cooing.

"I told you that your sweet meat would be mine someday. I told you that your sweet meat. . .."

A telephone call roused Grender from bed. It caused him to throw off his oversized bed shirt. As it cascaded to the floor, it filled with air like a sail cast to wind.

Train was holding the whore. They had her at a dilapidated house in the inlet section of the city, which was awaiting a wrecking ball. The entire block was slated for demolition. New moderate-priced housing would rise, financed by the Casino Redevelopment Authority for middle income casino employees. Meanwhile, the old homes were shooting galleries for druggies and seedy habitats for squatters. Grender would find her, there. His new friend had even promised him a treat. Prell would be his special date.

Grender jumped into his county car and checked his wallet for his badge. His pistol was with him, too. He'd need both for the trip he was taking. He started the Chevy and screeched.

"I'm in sleaze up to my knees—and lovin' it!"

Prell tugged on handcuffs that bound her wrists to the bed's wrought iron headboard. Poon Tang Train pulled out his steely pal. With a swish the knife's blade sprang open and Prell's eyes bulged. He lightly traced where he would place his mark, the knife's tip delicately running the length of her nose, then crossing her eyebrows. The touch was too light to break her skin but forceful enough that she knew what he had in mind.

"What are you gonna do with half a face?" he tormented her. "You sure won't be attracting men head-on."

She couldn't stop trembling. Her eyes darted around the dilapidated bedroom. Windows were boarded from the outside. Faded wallpaper was coming down at the seams. The plaster ceiling showed water marks from a roof leak, telling her that she was on the top floor.

"Meet your new girlfriends," Train said, "while I let my homeboys downstairs go for the night."

Two women entered. Prell had met both on the strip and recognized them as street trash.

Maybelline had a pocked face that heavy makeup couldn't conceal. She lived under a thirty-five-dollar wig when she walked Pacific Avenue and scratched her head incessantly.

Chanel had grown up on rough Bronx corners. Her face was like the United Nations, displaying a mix of ethnicity. Her delicate nose and slanted eyes that would have been exotic if they weren't glazed over. Track marks on her arms looked fresh and sore.

The women removed Prell's clothes. She tried resisting until Chanel slapped her face.

"Don't be givin' us no hard time," she warned.

Then, the two women chatted as if Prell wasn't there, conversing about where to stick needles to hide marks in case they were arrested.

"Under fingernails, that's where we should be doin' it," Chanel was saying. The two whores admired Prell's shoes and dress as they took them and prepared her for her new role.

"The life you knew is over, Girlfriend," Chanel said. "You're going to be one of the Train's ladies now. He can be mean, but he can be good, too. Your new name is Cover Girl. Do as he says or he'll rename you Scar Face."

Prell heard a knock on the door downstairs, then sounds as if Train had let someone inside.

"Time to take your medicine," both women sang to her.

Chanel grabbed her ears as Maybelline tried forcing pills past locked lips.

"They're just roofies and a little somethin' to punch them up, Honey," Chanel said. "Gonna take you on a nice trip."

Prell had heard of the drug that had a reputation for relieving sexual inhibitions and giving an overall feeling of tranquility.

"She's not cooperating," Channel called downstairs.

Footsteps pounded up the stairs. Train entered the room to force-feed Prell. He stuck pills in her mouth and Prell spit them into the air like a medication geyser. Then, the swish of Train's switch blade made everyone freeze. Slowly, he approached Prell, pills in one hand and the blade in the other.

"Which do you want?" he sneered.

Prell slowly opened her mouth.

"That's a good bitch. Open wide for your man."

Train stuffed pills down her throat the way a veterinarian force-feeds medication to an animal. She had no choice except to swallow or choke.

After minutes passed—maybe longer as Prell had lost her modest notion of time—hands that seemed to have no bodies stripped her remaining clothes. A squat Santa Claus, without a beard, said something.

Prell laughed.

He had Santa's body but Missus Claus' voice. She looked for elves, but her eyes grew heavy. Someone flipped Prell onto her stomach and she drifted to sleep.

Prell woke to see she was wearing beat up sneakers, foul-smelling blue jeans, and an oversized tee shirt: clothes Maybelline had worn. They made Prell itch. Someone had lice. Prell rubbed the top of her head and tried gaining her bearings. She saw a stainless-steel toilet across from her that had a sink affixed to the top. Steel bars confined her to the six by eight-foot quarters she shared with another woman.

"They brought you in last night," a woman called from the bunk above. "You were a sight to see. My Lord, girl! You were feeling no pain."

"I gotta call my lawyer's office," Prell said.

"Sorry, Dearie," her cell mate said. The guards told us no one from this wing can make a call for some reason. Maybe the phones are out."

Prell wondered why she was there. She tried standing and lost her balance. So, she laid on her bunk, scratching and feeling discomfort whenever she tried to sit.

Paul waited in his cell to be taken back to court. Whenever he had visited clients at the facility, guards warned him to avoid the toilets. They were landing zones for everything from crabs to infectious disease. Since his arrest, he had no choice. Guards kept him separate from other inmates due to the severity of his charges and his mini celebrity. Everyone knew Paul. He had been well liked as a lawyer but as an inmate, he was just another asshole.

Grender stole the driver's seat as the murder trial raced to the finish line. The prosecution rested and the defense case was winding down. All too soon, closing arguments would lead to an inevitable verdict to please him.

He also felt good about his evening tryst and knowing the defense wouldn't find Prell in time. Grender had asked her why the defense had identified as a witness . . . and she seemed to know something he also knew. In her drugged stupor, she had mentioned a mean man who had no name. That was all Grender needed to hear. He booked her on prostitution charges and locked her in the county jail.

She wouldn't have access to a phone for a week. He would keep her there, under wraps, until she was brought before a judge for arraignment. A few days was all Grender needed to keep her from testifying.

Train was mad about losing his goods, but he'd bail Prell out of jail, after her arraignment. AK would still be in the hospital with broken cheek bones and internal bleeding, giving Train time to introduce his new girl to Mister Smack. After she had a taste, Train knew, she'd beg him for more just as Grandmaster Flash rapped:

> Smack your arm, smack your head,
> And smack your ass,
> The pin's going stick you good, Sister.

A sheriff's deputy escorted Paul to his seat at the defense table. His business suit reeked of jail stench but seeing Mickey's face relieved tension that had manifested into a migraine headache.

A deputy allowed Boog to approach, apparently knowing him as a former cop. He told Paul about Prell failing to arrive at the bar.

"You can never count on a hooker," Boog said.

Paul knew better. If Prell had information, she would have met Boog unless something happened to her. He thought about the young woman, realizing time was running out, and wishing he was free to find her.

Across town another woman searched for someone. Her feet pounded planks on the boardwalk. She dropped into familiar haunts, looking for someone who might help if only she could find him.

She stopped to catch her breath, then realized she had to keep moving. Tired feet trudged. The woman was no whore working the streets. She was a Hiller from Chestnut Hill, cursing herself for being slow in arriving, and praying she wasn't too late.

Chapter Thirty-Eight

There's Something About an Old Love

AMANDA CAMERON JUMPED ONTO THE JITNEY. For seventy years, the minibuses zipped at breakneck speeds along Pacific Avenue as Atlantic City's unique form of mass transit. Their drivers delivered eight to ten passengers from one corner to the next. The ride cost a dime in 1953 when she was last in town. Today, at a buck the fare remained a bargain. The little bus dropped Amanda at her final stop of the day.

She had called her son, after learning of the charges against him, and offered to help. Yet, she couldn't think of anything to do. She couldn't bear to sit in the courtroom as the trial ensued. Instead, she followed the proceeding by calling Lee Gunther for daily updates. Finally, it had occurred to her. She could try something. It was a long shot and she hoped it wasn't too late. Amanda was searching for her hoodlum.

She walked toward the place she'd met him forty years earlier. So much of the town had been demolished for the grand new casinos that she didn't know whether the place was standing. Then, she spied the building though the business was renamed.

Amanda stood across the street from the former Rocket Club and checked her reflection in a windowpane. Forty years hadn't been as hard on her as time had been to that night club.

After a certain point, she thought, *old bars like old dames can use a face lift.*

Hers sheared years, then collagen plumped out wrinkles, which return as if they have a memory, while her former pixie hairdo became a flipped-out bob that remained blond by tinting away grey. When it comes to a youthful appearance, Amanda was living proof to the simple adage: money helps.

Her husband wasn't wealthy, but they were well situated, and had married without fanfare. Theirs was not the burning love she read about in romance novels; she and Ben had a sensible relationship that fit each other's needs. Amanda had known passion once in life, and decided she just wasn't wanton . . . though memories—being the indelible creatures they are—occasionally revived in unconfessed fantasies that still stirred her loins.

Perhaps those remembrances caused Amanda to pay special attention to what she wore that day. Her heels were high, her dress just shy of revealing. Amanda chuckled at herself. She had dressed with the enthusiasm of a schoolgirl preparing for a prom. After the passage of so much time, she wondered.

What will he think of my appearance? Can I still entice a man?

"Whoa, boss. Wake up!"

Tony roused from slumber. He was sleeping less at night and finding himself dozing during daytime. His office chair was a comfortable nest for a catnap.

"A woman at the bar just ordered a Stoli orange madras," the bartender said. "That was her choice after she found out we don't serve champagne by the glass. Classy dame. Asked if I know a gentleman by the name of Antonio DeBona. What do you want me to say?"

"Tell her you never heard of him." Tony crossed his arms and lowered his chin onto his chest.

"This one's a pistol, Boss," the bartender said as he walked back toward the bar. "Claims you're her hoodlum."

"Yeah, well, I'm everybody's hoodlum. I'm a fuckin' institution."

He took a deep breath and closed his eyes before it occurred to him. Only one person had ever called him "her hoodlum." But that was so long ago.

He lifted himself and stretched his limbs. Falling asleep in that chair was easy but it stiffened his frame. He walked into the bar room, then stopped to catch a glimpse of the woman, who faced away from him upon a bar stool, leaning from a drunk perched next to her. The lady was comically out of place for the room and needed help. Tony walked to her. His arched eyebrow sent the booze hound retreating.

Amanda looked up and Tony saw the unchanged face of the college girl he had saved in that place so many years earlier. Amanda just gazed, neither sipping nor setting down her drink. For a moment, they seemed to share lust-driven remembrances of the college coed and the hoodlum. Their silence grew awkward until Tony at last spoke.

"So, you graduated, I suppose."

Both laughed. Her smile told him she was enjoying the moment yet her eyes conveyed urgency.

What, he thought, *is the story of her life . . . and what brings her back?*

Tony ordered a drink for himself, lifted his glass, and inquired.

"To what shall we toast?"

"To our son," Amanda instantly replied.

Atlantic City has always been, and shall always be, a town chuck full of passions. Mister Shek was discovering his own. He left a baccarat table to join his casino host, Mister Nguyen, who introduced him to a lady that towered above Shek in her fuck-me-pumps. She was everything he desired from fresh pedicure to flaming red, frizzy hair. Whorezilla joined him for dinner in the casino's premier restaurant.

Shek tipped the maître d' and expressed interest in dining in the back of the room. They promptly accommodated him to the chagrin of a waiting doctor and his wife.

"Don't you know that table was reserved for Doctor Clemens?" the man's wife complained.

"So sorry," the maître d' solicitously replied. "It's a very busy evening."

Doctors may receive favored treatment in some restaurants but high rolling guests in casinos always enjoy preferential accommodation, for which they never receive a bill. Instead, they pay on play tables.

Shek and his dinner date sat closely. She stroked his shoulder with her hand and ran the tip of her shoe along his calf. When their main course arrived, she helped rearrange the napkin on his lap, her hand playing hide-and-seek underneath. Quickly, Shek directed their server to send two bottles of Taittinger Brut champagne to his suite, where they hastened.

The maître d' gave good news to the waiting couple.

"A table just opened."

In the suite living room Shek handed his supping partner a filled glass, then went to his knees to remove her shoes. Gently, he massaged her feet, then poured champagne for himself into a pump that seemed to hold half a magnum. Shek drank heartily before mounting her toes and indulging his fetish to fruition.

Spent and exhausted, Shek led her into the bedroom to tuck next to him in a cushy king-sized bed. His thoughts turned to the morrow, when perhaps he would enjoy her charms again . . . before dealing with that old Italian mob boss the final time.

Paul reflected on a hard bunk in his solitary cell. Grender and Lee had presented their summations, Judge Hastings had rendered his instructions, and the jury had begun deliberating behind closed doors. In the morning, deliberations would resume until jurors reached their final verdict.

He heard footsteps approaching from the far end of the corridor and was surprised to see a female guard approach the bars of his cell. Instantly, he recognized Mary from visiting clients in the women's wing. She had a plain appearance, like all women on duty, who dressed in the same uniforms as their male counterparts. Jail regulations forbade them from wearing makeup.

"How are you holding up, Counselor?" she kindly inquired.

"I've seen better days," he replied with the obvious.

"I'm bunking one of your clients in my wing."

Paul thought nothing of it. The county lockup served as a holding facility for prisoners awaiting or undergoing trial, and as a detention center for convicts sentenced to one year or less jail time. He always had a client there.

"This woman says she's been trying to reach you."

"Well, I'm currently unavailable to clientele."

"Her charge sheet goes by her alias. We have her booked under the name of Queen Victoria."

Paul leaped from the bed.

"How long has she been here?"

"A few days. They brought her here on prostitution charges after an arrest in Atlantic City. Something's funny about the bust, though. Instead of transporting her to Atlantic City Municipal Court for arraignment the next morning, we received orders from the County Prosecutor's Office to keep her in the remote holding area of the women's wing. We're supposed to keep her there until the end of the week."

"Grender," Paul muttered.

Suddenly, he knew why the defense couldn't find Prell. Grender had her under lock and key.

"Mary, can you do something for me?"

"Depends on what it is."

"Get a message to Carol Resnick at the Prosecutor's Office. Call on an emergency basis. They'll track her down for you tonight at her home."

Paul picked up a legal pad he kept by his bunk and wrote quickly as he could. He handed the message to Mary through the bars, then looked her into her eyes.

"And Mary, please do one more thing for me."

"What's that?" she asked, as she took the paper from his hand.

"Put Queen Victoria on the sheriff's bus tomorrow taking prisoners to the Municipal Court for arraignment. Let her get in front of Judge Light."

"I'd lose my job if I ever sent a prisoner to court without a transfer order."

"Mary," Paul said with pleading eyes, "please make a mistake tomorrow. Send her to the judge for his nine o'clock arraignment list. Tell her to talk to Judge Light on the record. Have her spill out anything she knows about my case."

"You know I can't do that."

Paul's eyes begged.

"I gotta go now, Counselor."

"Will you get the Queen on a prisoner bus in the morning?"

"I don't know," Mary said as she walked away, "but I'll see if I can get this message to Carol Resnick."

Paul tossed the legal pad to the floor and grabbed the bars with both hands, helpless to do anything else.

Tony waited in his office for his men. His college girl had gone, and he hadn't replied when she asked for help. He slugged a stiff drink. Whiskey, straight, burned his throat. That night, Tony would see his daughters, who were fully grown with families of their own. It might be his last chance to say goodbye and he had something for each. His estate could never pass through normal channels with concealed assets acquired during a lifetime of illicit endeavors. Each child would receive something. Tony always took care of *familiglia*.

In the morrow, he'd settle old scores or die. He picked up the telephone in one hand and held his drink in the other. Whiskey scorched his throat and ignited those dark feelings.

Perhaps, he thought, *it's too late to help myself or anyone else. It may be in the hands of fate to determine who lives . . . and who dies.*

Part III

Chapter Thirty-Nine

Fate Always Stirs the Quick and the Dead

FUROR STIRRED WHEN THE DOORS OPENNED. A crowd surged into Judge Hastings' courtroom expecting the jury to deliver its verdict sometime during the day. Those with press credentials sat on seats reserved for them but everyone else scurried for a vacant spot. Paul watched Mickey grab her same seat on the front row wearing black. He wondered if it was time for her to be in widow's weeds. Soon, he'd know.

Amid the commotion, a courteous sheriff's deputy ushered a big man. Despite the tension or perhaps because of it, Paul chuckled.

Only in Atlantic City would this happen, he thought.

Mob boss Tony DeBona was being ushered. Paul watched the officer whisper to a seated spectator. The man rose and removed himself to a seat in the rear of the room.

Paul wondered about the old man.

What's his game now?

Tony graciously nodded to the officer, who helped him. He was prepared to spend his day visible to the press as well as court officers. Later, they could verify his airtight alibi, when so much ensued on the streets. He looked toward Paul. Their eyes met only for an instant before he turned away. Tony wanted to say so much to the younger man but was helpless to impart a word.

Bobby the Brain was busy. While muscles in the family flexed, his mind engaged elsewhere. Since Tony had learned something of computers from dealing with the disks, he had sent Bobby to buy computer systems for each of his grandchildren.

"My young friend," he had said, "you know more about these fancy machines than me."

"Boss, we should get you a computer, too," Bobby suggested.

Tony laughed heartedly.

"No. I'm not ready to join you in the computer era. Here's the business card of a man, who sells at steep discounts. Assure I'm getting is state of the art. I don't want to disappoint my grandchildren with shit."

Bobby found it ironic that the old boss had asked him to run the errand. When he finished shopping, Bobby would meet someone else: the Vietnamese killer had approached Bobby with a deal. The man wanted to purchase another set of computer disks containing the same information Bobby had previously provided to him for Mister Shek.

By specially encrypting the data, he could sell it again. Bobby wasn't certain what had happened to the last set. Pepperman must have hidden them. Apparently, Mister Shek planned to turn the disks over to another law enforcement agency, which suited Bobby fine. They conveyed no information that implicated him in nefarious activities.

The data placing heat on Tony DeBona would allow the under boss to take charge of the family, while the old man defended himself on racketeering charges. Bobby had tired of waiting for his Boss to release control and had assured Tony's retirement.

Mister Shek woke refreshed. His bedmate lay face-down, snorting. He tapped the blanket that covered her and the big woman stirred, rising like a peak on the Rockies.

"*Whatcha* want?" she groaned.

Shek rubbed the palms of his hands together, ready to climb that mountaintop. Afterward, he'd have coffee before meeting his hired killer, who at long last was handing over the computer disks he was to have taken from Pepperman's corpse. Shek had also lost patience. If the killer failed to deliver that day, Shek would see to the execution of his executioner.

He who had no name was at the designated meeting place. The killer stood at the end of the boardwalk overlooking the Atlantic City inlet. He watched boats pass from the harbor to the ocean through swirling waters. Though the Vietnamese man had been born in hilly countryside outside Da Nang, following his parent's death he'd been raised by relatives, who lived on boats in the delta south of Saigon. He relived those days in daydreams, while waiting for DeBona's under boss to bring the disks he'd take to Shek.

The little game he played with the two mob families had him tightroping a fine line, working for while scamming both. He had taken the first set of disks from the commissioner's corpse and delivered them to DeBona for a comfortable profit. A small portion of those proceeds was purchasing another set from their maker to sell Shek, who would never know they hadn't come from Pepperman's pocket. The Asian crime lord would deliver them to authorities eager to pick up where Pepperman had left off.

Capitalism at its best, he thought, *assuring the end for the old Italian boss.*

Paul waited in the courtroom with everyone else for the verdict. He noticed Lee massaging his bad knee at the counsel table.

"That seems to have gotten worse," Paul mentioned to his friend to try breaking the tension.

Lee didn't look up.

"Banged it up on my own run to hell," he said. "Let's hope we pulled you out of yours."

Lee rose and shook his leg.

"I have to stand and walk a bit," he said, "to circulate blood."

As his friend moved around their table, Paul spotted Mickey. He would have liked speaking with her. Chatter would have relaxed him but the armed officer behind him wouldn't allow her to approach. Paul refilled his paper cup from the water pitcher on the counsel table. As he swigged, a court attendant brought news.

"The jury has a verdict."

She whispered first to Lee at the defense table, then to assistants at the prosecutor's table. Grender had left for a meal.

"They'll bring it out at one-thirty when the judge returns from lunch."

Sensing what was happening, eyes and ears in the gallery perked with anticipation. Paul felt his guts twist.

Bobby the Brain was making a stop on the way to deliver his disks. He always felt a thrill shopping in computer stores. That one was off the beaten track, but worth the trip. The old boss was right: prices couldn't be beaten. The shop sold stolen merchandise that was ripped off shipping trucks en route to retail stores.

Bobby introduced himself to the bespectacled salesman, who wore plaid pants and Hush Puppies. The geek led him to a display area in the rear and turned on a model with the works—Pentium processor, 540 MB high-performance enhanced hard drive, 64 MB of Ram, SoundBlaster stereo, and more. Bobby chuckled. He tried imagining the old man deciphering the technical language that gushed from the salesman's mouth. Quickly, the geek convinced Bobby to buy a unit for himself, too. How could he go wrong at those prices?

"Try the demonstration program," the salesman suggested. "We have a great game on it that shows the quality of the system graphics and sound features. Just click the mouse button to start it."

Bobby sat before the model and studied its monitor displaying the words, "Special Demo." He joined his hands to crack his knuckles, then grasped the mouse and clicked. The program started and the screen flashed the word, "Bang." Nothing else happened.

"What's with this?" Bobby said, concerned that the machine wasn't all it was cracked up to be.

The salesman adjusted his eyeglasses on the bridge of his nose and tilted his head uncertainly.

"Try clicking the mouse button again," he suggested.

Bobby clicked. The screen went blank. Then, the word, "Bang," reappeared. He looked up at the salesman, who shrugged his shoulders.

"Try again. You should get a blast from the sound system."

Bobby clicked the third and final time. In bold letters the screen displayed: "YOU'RE DEAD!"

Computer sounds never reached Bobby's ears. The last thing he heard was a blast from the nerd's revolver that blew his brain across the screen.

The salesman reached into Bobby's pocket and removed what Tony had told him he would find, then placed the two disks into the computer. The Pentium processor zipped as all evidence against Tony and his family erased. Bobby would've been impressed . . . if he wasn't so dead.

Mister Shek and his overnight guest partook a late brunch at a table for two in the suite living room, served by a dithering waiter. Lacking patience, Shek would report the elderly man's incompetence to hotel management.

They should fire the old sloth, he thought.

"More coffee?" Shek said to his guest.

She shook her head, while her lips never left the glass rim of her Mimosa.

Shek snapped his fingers and pointed to his empty cup. The thought flashed.

Can't the fool see that I need more?

The waiter teetered over with a coffee pitcher but Shek demanded a fresh cup and saucer. He took satisfaction watching the frail man return to the serving cart, pour coffee into clean china, then return with hands shaking as he struggled not to spill a drop. Shek swallowed.

"Crappy coffee," he cranked.

As Shek finished the cup, he felt body discomfort, then sheer pain assailed. He convulsed as stomach spasms balled him over. Shek let out a cry and fell to the floor at a pair of size thirteens. Too late, he understood. The waiter, who had just poisoned him, and the whore with whom he'd slept, worked for DeBona.

He died with satisfaction they didn't know what he had in store for the old man, who called himself the Boss of the Boardwalk.

"Will there be anything else, Madam?" the waiter said.

"Well, not coffee," she answered.

Then, she emptied Shek's plate onto her own, knowing breakfast is the most important meal of the day.

He who had no name still lingered on the boardwalk, when he spied a diminutive black man coming his way, walking with a limp and wearing ragged clothes. Homeless people strolled that end of the boards at all hours of the day, but they were no threat. The killer turned his back and watched an unrigged sailing ship slow motor through the choppy waters.

Suddenly, he felt a poke in the back from a gun barrel. The homeless man wasn't what he appeared. He was a cop, quickly joined by fellow undercover officers, who raced to the boardwalk from all directions. Marked patrol cars dashed to the scene with their overhead lights flashing and sirens blaring. The trap had sprung.

The arrest team worked at the direction of Carol Resnick, who had received a tip from someone she only referred to as a "reliable information source." They handcuffed the hit man before he could even react. He who had no name would be booked, then taken to the county jail and held in a special cell.

Paul watched the jurors walk into the courtroom in single file. As they took their seats, Miz PMS gave him a sneer, a troubling indication that could mean they were delivering bad news.

"Sir," Judge Hastings called to the jury foreman. "I understand the jury has reached a verdict."

The thin man rose. Ever so slightly papers shook in his hand. His voice quaked as he spoke.

"Yes, we have, your Honor."

He shuffled his feet, then dropped the jury ballot forms and they sailed across the floor. Murmurs filled the room as he retrieved paperwork and nodded to show he was ready again.

Judge Hastings said, "Bailiff, you may begin."

The court officer in a navy blazer cleared his throat. Silence enveloped the room. Then, the officer trumpeted, "How do you, members of the jury, find the defendant . . ."

A loud commotion came from outside the courtroom doors.

". . . Paul Cameron . . ."

Voices heatedly argued.

". . . upon the charge of murder in the first degree?"

Judge Hastings pounded his gavel.

"Bailiff," he called out, "I want it quiet out there before we continue."

The bailiff hustled toward the doors. All heads turned to the entranceway as the voices grew louder still.

Outside the courtroom, two deputies were guarding. Under strict orders from the trial judge, no one was to enter the packed courtroom during the reading of the verdict. They had been instructed to exercise force, if necessary, and the deputies were prepared to use it. On the other hand, they weren't accustomed to having their authority challenged by so formidable a pair of gate crashers. Carol Resnick flashed her badge. Judge Light hadn't even taken time to remove his judicial robe when he had rushed from his bench at Atlantic City Municipal Court. Both demanded to enter.

The deputies didn't know what to do until Boog approached. Unable to find an empty seat in the courtroom, he had been waiting in the hallway. Sensing good might come from assisting, he warned the deputies.

"Let 'em into the courtroom fast or your asses will be on the line."

Recognizing Boog as one of their own, the deputies allowed all three to enter. They dashed past a bewildered bailiff just as the jury foreman continued reading the verdict.

"We, the jurors, find the defendant, Paul—"

"Objection, your Honor!" Carol shouted. She reached the bench with Judge Light and Boog beside her.

Everything in the courtroom stopped dead, including the foreman's mouth, which just hung open.

"Miz Resnick, you're disrupting this court!" Judge Hastings roared. His eyebrows twitched and his face flushed. "I'm going to have you cited for contempt."

"No, you're not," Judge Light called.

"Sir," Judge Hastings said to his colleague from the lower court, "I recognize you and Miz Resnick but neither of you may say a word in this courtroom until the verdict is read."

Carol was undeterred. She didn't earn the reputation of being the Mistress of Major Crimes by treading softly.

"Your Honor," she continued, "I'm here to report prosecutorial misconduct in this case and to recommend that the Court immediately declare a mistrial."

Horace Grender jumped to his feet and screamed with indignation.

"Judge, I don't know what she's talking about. This woman isn't here with the authority of my office. I ask that she be taken from this room, gagged and in handcuffs, if necessary."

Flabbergasted, Judge Hastings directed himself to Judge Light.

"Sir," he said, "perhaps you can enlighten me."

"This morning," Judge Light began, "a young lady appeared in my courtroom. Her case wasn't on my list for the day. She had found her way onto the sheriff's bus by some kind of paperwork foul up at the county jail. She screamed in our lockup facility until I brought her into my courtroom to charge her with disturbing the peace. When the young woman came before me, she told me something that a call from Miz Resnick later confirmed. It seems Mister Grender locked up the woman, who was identified as a defense witness in this trial, to keep her from rendering testimony."

Judge Hastings glared at Grender, who was clutching his hands together. They detectably shook.

"It also appears," Judge Light continued, "that Mister Grender abused the power of his office by manufacturing charges against this witness and depriving her of the right to speedy arraignment. She's been concealed under special orders in the women's wing of the county jail. The young lady had information that would have led the defense to another suspect in this murder case."

"Your Honor," Carol interjected, "I just received confirmation of that woman's claims from an independent source, who has provided reliable information to law enforcement authorities in the past. This has resulted in the arrest of an organized crime figure for the murders of Sarah Cameron, Doctor Emile Ricardo, and Casino Control Commissioner Rolland Pepperman. The man is also wanted by federal authorities for racketeering and has outstanding warrants on murder charges in two other jurisdictions."

Carol turned to her boss with contempt radiating from her eyes.

"My office has also learned that much, if not all, of this was known to Mister Grender. It's my duty to report that the County Prosecutor has breached his professional obligations under the Code of Professional Responsibility and as mandated by the Rules governing practice in this court. He blatantly failed to give the defense full, fair, and legitimate discovery. His conduct is tantamount to obstruction of justice."

Judge Hastings was stunned.

"If I may reply," Grender began.

"You may not," Judge Hastings said. "And who might you be?" He focused on the burly man who had burst into the courtroom with Carol and Judge Light.

"I'm the Boogster," came the prompt reply.

"Indeed, you are," Judge Hastings said before turning to Lee. "Do you have anything to say, Mister Gunther?"

Lee just smiled. He was a man of no words when none were needed.

Judge Hastings swallowed. His Adam's apple bobbed. Then, he ruled.

"I have no choice but to declare a mistrial. I further release the defendant from all requirements of bail. The prosecutor's office has a suspect in custody for three homicides, including the murder for which this defendant is charged."

Turning to Grender, he added, "You'll have a lot of explaining to do before the Ethics Board. I suspect they'll refer the matter for investigation to determine what charges should be brought against you for misconduct in office."

Judge Hastings shook his head with disgust as he pounded his gavel for the final time in the case.

"A mistrial is declared. The defendant shall be immediately released. Court is adjourned."

"But," protested the jury foreman, "we found the defendant—"

"Don't say it," fumed the judge, "you son of a—"

Courtroom clatter covered the uncustomary utterance.

Lee chuckled and offered: "What did we just hear?"

"Can't tell," Lee replied, still shell shocked.

It seemed like a thousand voices rose at once to fill the courtroom. Reporters scurried to telephone the news to their offices. Outside the courthouse, a camera crew from the city's only television station was waiting at the direction of Grender, who had expected a different kind of day.

The Boss of the Boardwalk sat calmly on the front row. His eyes studied Paul and he liked what he saw. How could he not? In the young man he observed so much of himself. Someday the young man would learn why. Someday, not that day.

He rose quietly. Tony strolled from the courtroom, satisfied the call he had placed to Miz Resnick, as her "independent source," produced his intended result. Amid all the commotion, he left unnoticed. Tony felt compelled to be elsewhere.

Lee leaped toward Grender's desk more agilely than he had moved in years. Oblivious to the stiffness in his knee and too pumped to feel pain, he asked Grender something at point-blank range.

"How's it feel to get dicked up the ass?"

The squat man never answered; his face never flinched. He rushed from the courtroom, slinking past the press and offering a squeaky, "no comment," to the waiting television news crew.

Carol turned toward Paul. Barry's engagement ring had never wrapped her finger and she wanted to grab the opportunity with Paul that they always seemed to miss.

Disappointment bit her when she saw him leaving with Mickey. The paralegal held his arm with her head against his shoulder. Maybe it was time to wear that ring, after all.

She consoled herself by talking to Judge Light who, she realized, was about to realize his own ambitions. Horace Grender had let his office run out of control too long. Judge Light was ready to step up from the Municipal Court judgeship to the job of Atlantic County Prosecutor. Politicos had already considered the jurist as a possible successor to Grender and it was obvious that the time had come.

Reverend Rich heard the news in his church. He had waited for it with the woman Paul had once saved from the deadly forces of organized crime. God had answered their prayers and it was time to express gratitude. Their knees kissed the carpet; their hands clasped. Before his eyes closed, the Rev turned to Anise and his bellowing words filled the chapel.

"Fear may keep us up all night, but faith makes one fine pillow."

A lesson, he realized, the lawyer had paid a high price to learn.

In a six by eight-foot cell at the Atlantic County jail, he who had no name tied a knot. He pulled it tight in the bed sheet that he had fashioned as a noose around his neck. Next, he tied the other end of the sheet to a steel bar running across the ceiling. He stood atop his bunk testing the strength of the knots at both ends. Then, without fanfare, he threw himself down.

The noose slowly strangled him. His face turned blue and his legs kicked. With eyes bulging and tongue extended, he looked like a grotesque marionette. Death came slowly. In his last earthly moments, he saw the same Viet Cong officer from his youth staring at him. A pistol was in the officer's hand, still smoking from the murder of his parents but that time the Viet Cong officer wasn't smiling. He who had no name would be tormented no longer.

Prell knew what to do when Judge Light released her from jail: she ran to AK. He was in no condition to leave the hospital but her fresh face was all he needed to find strength. Prell helped him into a wheelchair, pretended she was his private duty nurse, and sneaked him out of the hospital without a formal discharge.

She laid him in the back of their Beemer and started the car with a roar. They headed wherever they might find a home. AK was ready to leave the life. He would marry her and Prell was ready to be his baby alone. They were leaving the streets to the likes of Poon Tang Train and Smitty, whose likes would always haunt there.

Tony was ready to make rounds. Sammy Smoke, whom he had groomed with Bobby so either might someday reign over their crime family, offered to accompany him but Tony stole away alone, promising to find one of their boys to watch his back. His words came as a necessary prevarication, knowing his trip must be taken alone.

First, he strolled the boardwalk where he handed an envelope to Amanda, who had remained in town through the trial. Then, he went to Lena's grave, where he lifted a flower, and spoke from his heart.

"*Mia cara moglie, mia amore,*" he began, "my dear wife, my love, this day I have broken the old curse: my son won't fall prey to the sin of his father, committed so long ago on our wedding day. The wellbeing of our children and grandchildren is assured and I leave no business undone."

Only for an instant did Tony hear gunfire blast across the cemetery. It caught him by no surprise. Lead didn't rain because he'd become careless or predictable. This was his premeditated adieu.

The duo of Sheik's henchmen, who rose from behind gravestones, pumped full clips from submachine pistols into his large frame. The impact shoved Tony against Lena's headstone, his blood smearing her name as he slunk to his knees. Led sheared his flesh yet brought serenity nigh, as if each bullet taken shed the sin of each he had ever fired. His assassins ran, leaving the Boss of the Boardwalk the only place he wished to be. He and Lena were together again.

Fresh flowers are still delivered there. They come from the college girl, who will always be in her hoodlum's debt. Someday, she would hand Paul the note her hoodlum had asked to be given to his son after he was gone. Sketched with a paucity of words, it came straightforward and from the heart. Tears in Amanda's eyes would let Paul know that all his father wrote was true.

At last Paul was free to start life anew yet something bothered him. Something still didn't toll veracity's bell.

Chapter Forty

Boardwalkers for Life

CAROL PULLED HAIR BACK FROM HER FACE. The long night had been a good one. She would be the new First Assistant County Prosecutor under Acting County Prosecutor Clarence Light soon as Grender cleaned out his desk. So, she helped him pack.

Grender removed his personal belongings from the office after hours to avoid embarrassment in front of former staff members, who were glad to see him go. His resignation came as no surprise and they exchanged no words as the man waddled out for the last time. She lingered in his empty office and soaked in the feel of a room that might someday be hers. Carol had her own ambitions and looked forward to working as second-in-command under Clarence Light. She had broken off with her car dealer and was ready to delve into her career.

"There's a call for the County Prosecutor," a member of the small night staff called into the intercom. "Do you want to take it, Miz Resnick?"

Carol thought. She had put in enough time for the county. Time to head home, she figured.

"Mister Light starts tomorrow," she called out. "He can take the call in the morning."

Carol began to leave when the woman called back.

"Miz Resnick, this gentleman is from the FBI, and says his call is important. It has something to do with the Sarah Cameron murder. He insists on talking to someone, right way."

Why is the FBI calling about the Cameron case? she wondered.

Certainly, it was a local matter outside federal jurisdiction.

"I'll take the call," she said more out of curiosity than anything else.

Carol picked up the phone. What the federal agent said chilled her.

Paul had placed his Brigantine house under Contract of Sale, wishing no part of the place, and selling it furnished. His realtor scheduled a fast approaching closing date, where he'd turnover keys to the new owner. Paul returned to the house only to assure he was leaving nothing wanted behind. The mission had been Mickey's suggestion, which he endured with discomfiture.

Equally discomforting was the relationship with Mickey that had somehow engaged the day he was released from Judge Hastings' courtroom. They had gone to Boog's bar where drinks were on the house for Paul's well-wishers. She attached herself to him and they had become something more than coworkers.

Yet, she seemed intent to pursue him for the sake of capture, rather than genuine affection. The only way to handle a compulsive relationship, he realized, is to enjoy it—or to sprint away fast and far. By definition, there's no way to lighten obsession.

Still, he wondered: *How can I run from an assistant I see every day in my office? Can I fire the woman who stood so steadfastly by my side?*

Jail had given him pause to reflect. Recognizing for the first time how easily life's thin thread can snap, he realized the old mob boss had been right. Young people don't know enough about love. He also considered lingering words from the note his mother had given him. Now more than ever, Paul longed for the woman he had always sensed felt the same about him.

Something else also troubled him. The murder trial had reached an uneasy resolution. The jury hadn't acquitted him by rendering a "not guilty" verdict. Instead, Judge Hastings had dismissed the charges when he found grounds for a mistrial. The difference is fundamental. Prosecutors could never try Paul again on the murder charge, if he had been found not guilty. Double jeopardy constitutionally bars a retrial after acquittal. Yet the doctrine doesn't bar a second trial where the court dismisses the case without a verdict. The State could indict Paul and retry him anytime. That seemed unlikely in view of the arrest and suicide of the Vietnamese hit man. Still, Paul felt uncomfortable because everything didn't add up.

Why hadn't they discovered the identity of Sarah's boyfriend? Why did a hired killer brutally murder Sarah and Emile? Paul remembered his troubles with Tony DeBona. The man had a vicious reputation. Did the mob boss orchestrate a double homicide to pin on Paul for the sake of vengeance alone?

Clearly, Tony Quick Fish would've killed the witness in his fire insurance case, if Paul hadn't interceded. Perhaps the notion that the mobster would have Sarah and Emile killed, too, wasn't far-fetched. Happenstances that spared him from a death sentence left many questions unanswered.

Mickey interrupted his thoughts. "Got a light?" she said.

Paul reached into his pocket for the lighter Boog had purchased from Jagan when it had seemed so significant to his defense. Paul occasionally lit a cigar and had thought he might feel compelled to do so after cleaning out the house.

He lit her as his cell phone sounded on the bedroom dresser where he had set it down. The ring of little Motorola surprised him. Most cellular phones were installed as larger car units and he was still getting accustomed to carrying the newly released smaller device.

"Aren't you answering your cell phone?" Mickey said.

He shrugged. *Oh, why not*, he thought, as he grabbed it too late.

Minutes later, the phone sounded again. That time Paul wasn't answering. Whomever was calling could reach him at the office in the morning.

Mickey emerged from the master closet as the phone rang again. She answered this time and handed the phone to Paul with a smirk.

"It's Resnick," she spit.

Mickey walked into the bathroom as Paul took the call. It perturbed her that he should receive calls from other women late at night. She'd seen the tall blond and didn't want her turning that into a habit.

Maybe, she thought, *Paul and I should set ground rules*.

Knowing titillation can be a great ground breaker for that kind of conversation, she stripped and returned wearing only an oversized bath towel that covered her from neck to thighs. She caught his eye from across the room.

Time, she knew, *for a strip tease*.

Ever so slowly she lowered the towel down her shoulders, then further, just to the top of a generously fashioned breast. Slowly, she uncovered the other, stopping at the pinkish rim of her areola. Her eyes bore into his, pouting lips inviting. She turned to face a wall, dropping the towel to massage swaying buttocks.

"Oooh," she purred.

Paul's attention tugged in two directions, but something born within him dispelled passion . . . and focused on Carol's words.

"I received a telephone call from an FBI special agent tonight who has information on Sarah's murder," she said.

Paul didn't like what he was hearing and glanced down to concentrate. Perhaps Carol was calling to warn him that they were reinstating the murder charge against him. Maybe the call was a sympathetic gesture to make it easier for him to surrender.

"The agent," Carol continued, "met Doctor Ricardo in Washington at a seminar just before he was murdered."

That must have been one of the people Emile had mentioned to Anthony, Paul realized. What could the agent have learned about his case that Emile had found so compelling?

"He told me Doctor Ricardo was using criminologists there as a sounding board for his theories in your case. Someone at the seminar introduced him to this FBI agent, who had quick access to Bureau records. The agent did background checks on some of Doctor Ricardo's suspects. Tonight, the agent called for Doctor Ricardo to see if the information had been of any value and learned the doctor had been killed. The agent thought about his death and decided he should call our office."

Where is this going? Paul wondered.

"Ah," a breathy moan beckoned from across the room.

He looked up to see Mickey still facing the wall, one hand probing her thighs.

"Paul," Carol asked sharply, "how much do you know about your paralegal's background?"

The thought stunned him. He turned away from Mickey and realized he knew very little. She had slipped into his life and made herself indispensable to his law practice. They had worked together a few years, but Mickey rarely spoke of her past. So much like Sarah, she seemed to have none. As Carol continued to speak, pieces of the puzzle began to fit.

This is a Goddamned insult, Mickey realized.

Annoyed that the call consumed Paul's attention, she dropped the towel and strutted to the bathroom, searching for something else to entice him. In the linen closet she found a special toy on an upper shelf. When she returned to the bedroom, she went to Paul, took the phone, and disconnected the call.

"Time to try something," Mickey said. "You're going to like this."

Paul stared. When he saw Mickey dangling handcuffs, he knew for certain.

"Hold out your wrists," she said, peering with her cross-eyed gaze. "Just relax and let me do all the work."

"You knew exactly where to look for those things, didn't you?" he said, gesturing to the cuffs.

"I just saw them in the bathroom while I was looking around."

"No, you saw them before that. You've been here without me."

"What do you mean?"

"On the night of Sarah's murder an anonymous caller notified police of the killing but didn't use their nine-one-one line or the main telephone line that would have been recorded. Whoever made that call knew something about the inner workings of a cop shop. That telephone number is in our office directory."

"Half the lawyers in this county have that telephone number in their office directory."

"Not that many."

Paul paused as he pulled things together.

"The night cops arrested me with Boog, someone must have tipped them that I was here. Who would have known?"

Mickey raised another cigarette to her lips and waited for Paul to light it.

He pulled out the lighter, looked at, and stopped.

"The engraving on this lighter," he said.

"What about it?"

"This initial isn't for the last name of Sarah's lover."

"What do you mean?"

"The 'M' is for her lover's first name, isn't it, Mickey."

"I don't know what you're talking about." Mickey huffed. "If you don't want to light me, I can do it myself."

She reached into her handbag.

"You know," Paul mused, "I never really enjoyed the kinkier aspects of Sarah's sexual appetite. My lovemaking's less complicated."

"Maybe you never tried it with the right person," Mickey said, holding the handcuffs high. "Let me try them on you."

"You knew where to find those things because you used them here on Sarah, didn't you?"

Paul asked as if he were cross-examining a witness. He thought about the other things that had troubled him. Everything was becoming so clear.

"When I came here that night with Boog and saw my photograph with Sarah on the mantlepiece, I knew something was wrong. The only way she would've put a picture of me on display would've been by cutting out my head or blackening my teeth. Sarah took my photo off the mantlepiece, alright, but you knew where to find it, and put it back. Sarah always had snapshots taken of herself with friends. How many Kodak memories of you were on that mantle before you hid them?"

"Paul, listen to yourself. None of this makes sense."

"Sarah was sexually adventurous and you're no stranger to prurience. You were her lover, weren't you?"

Mickey was still looking through her purse. "Are you going to light me up or not?"

Paul just stared at her.

"The beer in the refrigerator that Boog found the night police caught us here was yours, wasn't it, Madame Brewski? The legal advice Sarah was getting about the divorce case. Who better to provide it than her husband's paralegal?"

Mickey continued to rummage through the large bag. Her hands trembled.

"You knew Emile Ricardo would be waiting alone for me in his apartment the night he was killed. You even knew I would be late. You got there ahead of me, didn't you?"

Mickey's chest began to heave as she breathed faster.

"Even the alibi you offered to give me when you thought I needed one. You weren't looking to give me an alibi. You were looking to give yourself one."

Mickey pulled something from her bag, a small pistol that she cocked, and trained on Paul's face.

"Sarah was mean to you, Paul," she said in a quaking voice.

Paul jolted, aware of how easily she could pull the trigger. He remained facing her but backed away ever so slowly.

"She left you, so I went to talk to her. I wanted to tell her what she was doing to you wasn't right. I've always looked out for you, Paul. You know I've been loyal."

From the corner of his eyes, Paul looked around the room for a way to escape.

"Sarah invited me here to talk," Mickey continued.

Paul edged toward the bedroom door.

"She knew all about men. Men are so easy to manipulate. You can always outsmart a penis."

The doorway was still ten feet away. Paul wondered if she noticed he was close to making a getaway.

"Get away from the door!" she screamed, steadying the pistol with both her hands and pointing it directly between his eyes.

Paul jumped away from it fast.

"Down on your knees. Now!"

Paul lowered himself to the floor as she continued.

"I could tell she was attracted to me. When I discovered what she liked in bed, I catered to her needs. Sarah needed to be controlled and I liked it, Paul. I played her games and gave her love the way you couldn't.

"She would have never died but she was going to leave me, too. Sarah told me that she was tired of playing our games. She was dumping me just like she dumped you. I couldn't let her do that. I had to kill her for both of us. You understand, don't you?"

Paul needed to buy time until he could figure a way out. He looked up and spoke.

"Emile found out about your past, didn't he?" Paul said. "He suspected you. To his trained eye there was something about you that made him get a criminal background check. It revealed information you didn't want disclosed."

"That's my past. I'm not that person anymore."

"No," Paul said, having just learned from Carol. "You're the same little girl, who was raped by her stepfather while her mother watched. You're the same child, who couldn't stand the touch of her stepfather's hands in places they didn't belong, so you stabbed his groin. You were taken away for psychiatric confinement, weren't you, Makayla."

Tears welled in Mickey's eyes.

"Don't ever call me by that name. I'm not Makayla, anymore."

The gun in her hand shook. Her fingers gripped tightly around the handle and over the trigger as Paul pressed.

"Back then, they didn't treat victims of abuse the way they're handled today. It wasn't easy for you, was it? But they seal juvenile records. Few sources would ever learn what you did. Local authorities would have trouble gaining access to those records, but Emile found someone at the FBI, who confirmed what Emile suspected about you. He knew. That's why you had to kill him, isn't it?"

"What difference does it make? You got off the murder charge and look at how much better off you are financially. Sarah would've taken you to the cleaners. I helped you. You owe me, Paul. Don't tell me that you're going to reject me, too. Don't make me do something to you. I won't let you hurt me."

Her breaths came shorter and louder as her words sped. Paul knew he had to help her regain composure or she'd kill him in a psychotic rage. He held out his wrists and closed his eyes.

"Bind me," he pleaded.

Mickey looked uncertain. Her bosom heaved as she fought for air.

"Chain me the way you chained Sarah," he begged.

Her head spun as she dangled cuffs in one hand and aimed her gun in the other.

"Look at me," she ordered.

Paul tilted his eyes upward and Mickey felt the rush, the old feeling that came when she was in control. She would handcuff and bind him. Then, she would do what she had to do. He deserved it. They all deserved what she had done to them.

"Tell me who's going to do this to you."

"You are," he said.

"Who?" She screamed.

"Mickey is doing this to me," he whispered.

His pale blue eyes bespoke an innocence they'd soon lose, she realized.

"Stay on your knees," she ordered, "and tilt your head toward the floor. That's right, lover. Close your eyes."

Teasing them then hearing them beg roused her passion. Paul would die, just like Sarah. After he was bound, she would find a knife in the kitchen. His cries would amplify her pleasure.

But first they would talk. She'd explain how he had taken her for granted and mistreated her. There was no hurry. The night was long and, in the morrow, she'd be gone.

She spoke and he listened with head cast low, until she planted a kiss on his forehead to reward his submission.

Paul felt moist lips and swung his fists without looking. He caught Mickey under the chin and sent her reeling. The pistol flew across the floor.

"You bastard!" Mickey screamed as she scurried on all fours along the carpet. "I'll blow your balls off for this."

Paul bolted for the gun, but Mickey reached it first. Before she could shoot, he jumped on top of her, grabbed the cuffs, and clicked one around her left wrist. Then, she fired. A bullet whizzed by his ear. He backed away stunned, knowing her next shot would kill him. Mickey aimed to pump the remaining five rounds into his groin.

"Die, you fucking bastard!" she screamed, as gunfire filled the room.

Carol drove up to the beach house, finding a scene all too familiar. Overhead lights on patrol cars flashed in the night. An ambulance waited to remove the body after the coroner completed his work.

"Ah," called out the cop standing by the front door. "It's the Mistress of—"

"I beg your pardon," shot the First Assistant County Prosecutor.

"I'm sorry, Ma'am," came the officer's embarrassed response.

Carol had shed her former nickname and became accustomed to respect that was her due.

Cops had already taken their familiar seats in the family room on the first floor to watch TV. She ran up the winding staircase to the second level. Boog Johnson was waiting with an open beer bottle in his hand.

"Good evening, Counselor," he said.

Carol's heart sank as she realized she had been too late. She had called the Boogster after Paul's phone seemed to disconnect. He had told her what Paul was doing, and said his bar was only minutes away so he'd check it out. The next call had come from police, whom Boog called for assistance, and they alerted her.

She walked to the bedroom. The body was covered, and her investigators were busy.

A hand rested on her shoulder as she tried to think of what to say or do. Never had Carol felt so lost at a crime scene. From behind came a voice.

"Thanks for calling."

Carol spun around to stare into Paul's blue eyes, then looked back to the covered corpse.

"It's Mickey," he said.

The Boogster walked toward them.

"I rushed here with my old service revolver, and had to use it," he explained. "I've turned the gun over to your people and gave them a statement."

Carol stood with her mouth open. Boog was the only one who seemed able to talk.

"I just told defense counsel that *first* you get their weapons from them. *Then* you cuff 'em. Don't they teach you people anything in law school?"

Without a word spoken, Carol wrapped Paul in an embrace she never intended. His arms responded naturally, yet only for a moment, as Carol excused herself to direct the scene.

Paul gave his own statement to a police sergeant, then found a quiet corner to pull something from his pocket. Unfolding the note his father had penned and his mother had tendered, he read once again:

> *Mio Caro Figlio,* My Dear Son, *verso il mio sangue per il mio,* I spill my blood for my blood, knowing what runs through your veins.

Paul reflected upon their first meeting: that day in his law office discussing a fire insurance case, when a stranger shared words that seemed fatherly. Their talk had even turned to Paul's lack of children. Had the man somehow sensed what his mother shrouded as her secret? His eyes lowered to his father's valediction:

> Ours are separate journeys. With each step know life casts travails yet solace abounds. Find it in the pure and endless surf that is our reminder of sanctity and hope. Allow this to open your heart and waken your soul.

Forget not, *mia figlio*, who and what you are.

Paul's hands didn't release the missive until all overhead lights from emergency vehicles dimmed and death's cleanup crew departed. It was then he knew—when he and Carol were at last alone—that no more time between them would be lost. Deep feelings displaced conjecture and consumed him with self-awareness.

Paul was the progeny of a man, whose capacity for love concealed soullessness, and a woman, whose piety kept passion at arm's length. Yet, he found an awakening of his soul and an opening of his heart, which his mother sensed, and his father promised.

Paul and Carol joined hands. Their touch seemed to set the world ablaze as they became aware of sunrise glistening where blue sea and blue sky met, announcing dawn that brought more than a new day.

"We may have some professional conflicts of interest," Carol bantered.

"Overruled, Counselor," came Paul's repartee. "Besides, I'm considering some changes, perhaps focusing on something else. Let's just call it civil practice for now."

"And leave your criminal practice behind?"

"Not entirely but Lee and I have been talking. Something on the horizon is calling us. Something . . . ."

Paul's voice trailed, as if for the moment consumed by a thought not ready for pronouncement.

"Something on the horizon is calling me," Carol said with eyes trained on the sea."

Paul's eyes followed her focus and his heart concurred.

The son of the Boss of the Boardwalk and the former Mistress of Major Crimes departed for Atlantic City. After all, it was a day befitting a stroll for the boardwalkers.

"Devilish adventure . . .
with room for romance."
Philadelphia Out on the Town News

A Run to Hell

Second Edition with Epilogue

JOIN RECOGNIZABLE FACES IN A HISTORY MYSTERY that reveals the CIA operation to snare or kill ruthless dictator and drug kingpin, General Manuel Noriega, who turned a nation into Satan's dominion, and the Mafia assassination of Oscar-winning best actress Grace Kelly, after becoming Princess of Monaco.

Sprint from a city alley paved with brimstone to exotic locales in Monaco, Miami, the Everglades, the Baja Peninsula of Mexico, and Panama. Along the way, descend into the world of the notorious Philadelphia Mafia family, and wonder whether a mob *capo* is covering your back or looking to whack you.

Pack light. You'll be moving fast through perfect reading for any beach, hearth, or comfort zone.

The "Second Edition with Epilogue" is overwhelmingly recommended. *Schof*

More Praise for *A Run to Hell*

"This exciting tale grabs you the first page . . . packed with secrets, intrigue, and adventure—something for everyone."

—*Book Dealers World*

"A spellbinder." —*The Tampa Tribune*

"Tom Clancy and John Grisham fans will REALLY love this one! Fiction and fact are mixed so well that I cannot tell where the truth ends and lies begin. HIGHLY RECOMMENDED READING.

—*Huntress Book Reviews*

"A great mix of fact and fiction, thriller and history."

—*Naples Daily News*

"It's the way the mob stuff really ran."

—"Fat Joey A" Altimare, longtime alleged and prison-pedigreed Philly mob member

"Recommended reading."

—*Royalty.nu,* The World of Royalty

"A Run to Hell jabs like a pitchfork through your heart.

—Don Cannon, *WOGL-FM, Philadelphia*

"*A Run to Hell* mixes a Grisham-style law story with the intrigue of organized crime, with a romantic subplot."

—*Ambience Magazine*